Marconics
THE HUMAN UPGRADE

VOL. 2 Angels of Atlantis

Alison David Bird, C.Ht. & Lisa Wilson, L.M.T.
Grace Elohim & Archangel Ariel

BALBOA
PRESS
A DIVISION OF HAY HOUSE

Balboa Press books may be ordered through booksellers or by contacting:

Balboa Press
A Division of Hay House
1663 Liberty Drive
Bloomington, IN 47403
www.balboapress.com
1 (877) 407-4847

Because of the dynamic nature of the Internet, any web addresses or links contained in this book may have changed since publication and may no longer be valid. The views expressed in this work are solely those of the author and do not necessarily reflect the views of the publisher, and the publisher hereby disclaims any responsibility for them.

The author of this book does not dispense medical advice or prescribe the use of any technique as a form of treatment for physical, emotional, or medical problems without the advice of a physician, either directly or indirectly. The intent of the author is only to offer information of a general nature to help you in your quest for emotional and spiritual well-being. In the event you use any of the information in this book for yourself, which is your constitutional right, the author and the publisher assume no responsibility for your actions.

Any people depicted in stock imagery provided by Thinkstock are models, and such images are being used for illustrative purposes only.
Certain stock imagery © Thinkstock.

Print information available on the last page.

ISBN: 978-1-5043-8681-4 (sc)
ISBN: 978-1-5043-8680-7 (hc)
ISBN: 978-1-5043-8679-1 (e)

Library of Congress Control Number: 2017913392

Balboa Press rev. date: 09/12/2017

Contents

Preface

It is often said that 'truth is stranger than fiction', and in our case, this is no exception.

As we began writing this book, we deliberated on how best to share this information: as non-fiction or fiction. Hours were spent reviewing 'volumes of material' in the form of channelings and hypnosis sessions. Ultimately we decided that either format would require you to suspend your beliefs and take the journey with us. Either format would resonate with the vibration of truth for the light workers, the truth seekers, and the way showers.

The fictional format provided us with a unique opportunity to share our galactic experiences with you in the way our Galactics share them with us. Though we have used a narrative framework, it will be up to you to discern truth, like recognizing your own reflection in the mirror.

Grace had pointed out at the beginning, "For some these would only be stories."

In the summer of 2016, while sequestered on a campground in Vermont for a writing weekend, Ariel paid us a visit...

> "We're very pleased that you are finally writing these pieces of the story.
> "It has been entertaining for us, to have you... cobble it together, as you are retelling it and sharing it with one another

and finally going back and listening to the volumes of material that you have. You are connecting back with us in those moments in space and time.

"This is very enjoyable because you know we exist in the 'now moment', so it enables us to transport there with you and strengthen those connections. For example, as Lisa was writing her view of my experience with Grace at the table with the small council... I can feed her that information because our connection is so much stronger now. And Grace can do the same thing for you, Alison.

"So as you let go of your concerns around 'what is the story?' and 'how do you tell the story?'... you can just tell the story.

"We are so happy to fill in the blanks. It is enjoyable for us because your knowledge and experience and belief system has expanded to such a degree, we can share this information with you and you can take it on board without the previous filters...

"Go back two years... Neither of you would have really been able to accept the full scope of those truths at that time. We've had to put it into human constructs so you can understand it.

"That is the frequency we can pour down for you in terms of how we interact with one another now. It is pleasing for us to be able to share more of that bigger picture with you. We believe too, that this gives you a greater understanding of the other side of the coin.

"It will also help expand the belief of your students and those that are still to come through. It will also give them the unique opportunity, now, to be able to look back at sci-fi messages that have come through mainstream media and be able to glean the nuggets of truth from them.

"You know those things don't get there by accident. You've shared that so many times with your classes. This will start to create the bridge for some people that 'IT really is true.' And that is going to create 'new imagination pathways' for the Higher Aspects of those individuals to reach back to their incarnates to help them Ascend."

In peace,
Alison David Bird C.Ht. & Lisa Wilson LMT

Message to our Lightworkers

"We are not strangers, we know you and you know us. We are your families. You do not need to fear us or be concerned about our intentions for you; nothing happens here that you have not already agreed at our council meetings here in the Higher Realms. You approve it here, and we move to manifest it in the physical.

"We are here with you and you are there for all of us.

"You are honored for all you have done and all you will achieve. It would be easier for you if you lay down your shields and your spears, and allow all that can flow from us to you to manifest, in an atmosphere of trust and love.

"The love we experience here in the Higher Realms is not that of rainbows, hearts and flowers as it is in your world, it's true. Love here comes from a deeper knowingness of who you are. Do not fear, know you are loved by those who, you would desire to be loved by."

Dedication

To all Guardians 'seen and unseen'.

Acknowledgements

S pecial thanks to 'The Medic' and 'The Commander'.

Prologue

"I could hear the Falcon's cry piercing the sky. The sun was hot and relentless. We had been walking for what seemed like eons. It was slow, torturous. Each step felt like an effort, as though we were walking through molasses. Members of my family were with me, a band of travelers looking for a reprieve. We had volunteered to come on this mission, we suspected but did not know for sure that we would be tied to the cyclical karmic fate of the dense Earth. I watched as the Falcon glided for a moment and then disappeared into the sun.

The lush valley sprawled out before us, rich greens bellied up to river banks. Palms swayed in the wind. I could see the progression of time speeding by as farmers, artisans and builders emerged from the local human stock – they cultivated the land and began building our cities. I watched as scaffoldings were erected and buildings constructed – it was happening within seconds, yet I knew hundreds of years were passing.

Suddenly everything was still. I heard the Falcon again and I looked up at my own reflection in a polished mirror. I was wearing a white dress and could feel the lightness of the linens against my skin. My bare feet flat against the stone floor. I leaned in to take a closer look. I picked up a paint brush, dipped it in kohl and began tracing the outline of my eyes. I stopped at the inside corner of my left eye and dragged the brush slowly against my skin, tracing the contour of my cheek bone. I repeated this with my right eye feeling each of the bristles, wet against my skin, marking me with the ceremonial makeup in honor and reverence for what I was about to do.

I picked up a golden necklace and fastened it around my neck. I lifted my headdress with both hands and placed it upon my head. The horns and the disk were made of gold. A green stone cut like an emerald glittered at the center of my forehead.

Slowly and deliberately I crossed the room, passed through a short corridor and entered an antechamber. I looked at the table to my right. It was perfectly laid out with golden instruments. I ran my fingers over them. I could feel my own heart beginning to pound against the inside of my ribcage. I paused over one that looked like a cross between a harvesting sickle and a scimitar. I breathed deeply and picked it up.

I opened the chamber room door and saw the being on the table waiting for me. I stepped forward and closed the door behind me." - Isis

Chapter 1

Outbreak

54 million BC

The High Commander of the Seraphiam Order kept a deliberate pace as she strode down the cobbled thoroughfare into the city.

She had slowed her vibration to take form and experience it. Now her senses were being assaulted by the sound of deep, raspy coughing, dark smoke and an acrid burning odor. In some, the cough had already progressed to a choking. From under the traveling cloak, her uniform, identity, and frequency masked, she could observe the melee as she maneuvered through the unusually crowded streets.

These people were sick and dying. Trying to make sense of it, she murmured to herself, "This isn't right..."

Rounding the corner, the Commander walked into an amassing crowd that had cornered a local official. He was trying to calm them and positioned himself on a large outcropping of rock adjacent to the building. Like a preacher in a pulpit, hands outstretched in a gesture that said 'settle down', he assured them he had seen the reinforcements with his own eyes; the Elohim had arrived earlier that morning and had set up an outpost to the west of the city. The Seraphiam had increased their presence as well. Help was here.

Her eyes narrowed as she surveyed the crowd. This did not match her reports. The dispatches said nothing of an outbreak. All of this was supposed to have been contained, yet at least half already had the markings; black and oily, like a tattoo. It was already too late for some. She could see the pooling of the blackness around their hearts and throats, and others carried the telltale track marks up the nose or into the corner of the mouth. She shook her head in anger; those would be lost.

A hand touched her shoulder. "Ariel?" She grabbed it as she turned around.

Aleah. It was uncommon for the Anahazi to take dense form, they preferred to stay in the Central City. Ariel was relieved to see her unharmed and gently released her grip. A thousand words passed silently between them.

Ariel followed Aleah through the throngs of people flooding the market place and making their way to the citadel. As they drew closer, she could see the sickness was more widespread. By her estimation at least three quarters of the population had been infected. It was far worse than had previously been reported. The virus was spreading rapidly.

They made their way to the stone archway at the city center and passed into the sacred healing grounds. The air was thick with the choking sounds of suffocation. As they approached the healing chambers Ariel was satisfied that anyone who could over hear them already knew what they were dealing with.

"How?" she demanded, "The experiments were no longer sanctioned. The Elohim forbade it, Grace forbade it."

Aleah shook her head slowly. "They had outside *help*," she said, not bothering to mask the inference of off-world interference.

"The genomes would have needed chemical intervention. The people here, they wouldn't have gone against a Federation decree. We have reason to believe it wants to access the gates."

Ariel's eyes grew wide with a mix of confusion and disbelief. A toxic form of dark matter had been deliberately quarantined within the cores of many planets. It was a relic from early creation in the Universe. "How could it possibly *know* about that? How does it *know* anything?"

Aleah leaned forward, touching her third eye to Ariel's. The frequency download of information and images came in an onslaught as Aleah shared all she knew; experiments conducted outside of Federation guidelines, and without the consent of the Elohim. The force itself was corrupting and corruptible, the quarantine should have enabled it to lighten and raise its vibration as the planetary systems came to higher light. After a moment she added, "It became self-aware... they thought they could control it." Ariel didn't need to ask how much time they had left. As they entered the city she realized that it was already too late.

Aleah led Ariel through an opulent water garden encircled by tall cathedral amethysts and fifteen-foot-high quartz points to a private chamber off the colonnade.

Alone, Ariel stood silently gazing out at the garden. She cleared her thoughts and focused on Grace Elohim. Telepathic communication was easier within the Seraphiam collective, but after eons of time together, she and Grace always managed to find each other. Stretching out with her mind she searched for Grace, locating her in the camp to the west of the city. She pulsed the frequency of her thoughts to Grace. The initial reports and subsequent dispatches had painted a far more optimistic prognosis.

She waited. After a few minutes her mind was flooded with Grace's frequency; she was shown a hooded figure traveling below the city center. She observed the figure make its way to the colossal quartz generator of the electromagnetic grid and set the charge in place. Ariel's heart sank. Then Grace's voice reverberated through her skull, "We have time."

Sensing Aleah had returned to the garden, Ariel pulsed back that she understood.

"Are they here?"

"Yes, this way."

The two women walked in silence to the meeting hall where the Seraphiam Order waited for Ariel. She turned to Aleah before entering. "Aleah, can you leave here?"

"Yes, I can return to the Central City... or enter a similar matrix in another system."

"Then don't wait, you should go now..." She touched Aleah's shoulder, and they nodded their goodbyes.

When Ariel entered the hall and pulled down her hood, the members of the Seraphiam Order rose to greet her in the traditional way; all at once, they raised their right arms to shoulder height, open palms facing out, followed by a nod – symbolizing the third eye to third eye connection – and then placed their left hands to their chests, *'so you know me in your heart.'* She returned the intimate salute in kind.

Ariel produced and then carefully opened a large leather satchel containing her orders from Grace. The Angelics observed as she took out a large pink quartz point and held it out before her. She was quiet for a moment as she decided how to continue. She placed the crystal atop its case and breathed deeply.

"This isn't going to be like the last time. Our orders are Extraction," she started.

They had all been at the close of the Luciferian project and it had left a deep wound on all of their hearts. They lost many of their brothers and sisters on that planet and even more in the ensuing Fall.

"Some of them can shed the density and Ascend out, or use the Gate," she continued. "The ones that can't, we will take."

Her brothers looked at one another and then back at her. Ariel's voice became deep and resonant, taking the double timbre of the Commander.

"We cannot take them all. If the blackness has them at the heart, in the nose or mouth, you must move past them. If they don't want to come willingly, you must move past them. We have time, but we must act with haste and precision – *there are many.*" She lay several smaller satchels on table, each containing orders.

"They can't be healed?" Gabriel interjected. They were all thinking it. They could heal almost anything. Extraction translated to retreat, defeat.

"We can't risk its spreading," Ariel said resolutely. "Our directive is to preserve as many of the souls as we can and to contain the Vilkriss." She hated to even name it. "It has awareness and given the way the virus is replicating, it's learning and adapting quickly. If it breaks loose, if it gets to the gates, what you see here will spread throughout the galaxy and then beyond."

Ariel waved her hand over the center of the table, a hologram of the city appeared. They divided it into quadrants, each taking a piece of the territory. She waved her hand again and honed in on an octagonal shaped building on the bluffs to the far eastern border. "Once you have covered your target areas, take the evacuees to the Gate facing the sea. We will be off-worlding them."

"Anything else Commander?"

"Save who you can and get out!

4

Chapter 2

The Fall

Above the horizon to the east a flash of light caught Grace's eye. The buttes in the distance shuddered momentarily, their distinctive silhouettes blurred by a veil of rising dust against the early morning sky, which then seemed to transform suddenly before her eyes into a burning sunset.

Grace watched in disbelief from the relative safety of the flat lands, miles to the west of the city. "No!" she gasped, and instinctively raised her luminous hand as if she could reach out across the plane and stop it.

In a moment, she saw the shock wave travelling faster than the speed of sound towards her. Beneath the planet's surface it lifted the dessert floor like a rug about to be shaken out. It seemed to slow down as she felt it lift her off her feet and slam her bodily to the ground before continuing to ripple outward in all directions across the landscape. Then came the unholy sound of detonation.

The groaning tremors emanating from deep beneath the crust forewarned of what was to come; the mantle was being rent asunder. The planet would be knocked off her axis and cease to spin, gravity would fail, and she would break apart. The electromagnetic Grid containing the living library of Tara along with the souls of millions of beings would be scattered throughout time and space.

In billowing, choking dust, Grace tried several times to get to her feet. The biological vehicle was destroyed. She initiated bio-transfer allowing the temporary soul carrier to fall to the ground like a discarded overcoat and she projected her consciousness back to the Halls of Amenti.

She flew through the ancient carved stone corridors with the force of a raging storm audible as a high pitch scream. She swept into the huge domed chamber and hovered above the floor beneath its oculus. As she looked up she could see the Pegasus Portal as it opened, and through it the signature rainbow energy field, shielding the waiting Anahazi ship, and in a moment she ascended into it.

She stood on the holographic deck as her etheric body stabilized within the matrix of the Anahazi ship. She was surrounded by projections mapping and recording the untimely catastrophe as it unfolded.

She viewed the data in turn. Ships led mass evacuations from the planet's surface just moments before oxygen rich environments ignited into firestorms. The great temples and emerald pyramids of the Atlantean citadel crumbled into rubble and were sucked down into huge chasms opening up beneath them. A chain reaction of volcanic eruptions spewed molten lava down the sides of fertile mountains. Tidal waves, miles high, swamped the coasts and engulfed inland towns and villages. Large sways of land and beautiful ancient monumental cities along the seaboards on both coasts sank into the sea.

She threw back her head and let out a sonic scream with the force of small, localized explosion.

The deck began to fill with an ethereal silver grey smoke, with tiny flecks of neon light flitting through it. She inhaled and drew the smoke closer to her and in moments it began to take form. Soon a silent, statuesque, hooded being stood knee bent before her and made no attempt to move.

"Ariel." Grace called, gently pushing back the hood of the travelling cloak as Ariel began to lift her expressionless face toward her, displaying all that she had witnessed like a movie running through her empty eyes. Men, woman and children fell lifeless to the ground in the streets, in their homes and in the market places as Ariel's Legions enforced Grace's command.

"Ariel!" Shouted Grace again. Ariel's eyes began to focus on Grace's face, which in this moment was as old as time itself. Wearily, she began to speak, pulsing scenes and images of the destruction she had wrought directly into Grace's mind. "We saved as many as we could," she said, "but it wasn't enough."

"Where are the crystals?" Grace demanded.

The Seraphiam Commander retreated into the sanctuary of her hood. "They are on Tara, Grace. You said we had time…"

The weight of the loss of an entire planet and millions of souls at the peak of Human evolution was unbearable. The destruction of the Taran grid, the library of consciousness, and the Amenti Star Gate – which would now be pursued by those not worthy of access to such power – and even the loss of crystals themselves, crushed them both.

Grace turned back to the holographic images as this grotesque distortion blew holes in timelines up and down the continuum. Large portions of the planet were breaking away and being drawn irresistibly toward the sun. Soon they would enter the gravitational pull of a black hole and be sucked into a completely different set of galactic co-ordinates; falling into lower, denser, harmonic structures from which they could not be redeemed. Her voice grew low as she spoke her thoughts aloud, "They will have to let us go back up the timeline to get them."

"Yes," said Ariel rising to her feet, "We can do that!"

But as they turned to face each other they could no longer disguise with nuance of look or tone, the gravity or magnitude of what had happened on their watch.

They had once again become the Destroyers of Worlds.

*   *   *

Deep in Tara's core, now a cauldron of liquid magma, the dimensional walls were breached. As the Amenti shields failed, a tall muscular male figure in ceremonial attire entered the domed chamber through a narrow archway, above which was carved the inscription "Thoth." He moved slowly and deliberately as the stone floor trembled under his bare feet. Carrying a portion of the Taran records in his arms he walked purposefully toward the hexagonal platform etched with intergalactic symbols and stood at the entrance to the unstable Star Gate.

Chapter 3

Khem

26,000 BC

G race's hand slid slowly over the smooth, black surface of the obsidian statue of 'Bastet.' The sleek, black cat had been sent to her by Isis from the outpost of Khem, on Earth.

If Grace had been more successful with the manipulation of the timelines on Tara, its destruction may have been prevented. There would have been no necessity to send Isis, Horus or any of the Pantheon across the Arc Portal Bridge from Gold Andromeda; there would have been no need to settle a new civilization in that dark region of space. She would not now be standing here having to defend this advancing culture, and the statue would never have existed at all.

She admired the bejeweled collar around its neck, as it was a testament to the artistry and ingenuity of this new race of creative, physical beings. She pondered how the Tribunal might judge 'success' or 'failure'. The loss of Tara could be seen as failure, while the saving of a solar system and the seeding of a new species could be classified as a success. It would be viewed through the prism of Galactic Law.

She stood in silence and viewed her reflection in a mirror across the room. For the occasion, she honored the efforts of the Pantheon she would be lobbying for by donning Egyptian robes; a simple white, pleated cotton shift, pulled in at her narrow waist with a gold rope and tassel. Her black hair, severely cropped at the shoulders and over her eyes, was decorated with a row of small seed pearls collected from the Red Sea. A gift from Horus.

Before she could hear the approaching guard, she could feel their vibration beneath her feet. She steadied herself against the buffeting she would feel from their energy as they entered the room.

The gravity of this planet made it heavy and uncomfortable for Grace's body to move without assistance. The Priests of Ur had arrived to escort her to the Tribunal, where she would state her case in her own defense and give evidence against those closest to her.

Two Seraphiam adjutants flanked her on either side as the procession moved slowly from her chamber. They led through the ornate, narrow hallways and upwards into the uppermost circle of the ancient auditorium to take her seat overlooking the proceedings, which were already underway on the stage below.

She could make out the boyish curls and the decorative ceremonial body armor, of Archangel Lucifer. He had just completed presenting his petition to be allowed to continue his experiments with a structure that would enable Angelics to incarnate into physical form. Many thought his plans were dangerous and could create instability within the universal structure.

He had argued that if formless consciousness could be housed in humanoid vehicles, as were already successfully being used in evolutionary projects throughout the universe, then Angelics with their superior qualities and capabilities could achieve a great deal in physical form. They could be of greater assistance to all life forms, which could only enhance the evolution of the Free Will Universe at large.

While his intentions were respected, there was concern that artificial soul carriers, created to house Angelic light forms, could interfere with the more natural Spiritual progression of all beings in the Free Will Universe. It was a directive of the Divine Office, that beings must experience genuine evolution of the soul in order to co-create the ladder of Ascension to the God State.

Up until this point, his plans were the cause of a great ongoing debate and had resulted in a schism within the Elohim. They had split into two factions with the Elohei rejecting all suggestion of interfering in the natural progression of any species.

The Council seemed to converse with each other for a few moments before announcing that Lucifer's plans would be shelved until further data had been submitted for their consideration. The Chairman called the next item on the docket. The Earth Project.

Finally, Raffé Elohim, Grace's Seraphiam General and most trusted advisor, stood up from somewhere close to the front and stepped on to the dais.

Grace shifted uncomfortably in her seat. It was nearly time.

The auditorium waited quietly and attentively for him to begin. After a few moments, he waved his hand and raised the unilateral holographic presentation to full height. The front rows were almost engulfed by it.

Grace watched herself in the images as the last hours of Tara unfolded below. She remembered how hopeful they had been at the beginning of that mission. She saw herself receiving dispatches from Ariel on the Taran surface before she realized it was already too late. There was sadness as she relived the detonation and the evacuations through the holographic representation as had been witnessed aboard the Anahazi ship. Ariel's Legions moving like smoke through the populations and snatching the souls they could retrieve, and the ultimate retreat.

The great hall fell quiet and still as Grace rose to her feet and was led to an enclosed platform, which descended into the arena below.

A Seraphiam technician took over control of the hologram and Grace watched as a new projection began to run.

A quasar shot out from the blackness of space as the conscious projection and particulates of what remained of Tara exploded into the empty expanse of the Solar system on the edge of the Milky Way. Molten fragments of rock containing electro-tonal frequency of the Taran morphogenetic field collided together, swirling like a gyroscope. Larger pieces calling to them smaller ones, as they spiraled and adjusted, harmonizing with the gravitational pull of the local Sun. Twelve planets in all being formed and molded as hundreds of millennia passed by in seconds.

As they marked the passage of time, two of the planets collided, one creating the satellite moon of the 3rd density Earth and the other forming an asteroid belt. A third was knocked out of orbit into a wider arc around the sun. Nibiru.

"Why are we seeing a molten planet? What relevance is this?" asked the Tribunal leader, an Elder from the Melchizedek Cloister.

"Another intervention," Grace answered. "It was necessary to recalibrate the planet itself in terms of the gaseous and noxious emissions; the ratio of water to the landmass, the condition of the water, the population and the quality of the atmosphere for breathing. What may have been appropriate conditions to support life for some were poisonous for others. A reset was required to make adaptations to the planet's DNA."

The Elder nodded for her to continue.

"It has occurred multiple times. Numerous times. This is a very efficient way to reset the planets," the hologram flashed other worlds, other creators doing the same, as though to remind the entire Federation that this was, in fact, their way.

The potential for cataclysm of 5th density Tara had been foreseen by the Councils, but the timeline existed as a low probability. The Elohim had petitioned early on for a fallback position, should the unthinkable happen. The 3rd density had been prepared for other projects, and contained early Sirian, and Dracon seedings, as all had dominion over 3rd density at varying points along the time track. The Elohim were having much success with the Tarans, they had been evolving peacefully and preparing for Ascension to 7th density. The Elohim petition had been granted to prepare the 3rd density Earth to receive Taran survivors should the cataclysm be realized.

Of the 2,500 races that had come together under the banner of the Galactic Federation of Light and The Alliance of Free Worlds, each contributed genetic and biological materials to life on the New Earth Project. The hologram lurched forward to reveal teeming seas and skies, flora and fauna as diverse as the Federation itself.

With a wave of her hand, Grace drew their attention to the continent that would be known as Africa. The first human prototype, a mostly naked and hairy being, loped across the open planes of the Serengeti. Human 1.0.

An Elder of the Ur Council interrupted, "Your request for a team to go to ground was granted and overseen by the Covenant of Palaidor, can we please move forward to the retrieval mission?"

Grace nodded respectfully.

The Falcon's cry echoed through the great hall as they watched him soar upward and disappear into the sun. Waves of heat shimmered on the sands.

The Tribunal observed the Pantheon following Horus through the vast wasteland on planet Earth. The Tribunal members could empathize, those of them that had descended into density understood the discomfort experienced when submerged in that gravity. The slowing of their vibrations into lower dimensional reality meant each step felt like an exhaustive effort, as though walking through chest deep molasses. There was a ripple of compassion throughout the hall, as it was plainly visible that their progress was torturous. This soul group had volunteered for the first rescue attempt of the lost Atlantean souls by beginning the DNA seedings in Khem.

Grace paused, "As you observe, they were more etheric in form than anything else around them, which made it very difficult for the Pantheon and those that accessed the Star Gates to navigate their way in a denser matter based world."

"And what of the crystals?" The Elder inquired.

"They could not find them as Etherics. The crystals took on density. It was necessary to create a race of workers from the local population, who could be their hands and their feet on the ground; who could do the work that was necessary to create a new community and infrastructure. That took time. The blended essences of the Tarans into denser form could only be done through the local indigenous peoples. Crude attempts... Crude attempts at hybridization were made..."

"Who sanctioned this?" One of the senior Ur priests demanded.

"I did," Grace responded, her voice strong and powerful.

Someone whispered 'Nephilium.'

Grace whipped around, "It wasn't simply a matter of blending with local human life forms. The population at that time was as primitive, animalistic. And so the blending of DNA and essences of the population took place in the hope of being able to create a vehicle that could achieve multiple tasks and provide the necessary conditions to sustain and hold the higher light vibrations."

The Tribunal observed the emergence of a fertile valley sprawling out from the monochrome desert; rich greens bellied up to riverbanks. Palms swayed in the wind. They could see the progression of time speeding by on the hologram as the Pantheon manipulated the local human stock, corralling farmers, artisans, and builders from the most promising of the specimens —they cultivated the land and began building the physical cities. These were not slaves, they were skilled workers bred and raised.

The hologram played on.

Scaffoldings were erected and rudimentary wooden buildings constructed, then torn down and rebuilt in stone... each one more impressive than the last. Great temples to Horus, Isis, Osiris, Ramses and others of the Egyptian Pantheon were raised. The same stones disassembled and rebuilt again, grander and even more ornate. They witnessed the great river swelling and shrinking with the ebb and flow of seasons, altering its course, time and time again. They watched the progression of human evolution silently; it was happening within seconds, as linear years sped by.

Glances were cast between the Tribunal members, surprised at this development. The Pantheon had needed to enlist the physical help of the humans. Their intervention through DNA enhancement upgraded the local population into Human 2.0. This evolution resulted in a master and savior paradigm as humans began to worship the Pantheon in their light forms. The Tribunal had not anticipated the potential for spiritual awareness or awakening in beings from such intense density.

Then the realization dawned, the locals could not explain the superiority of the Pantheon. They appeared to them as gods and were treated as such. They were to a degree controlled through the worship cycle of fear and reward.

Suddenly everything was still. Grace had selected a 'now' moment to display.

The Falcon's cry echoed again through the hall. This time the incarnate Isis was standing in the hologram, staring at her own reflection in a polished mirror. Barefoot, and clothed in a white linen shift, they observed as Isis selected a paintbrush, dipped it in kohl mixed with sweet almond oil, and began tracing the outline of her eyes. She stopped at the inside corner of her left eye and dragged the brush slowly against her skin, tracing the contour of her cheekbone along the side of her nose. She repeated this with her right eye, marking herself with the ceremonial makeup in honor and reverence.

Isis picked up a wide golden necklace and fastened it, then lifted a headdress with both hands and placed it upon her head. The horns and the disk were made of gold. A green stone cut like an emerald glittered at the center of her forehead.

The Council looked on as slowly and deliberately Isis crossed the room, passed through a short corridor, and entered an antechamber. They could see that she was surveying a table full of surgical instruments that had been expertly forged in gold, running her fingers over them, she finally settled on one that looked like a cross between a harvesting sickle and a scimitar. They observed her breathing deeply as she picked it up.

The Melchizedek Emerald Order and other Council members shifted uncomfortably in their seats. There was a loud whisper of unsanctioned experiments.

Isis opened the chamber room door, acknowledged the being on the table waiting for her, stepped forward and closed the door.

Grace could sense the change of energy in the hall. Their suspicions were being confirmed. The rescue mission had been given too much leeway and was now out of control. She moved the hologram ahead slightly. Attendants were caring for a beautiful being that was laying supine on a vast marble table. She appeared calm and peaceful.

Isis's steps on the marble floor echoed from the hologram and reverberated throughout the arena. They watched her crossing the room. The being on the table was beautiful; her light extended beyond the physical vehicle.

They could see her orb like chakras pulsing out light and frequency, gently rotating like mini celestial bodies, in rhythm, in unison. The white and gold light coursing through the lines around her and through her body illuminated her further. She was alive, but sedated.

"Calliope," Grace offered, "A volunteer."

The hush of the hall had been replaced with a din of whispers as Isis blessed her, kissed her and placed the blade tip to Calliope's skin, hooking in just above the collar bone. Whispers gave way to gasps as they watched

Isis slowly and methodically draw the blade down through the body to the root, opening Calliope's physical and etheric form.

Stunned, the Tribunal watched on as Isis raised the golden sickle and began hacking, slicing and cutting. It was extremely physical and forceful as Isis drew back the blade over and over again. She moved through the chakras, energy field, and aura like a butcher, placing pieces of the fractured energy field into the sacred jars.

They watched Isis contort her face in an effort to fight back the tears as she clipped the golden etheric filaments free from the unified field, stitched the gaping holes in Calliope's aura, capped and sealed the raw and broken chakras. Calliope was now quarantined, unable to draw down higher light, unable to access the electro-tonal frequencies of the 5th density harmonics or beyond.

Grace motioned for the hologram to stop. She spoke in a deliberate and calming voice, "This is what had to be done. The lost ones were too light to function in density. They needed to be dumbed down."

"Surely, the level of disconnect here is too great! This is not what was agreed upon in the beginning of this operation," called out one of the delegates from Corlian in a tone of condemnation.

And there it is,' Grace thought.

"There were also enhancements introduced within the DNA of the local populations that were deemed not far enough along their own evolutionary path. They were enhanced to bring them more into alignment with the other seedings arriving on the planet, in a leveling. So, yes! Some were disconnected and others were raised up to be able to exist side by side on the same planet at the same point in time and space." She said.

The Tribunal members led by the Corlian delegation argued that the Pantheon interrupted the evolution of other promising seedings from the 5 root races. When they descended through the Arc Portal Bridge, using the Falcon Star Gate, they arrived fully formed and as highly evolved beings. The Pantheon, as the first humanoids, observed prehistoric Human 1.0 organizing himself in a rudimentary civilization for survival and took liberties with experimentation and DNA contributions. This, they claimed, was a violation of the Free Will Zone. The artistry, industry and ingenuity demonstrated by the evolving Human 2.0 under Grace's direction was overshadowed by the outrage drummed up by her opposition over her approval of the unorthodox methods employed by the Pantheon.

Grace had countered that the existing population was never going to evolve quickly enough. The Pantheon merged with the humans to create vehicles of a higher vibration that could house spirit of a higher vibration. It was an intervention to enhance evolution – it was intended to speed things along. They accused her, instead, of bypassing evolution. She knew this was exactly what the Central Race was afraid of, and the reason they were not keen to allow Lucifer's grand design for the creation of Angelic soul carriers. The mood in the amphitheater shifted and the Council were conferring. She must turn this around before they demand closure and reclamation of this project.

Chapter 4

Concessions

D rawing their attention away from the hologram, Grace moved to center stage. She stepped up onto the platform, and at her will, the dais rose into the air and began to turn slowly and deliberately in a full circle. Scanning the faces of everyone present, she would appeal to each of them in turn.

They watched her in silence, as an air of expectancy descended over the auditorium.

The balconies and galleries of tiered seating stretched upwards, towards the oculus in the center of the great dome above. Dignitaries, ambassadors, delegates and representatives from each quadrant of Free Will Universe One were seated and standing, ready to stake their claim.

Many respected Grace and were interested to hear the Elohim perspective. Others saw her as a stubborn obstacle on the path to achieving their own goals.

But no one would underestimate her; that would be to their detriment.

Taking a leaf from Lucifer's book, she made the most of the dramatic pause to be certain she had their full attention, before making her announcement.

"The Taran Crystals have been found!"

The assembly's astonishment was audible. Many had believed the crystals had never made it to Earth in the first place, and secondly, if they had, they would be part of the crystalline structure of the planet itself by now, hardly likely ever to surface or be found.

The news gave rise to loud murmurings and exchanges between interested parties. Grace paused again and after a few moments the noise died down and one singular voice spoke the thoughts of the rest.

"The Egyptians found them?"

"No" said Grace. "They are found much further along the time track; towards the end of the next planetary cycle, in its final millennium. This is why we must have dispensation here to continue along the timeline, and even enhance the evolutionary scale developing here. These are the beginnings of a civilization that will influence the entire planet; a planet, which through such diversity of seedings, would provide an opportunity for greater collaboration between contributing factions within the Galactic Federations. There would be great potential for the evolution of new, hybrid species that could become classified in future as valid races".

Vocal rumblings intensified. That was provident indeed. The end of the cycle would bring the planet Earth back up through the photon belt, marking the conclusion of the three-dimensional experiment. After closure and reclamation, there were plans to re-categorize the 3D planet as prime real estate, which meant it would be up for auction to the highest bidder. The Free Will Zone would be relaxed. The crystals and their contents would be more accessible to the buyer.

This was not a positive in Grace's book. There would be many vying for possession of the crystals. They were extremely 'collectible', and in the wrong hands much damage could be done.

As she began to state her position she was met with resistance from several quarters, particularly those who were on the fringes of the Federation. The crystals were seen as an asset, another selling point.

But the Melchizedeks were aware of Grace's project from the outset. They had been active contributors with volunteers who had been on the surface since the beginning of the Taran rescue mission.

The planet was a commodity now, in a fall system at the brink of Galactic War. It was considered a rare jewel; one that should be snatched from the hands of its current custodians, who did not recognize nor appreciate its uniqueness. It was one of the most beautiful, temperate and diverse planets in the universe; rich in minerals, gold, water and chlorophyll. Now the crystals made it even more desirable. To remove that bargaining chip from the negotiating table could trigger a revolt.

Grace's voice remained calm and measured in tones that echoed clearly throughout the arena, "The crystals are the key to the Ascension of planets throughout the multiverses. I request dispensation of this Council to assemble a timeline of recovery prior to closure."

The Corlian delegate was on his feet, "How is that so?" He slammed his hand emphatically on the gallery rail in front of him as he aimed his comment directly at the Council, anticipating their support. "Anything that is on Earth belongs to those who inherit it." He continued. "That is the Covenant. Those are the rules."

Recognizing the Corlian representative's divisionary tactic, Grace ignored his interjection and continued to command the audience.

There were many present who felt they owed Grace for deeds of the past. She must lead them to the decision that would secure all their futures and not herald further destruction. She knew she had enemies in the room, but she also had old friends.

"Proceed," said the Ur Chairman.

Grace nodded in gratitude.

"We have seen these crystals recovered on one timeline only. A timeline on which cataclysm will render the Earth a desolate wasteland." She took another deliberate pause for effect before continuing, "There will be no 'reclamation'... no 'salvage'... no 'harvesting'... no 're-tasking'... no 'resources' to be had here." Her voice echoed through the hall. "The crystals will not be accessible along any other future potential that we have viewed beyond this singular event." She scanned their faces to gauge the mood of the forum. It was in her favor.

She took the opportunity to seek out Raffé, in the lower gallery with Ariel. He bowed his head solemnly, and she lifted hers to the higher echelons and girded herself for the final act.

"This timeline will evoke Galactic War. Central City *will* declare the re-set of Free Will Universe One to avoid it. This will mean the destruction of every planet and system in the entire multiverse and not one in this room will be able to ensure the survival of their own people."

There was silence, but for the dull thudding sound of beings who had been standing at the balcony rails falling back into their seats. The Corlian delegate was whispering to his Second in Command.

She knew the impact of what she had just disclosed. She knew what they were thinking and feeling in this moment. She had felt it too when she had viewed it on Orly, where they had synchronized the timelines.

This had been a narrow potential, an unlikely outcome at best. But the discovery of the crystals may now have just helped to solidify it in reality within the Earth time matrix.

It was long understood that, with the memories of the Lyran wars still so painfully fresh, the Divine Office would not tolerate the suffering brought down by another one. The fact that another war was even possible within the Galactic structure implied the failure of the evolutionary experiment on a macro scale.

The closure and re-set of a dysfunctional Universe, or an unsuccessful project was not unheard of.

She had given them a moment to assimilate the information. Now, she could look the Corlian delegate in the eye as she slowly and deliberately delivered him her coup de grâce, like a smiling knife.

"With the crystals reclaimed for Tara, we perceive the creation of a timeline of potentiality where it may be possible to launch a rescue mission of beings throughout the condemned dimensions within this multidimensional structure."

Grace instructed the Seraphiam adjutant to raise the three-dimensional holographic representation of a humanoid, which stood from the floor of the auditorium almost level with the highest gallery. The Elohim were also humanoid, though etheric and more refined in features than the hologram depicted.

She began to speak, "We have seen the potential of the human prototype, as it has evolved in Egypt in the density of Earth, to be more than just a temporary soul carrier for visiting extra-terrestrials; and more than a subservient slave race. The rudiments of evolution are already inherent within the design of the operating system of the vehicle. It is designed to be independent of thought and therefore, is conscious. It is sentient and fast becoming self-aware. Physicality allows for extremes of sensory experience on a scale between pleasure and pain enabling discernment. The ability to make choices is the definition of intelligence.

"As you know during the various phases of the Earth project, we have intervened in the development of this prototype to enhance certain abilities, such as communication, through the introduction of speech encodings within the DNA.

"In the density of the three-dimensional planet this version has strength and agility, but is also capable of compassion and even mercy. We observe that it can perceive beauty and translate it into imagery with the mind, then project it into form through multiple mediums. It is not just communicating, it is sensing and articulating. It is creating!

"The egocentric low soul – an integral part of the operating systems – has mastered the nuances of the biological vehicle itself to be able to use the body in unusual and skillful ways. It seeks out pleasure and enjoyment because it can exercise judgment.

"Some of these models are actively pushing the boundaries and going so far as to experiment with tools and producing results through what can only be described as ingenuity.

"We think there is an opportunity here to take it to the next phase, experimentally, with a re-tooling of the vehicle itself. Without upgrades to the physical body, any attempt to advance the purpose of the human model 2.0 beyond the limits of its original design will result in its destruction.

"We propose an upgrade to the biological vehicle to enable the assimilation of higher frequencies for the assembly of spiritual DNA. We believe the Human 2.0 would then have the potential to expand its consciousness beyond its own physical reality. If this proves to be the case, we could orchestrate a timeline of awakening to coincide with the enhanced stellar energies in that solar system towards the end of the final cycle, when the planet ascends into higher frequency.

"If this can be achieved it would be possible to retrieve them all – every soul lost in the cataclysm and in its aftermath, could be redeemed and returned to point of origin!"

The Council addressed her. "At the end of this cycle the Earth is scheduled to be wrenched away from three dimensional frequencies. Tara has requested that the 5th dimensional version be returned to its original pre-cataclysmic Ascension path to 7th density. The three-dimensional planet will fall. Are you proposing that this new race will survive a planetary transition of this magnitude to ascend into 5th to Tara?"

"It is impossible," the Corlian interjected.

"Not impossible, just unprecedented," Grace retorted.

"Hybridization!" Shouted the Corlian in an attempt to elicit response from the assembly.

"Yes!" Grace spun around and addressed him directly. "Don't ignore the implications here. There is potential for expanded hybridization programs to be created throughout the sub universal sector, making higher evolution accessible to many and even Ascension out of a doomed matrix." She turned back to The Council, "We suggest an upgrade in the design of the soul carrier could allow for intelligent re-programming. We could take control through the DNA and modulate their capacity for evolution along a specific timeline. They could be made ready for Ascension into the higher frequencies of Tara."

The Council responded via the chairman, "This is your rescue plan? This is unacceptable. There are agreements in place that must be rectified in the allotted sequence. Alliances rely on the promises made by the Covenant of Palaidor."

"The Covenants and agreements will still stand," Grace assured them. "Access to the Free Will sector cannot be gained until the planet returns to the Galactic Core. I am not requesting an extension. I simply ask for the opportunity to use the period of planetary Ascension to sling shot the evolution of what could become an advanced hybrid race. At the same time as the planet is moving into higher bandwidths of frequency and approaching the center of the Galactic system, we could attempt to recover the living library of Tara's Atlantean civilization."

Some were visibly moved by the prospect, though not the Corlian. He stood at the rail and barked down, "And if you are not successful with your spiritual DNA, what happens then to the new – what are you calling them? Human 2.0?"

"3.0" Grace corrected, "If the new race has not evolved to a point where it can ascend out of the matrix, then it falls collateral."

"To be inherited?" The Corlian demanded.

Inherited was another word for "owned", in this case by the planet's new landlord.

Grace bowed her head. "Agreed."

He continued, "But what if they do evolve, as you say, but not far enough for Ascension. You may have created a formidable and adversarial race that could resist us!" He had shown his hand and immediately took steps to correct himself. "Or whomever takes over the sector. We could have a replay of the Sirian resistance."

"Remember the timeline," Grace prompted. "The collapse of Free Will Universe One means the loss of trillions of souls. This project is the only one with potential to provide retrieval. Yes, it is a long shot, and there is only a narrow window of opportunity. But if it is successful to even the smallest degree, we will all be winners."

The Corlians could see they were losing ground as other delegates and ambassadors were already casting their votes.

"If this is even to be considered, we demand a say in how this race is designed… It shouldn't be left to the Elohim to have dominion over a race which is most likely going to fall under the control of whomever becomes planetary custodian."

Another euphemism not wasted on The Council who conferred for a few moments before concluding.

"It is Sanctioned."

A mummer of enthusiasm, peppered with disgruntled disillusion moved through the hearings like waves on the surface of the sea.

In continuance, The Council imposed three caveats:

The first: To remain in alignment with Divine Directive, the Egyptian humanoids must be allowed to evolve naturally as co-creators and no longer perceive that they must be subservient to a superior being. It would be a protected Free Will Zone.

The second: To satisfy the requirements of the Federation, there must be a competition for the design of the new soul carrier hybrids, open to anyone who would agree to contribute to the New Earth project and its protection until it's conclusion.

The third: Due to the linear progression, the Arc Portal Bridge and Amenti Star Gate would be vulnerable. The Covenant would be relaxed. The Arc Portal Bridge withdrawn. The Sphere and the Flame removed.

The third was met with mixed emotion; Ariel slammed her hands on the gallery rail and rose to her feet. Grace nodded stoically and telepathically pulsed to Ariel, 'Stand down.' She read the slight tilt of Grace's chin as acceptance, though definitely not agreement.

The crystals would now be even more vulnerable without boots on the ground, and a show of force or act of defiance would not serve their mission. Ariel left herself open for her brothers to read the frequency of Grace's request to stand down. Now they only had time for immediate extraction and retrieval of the rescue teams.

After entering Earth's density, it was unknown if the Pantheon would be light enough to shed their semi dense soul carriers and transit back through the Arc to return to the Red Spiral Galaxy from which they had come as volunteers, or to use the Falcon Gate before the Sphere of Amenti was removed. Those that could not would be lost.

It was a fate worse than death. Without the Arc Portal Bridge there could be no ascent back through to the multiverse structure; and without the Sphere, the Gate would not provide access beyond the 12th dimension of the planetary grid. The Pantheon and other volunteers, who had arrived from much higher vibrations, would be trapped in the density of a three-dimensional planet until their altered vehicles decayed. Then they would be lost to a matrix, which could not support them in an evolutionary cycle or enable them to transit upward through the harmonic bandwidths. These volunteers would become disembodied consciousness, trapped and disconnected, unable to ascend or evolve, unable to return home.

There was blood in the water. The Pantheon were family, a collective in the same way as the Seraphiam saw themselves. To lose a member, was to lose one's self. Several other volunteer teams had descended through the Star Gates along the Arc Portal Bridge established through the Covenant of Palaidor at the same time; if not in support of the Taran rescue mission, then for various projects. Their founders, Melchizedeks, Bramans, and Hyperborean stood in disbelief and shock upon hearing their progeny would be condemned as well. While the Seraphiam under Ariel would remain allegiant to Grace and the Elohim Collective, other collectives and the Angelics sitting on the sidelines would not tolerate another loss reminiscent of the close of Venus, M51, and Mars.

The tension had become palpable.

Grace knew that the ruling to close the rescue mission would not be overturned, but she could not leave the volunteers, any of them, locked in a falling system.

It was a hard won concession. After much deliberation it was agreed that those who could exit their bodies would be allowed passage through the Star Gates and could return to their respective Galactic Sectors via the Arc. They would be spared an inquisition as the Tribunal had already passed judgement.

Those that could not be recalled would be given an option to enter a phantom matrix or would enter the matrix below the grid, ultimately tying themselves to the fate of the planet at the end of its last 26,000-year Ascension cycle. Upon their 'death', they had permission to both contribute memory, experience and knowledge to the pool of collective consciousness and they would remain within the harmonics of dimensions under the planetary grid. They would function like the Angelics and Ascended Masters had on other planetary systems, though they would not experience a personal incarnational or evolutionary cycle.

Grace and Ariel strode down the corridor in silence. They had been running a series of monotone frequencies to shield their thoughts since leaving the Tribunal hall. Now was not the time to be overheard. The human ability to progress enough to begin a worship program revealed potential timelines for spiritual evolution. They still had hope.

*   *   *

Ariel emerged from the portal of the Falcon Gate in Amenti. It took a moment to orient herself as she took stock of the density. Earth was beautiful but so supremely heavy; it was painful. She descended the stairs into the grand hall and was received by Isis and Horus. They were eagerly awaiting news.

"We did everything we could," she said hurriedly, "The Tribunal ruled against us. I've come to collect those of you who are able and willing to come back." Isis brought her hand to her heart; Horus lowered his head. They had lost. They had failed.

"And what of the able and *un*willing?" a sharp male voice called from the shadow of the arches.

"Ramses," Ariel nodded to him and decided to be economic in her relay of events, "The tide has turned against us. Grace secured dispensation for us to evacuate. They are recalling everyone and pulling up the Arc Portal Bridge."

Dozens of questioning and concerned voices echoed through the hall. Ariel could hear each one individually:

> *Surely they had misheard!*
> *Had the Tribunal forgotten they had been in density?*
> *What if they couldn't shed the vehicle?*
> *This was just like Tara, Bellock and Venus all over again!*
> *Were they about to be destroyed? Why else was 'The Butcher' here?*

Ariel raised her hand to silence them.

"How much time do we have," Isis asked.

"None, I've come straight from the Tribunal. You have to come now." No one uttered a sound. "Those of you who can step out of your soul carrier, go – go now before the Arc and the Sphere are removed. Those of you who can't...I can take you, but I do not know how long you would remain in a phantom matrix... Or... you can take your chances here. We've been granted permission for you to enter the planetary matrix as guides and guardians. You can't have an evolution here, but you can exist etherically within the harmonic bandwidths under the grid."

"How long would we be here if we stayed?" Ramses asked.

"Through the end of the cycle," Ariel offered, "and it would be dependent on if *they* can make the Shift when the time comes."

It was unthinkable. The fearful humans, who until the Pantheon arrived, were barely more than hairy barbarians, would now anchor evolution in the multiverse. Their awakening would now be the key to Ascension?!

Ariel rose to the top of the stepped pyramid at the center of the hall. She closed her eyes for a moment to check in. "We must go now," she commanded in a clear and resonant voice. The Amenti Gate activated granting them access to portals to other worlds in time and space. In the center above the Sphere a beam of light descended.

When the last of the Pantheon had entered the Arc or accessed the Gate, Ariel pulsed out that it was done, she was returning. A small band had opted to stay in the density, none of them choosing the phantom matrix. They had fared better than those on the previous planets she had been ordered to on reclamation and closure missions, and for that, she was grateful.

She entered the beam of light and felt the departiculation begin. Ariel noted how beautiful the Arc looked in density, each photon had been affected and could be perceived as an individual rainbow pixel. When the vibration increased it would become a brilliant white light.

Those that remained watched her shimmer and disappear as the Arc Portal Bridge was withdrawn, taking with it the Sphere of Amenti. The weight of the density closed around them like a tomb.

*   *   *

Ariel found Grace pouring over a long scroll spread over a large table, head down and eyes trained on inky markings that looked like a family tree. Stepping up beside Grace she observed the firm set of her brow – Ariel knew that look, Grace had a plan.

Pointing to a large symbol heading up the branches of the 'tree', she could see Grace was focused on the one that looked like a cross. "So… what is this?"

"Religion."

Chapter 5

Valerie

1943, Great Britain

V alerie struggled to buckle her new shoes. She realized she should never have taken them off in the first place.

She watched enviously as some older girls drew chalk squares on the tarmac playground with numbers in each one and began hopping from square to square in a game of 'hopscotch'. She couldn't wait for the day when she would be a big girl.

At seven she was still in infant school. She had mousy blonde hair and hazel eyes, but she was a pretty little thing. "It's her bone structure," her father would say. She had high cheekbones and 'smiley' eyes, just like her mother. She was prone to be a little on the chubby side, she wasn't wasting away like some of the kids, with families whose ration books couldn't stretch the week. Her father was a butcher, there was always a little something passed his way in payment.

When he wasn't doing that he was a volunteer fire warden. He would sit perched on the wooden gate at the end of their garden path, every night during the bombing blitz and watch for fires.

A deep rumbling in the distance, which had grown steadily louder, made her look up. Shielding her eyes against the brightness of sunshine, she suddenly saw its outline silhouetted against the morning sky.

"It's an airplane!" she shouted, jumping to her feet, one shoe still not properly buckled. Whenever she saw an airplane she would wave her hands over her head as big and wide as she could. Uncle David was a pilot in the Royal Air Force and he said if he ever saw her waving, he would 'waggle' his wings. He did it once, returning home from a raid over Germany. He passed right over the garden.

Mrs. Vaughn, the English teacher, came running out of the old Victorian red brick school house and into the playground, ringing a hand-held brass bell for all she was worth. "Children! Come inside, quickly! Quickly, now! RUN!" she shouted, in every direction.

The rumble of thunder grew louder as the plane flew directly towards the school. It passed for the first time right over Valerie's head and she had to clamp her hands over her ears because of the noise. It was so low it blocked out the sun, causing a monstrous shadow over the playground. She could make out the black and white cross, painted under its wing as the plane pulled up. Mrs. Vaughn shouted again, "It's coming back around, come on! Inside! inside now…Run!!"

She had seen those black and white crosses on a crashed plane in the cemetery that she and some older boys had played on and clambered over. Her father came to get her for tea one afternoon and had told them a German flight crew had died in it, and that had made it a war grave.

"It's a German plane!" Valerie shouted, as she turned and began to run towards the school door. At the same time, the Headmaster, Mr. Pritchard, ran out into the playground in front of her, he crouched down and beckoned to her to run to him. So, she ran as fast as she could – as fast as anyone could with one shoe not properly fastened. Waving his arms in the air he shouted, "Come on Valerie, come on!"

Children dropped balls and hoops and skipping ropes and fell off swings in the dash to reach the door.

A piercing screech from the 'shadow monster' overhead made her stop in her tracks, clamp her ears and shut her eyes. Then the loud crack of gunfire made her jump as it hit the tarmac playground in front of her, causing chunks of it to fly up in broken pieces. Then there was another and another, breaking up the ground between her and the Headmaster.

Her heart pounded in her chest and felt like it jumped up unto her throat and she let it out with a shrill scream! When she opened her eyes her head felt light as if she was floating, and she thought she was going to be sick.

She looked directly at Mr. Pritchard and as their eyes met he gave her such a strange look. He gripped his chest with both hands and dropped to his knees on the ground. "Go! Go!" he insisted in a small, strangled voice, waving her in the direction of the school building. The 'shadow monster' flew over the school just as she reached the door and this time it never came back.

The children were made to wait in the assembly hall while their parents were notified. Valerie thought they were all very over excited, as her Nana would say. Several of them had bumps and bruises from falling, Valerie had blood on her head where sharp chunks of playground had hit her in the face as she ran. One girl went into shock!

There was a lot noise and kafuffle as the teachers brought in chairs and pushed the seats together to make small beds for the younger children to lay down on, with blankets over them. They were all made to drink tea, which even had sugar in it. Grandpa said tea was the best remedy for shock, aside from a nip of brandy. Tea with brandy was even better!

She overheard Mrs. Vaughn talking to one of the other teachers who said that Mr. Pritchard's heart had attacked him, but Valerie didn't know what that meant.

All the parents seemed very upset and there were hugs and kisses and lots of crying. It seemed like a long time before Valerie's mother came to fetch her. Then they walked home together in thoughtful silence as they passed by shelled out ruins that had once been a business, shop or house.

Valerie's mother had tears in her eyes one day when she said they should always show respect as they passed the bombed out ruins of someone's home. She thought it seemed very odd how one day there could be a house there and then after the German bombers came, when they had all spent the night sleeping in the Anderson shelter in the garden, she would get up and there would just be a hole where the house had been. Where did it go?

Someone from her class had died in a house just three doors down from hers. The explosion had blown out all the windows in the front, and her father who had been fire watching that night, had been blown right off the garden gate.

On the way home they stopped at Sallyanne's Sweet Shoppe for some Gobstoppers, her favorite sweets. Her father said to her mother later, they had given the Ration Card a right bashing!

They didn't go down to the Anderson shelter that night, it had flooded when a water main got hit. Once when that had happened in the street, the family who were sleeping in it had drowned because they couldn't get out. She found it hard to sleep in her own bed, so she crept quietly out of her tiny bedroom, which overlooked the garden at the back of the house that Grandpa had turned from a lawn with decorative flower borders into one big veggie patch. She tiptoed onto the small square landing at the top of the stairs. The door on her right was her baby brother's room and the one directly opposite hers belonged to her mother and father. She trod very quietly as she came down the narrow staircase and sat on the bottom step, right near the sitting room door, so she could hear her mother and father talking. She found the sound of the announcer's voice on the news radio broadcast, and the gentle 'tinkle' of china cups and saucers very comforting. They were having supper.

"Such a shame," she heard her mother say.

"He was a good man, can't say fairer than that," said her father. "Bad luck so close to it all being over. Doesn't seem fair does it, to survive this long only to go from a heart attack just as it all ends?"

"It isn't over yet, Tom." Her mother said in her worried voice.

"I'm telling you!" Her father retorted. "You wait and see if I'm wrong! They just dropped a blooming great bomb – an atomic one – on Japan, Ethel. There won't be anyone left at this rate to fight any bloomin' war!" It went quiet, except for the calming voice of the man on the news, coming from the radiogram in the background.

Valerie suddenly felt tired and sad as she climbed back up the stairs to bed. *'They have children in Japan too, don't they?'* she thought to herself. She fell asleep thinking about Mr. Pritchard. She had known in her heart that he was dead all along, she had seen it in his eyes on the playground. She would miss him, he had always been kind to her, and funny. It seemed to her like there was always someone dying.

That night she was almost woken up, but not quite, by a strange feeling in her head and her stomach. She had tried to open her eyes but the light was so bright and she couldn't keep them open to see. There were children's voices but not loud enough that she could understand what they were saying.

Eventually, she could make out a face. It had big oval eyes, very blue and kind, and a large head that glowed whitish. Then she dreamed she was with this being who had long, spindly arms and legs, and they were standing in a very plain room with nothing in it except a bed and some toys. In her head she heard the being say, "This will be your little girl one day." Valerie looked but all she could see was a blue light floating above the ground in front of her. It floated towards her and was so close that it felt like it was all around her head! It felt very warm and lovely.

The next morning, she told her mother about the dream, but all she said was, "That's good, dear. Do your shoes up properly, we're going to be late for school." Valerie soon forgot all about the dream.

That is until almost 15 years later, when she was in the delivery room, at the maternity hospital, with her feet up in stirrups being urged by the doctor to 'push!'

"Valerie, this baby isn't coming out if you don't push!" He said again.

It felt like she had been pushing forever!

"Just get it out of me!" she heard herself yell. Her head felt light and strange and the room seemed to slip away as the doctor's voice grew faint…

"Doctor, she's going off," she heard the nurse say far away in the distance. Then blackness.

Above her she saw the luminous white face of the benevolent blue-eyed being she had seen as a child. She smiled in recognition and felt an overwhelming warmth and emotion coming from it. The kind gentle eyes seemed to smile back at her, then the luminous white face turned slightly to look at something above her belly. She followed its gaze and saw the beautiful, electric blue ball of light she had seen so many years ago. It seemed to speak to her in her mind and she felt herself respond.

Eventually it began to descend, slowly into her abdomen. She felt as though she was being enveloped in a warm blanket. Never had she felt such a sense of peace. But it didn't last long; as she came to again in the din of the delivery room she could hear herself screaming. She was pushing and pushing, and finally something slipped from between her legs and was caught by the arms of the waiting doctor.

"It's a girl!" he exclaimed.

"Good girl!" said the nurse, stroking Valerie's damp hair away from her face. "Daddy will be very pleased!" Squeezing her hand, gently, the nurse asked, "Do we have a name for baby?" Valerie had planned to call the baby Sheila if it was a little girl, after her best friend... but she said. "Her name is Alison."

*　　*　　*

Grace observed the scene as it unfolded from the holographic deck, on a ship stationed in the planet's atmosphere, ready to monitor fluctuations in the universal Akasha as they occurred. Nothing had changed.

"Do we have any readings at all?" she asked the technician.

"Nothing yet," he confirmed.

Grace looked at Raffé, "That's not possible."

The technician spun the projection 360 degrees and drew it up so big they were actually standing in the delivery room and they each began to study the scenario in detail. Where was the problem?

Then the nurse spoke urgently, "Oh, Doctor, baby is very blue." The doctor took the baby from her mother and lay it down on a nearby table, unwrapping the swaddling he lifted each of the baby's limbs and one by one let them go. They immediately fell limp at the baby's side. He gathered her up and sat back down on his stool, laying the swaddling blanket over his knees, he placed the baby face down and gave her bottom a loud slap! She didn't cry out. He took the blanket up in handfuls and began to vigorously rub the baby's back, legs and arms with it.

Grace watched with growing concern. Then when a few moments had passed with no response, she ordered the technician to create a 'glitch'. He looked back at her uneasily.

"That's an order," she re-iterated. He leaned forward hesitantly and began to remove the holographic plate from the console. He held it in partial suspension for a second then dropped it back in place; an intervention which, in his view, directly contravened the laws of Free Will.

The doctor felt the room tilt momentarily and put it down to low blood sugar, it had been a long night and he hadn't eaten. Valerie felt a wave of dizziness and nausea wash over her, which was totally acceptable under the circumstances, and the nurse registered the shudder through her feet. She had been suspicious of the building's structural integrity since the end of the war, when a German plane leaving the city at the end of a raid dropped an unexploded bomb outside the hospital doors. It had been buried under the rubble for years until it was eventually unearthed during construction work 6 years earlier and detonated in a controlled explosion by a bomb disposal unit.

Each passed the experience off as a personal anomaly and nothing more. But the baby jerked into life; she coughed, grizzled and began to cry.

"There we are!" said the doctor as though he knew all along that she was just taking her own sweet time.

Grace watched as tributaries spun outward from this new nexus point within the time torus and sent ripples throughout the continuum.

She smiled, nodded and said simply, "It's begun."

Chapter 6

Ghosts

1962 France.

"Where's Alison? Where's my little girl?" cried the English woman, her alarmed voice drawing attention from the other tourists.

Grace and Ariel watched the hologram, intrigued. "In their dimension, this structure is over 600 years old, and in ruins. Why does it hold such an attraction for them?"

The French tour guide stopped and stood for a moment with his mouth open. The woman was becoming very agitated, "She was right here!" she gestured to a spot at her feet. "Where did she go?"

"Pardon Madam…," said the tall, young Frenchman, clearly out of his depth. "She cannot be far," he assured her and responded immediately by gathering the tour group around him.

"Mesdames et Monsieurs, if we could all just move back a little?" He gestured with his arms for the foreign tourists to widen into a circle, which after some hesitation, they did. Then he turned back to the girl's mother. "Please, can you describe the little girl?"

A good looking man in an RAF Great coat, with a cow lick of dark hair over his forehead and piercing blue eyes, stepped forward and attempted to communicate in very poor French. "Elle est tres petites," he said. From the way he was gripping the woman's arm, it seemed clear to the guide that this was the little girl's father.

"I can speak English, Sir," he assured the man.

Relieved, the Englishman continued, "She's very blonde, almost white haired. Her name is Alison."

The guide gave out the description first in French and then again in German, and without being told what to do next, the assembled group spontaneously broke up into small parties and began to scatter themselves across the castle grounds in search of the three-year-old.

Her mother began sobbing softly, "She was just here! I had her hand one minute, and then she was gone!" Her husband grabbed her shoulders as if setting her in place in one spot and instructed her to stay where she was in case the little girl made her way back. Then he followed the French guide as they sped off across the grassy ramparts of what remained of the Medieval French fortress, in the direction of where they had just come. They spiraled down a worn, stone staircase and disappeared underneath the walls of the Keep and along a narrow, underground corridor flanked on either side by door-less rooms that had once formed the dungeons.

Faint voices echoed from above as the impromptu search parties called out the little girl's name. But it was the tour guide and her father who eventually found her standing alone outside a large empty cell.

With tears streaming down her face, she looked at them both and pointed at a heavy, iron studded, wooden door, "Why is the man in there screaming?"

The two men looked at each other and the tour guide finally spoke, "That's the old torture chamber."

"What is she seeing?" Grace asked, leaning closer to the holographic image.

The technician said, "She is touching in on the time track at around 1640 in Earth's history."

"So, she sees it as it was." said Ariel.

For Alison the castle wasn't a ruin, or an historical relic, it was real and alive. Blazing torches lined the musty, stone walls of the dank underground corridors, casting shadows over the wet, flagstone floor, running ankle deep with waste water and blood. To her it was dark, cold and frightening and somewhere behind that door, a man was dying.

"Humm?" Grace mused. "So, we have activations within the DNA already?

Raffé continued to study the data. "At this point she has the ability to at least see inter-dimensionally wherever the membranes are thinnest. There does seem to be a small harmonic rift here, the structure was erected on a point where planetary energies converge. It's no more really than a tear in the matrix, her connection is unlikely to be sustainable over time given the density of the parents. But it demonstrates that the mechanisms are in place. She should be able to remain hidden for a while longer though."

Smiling, Grace joined Ariel who was observing the other child through the second console, almost 15 linear years further along the time track. The small girl with long brown hair and deep brown eyes clambered into her pink ruffled canopy bed. After bed-time stories and 'lights out', they watched as she fell quickly into a deep sleep. This little one was sensitive; as they poured down the frequency in an attempt to make contact with her, she began to tremble, and her eyes popped open.

Lisa could see lights and shadows moving across her walls and over her bed. The shadows made strange shapes on her wall. They looked scary and she clutched her teddy tightly. The bed was beginning to move and shake. It was happening again! She wasn't allowed out of bed at night! So instead, she pulled the covers over her head. Too afraid to scream, she hoped that she would be invisible as long as she was completely hidden under her bedspread.

"We're terrifying her," said Ariel quietly, "can't we connect to her without waking her?"

"We've been trying different frequencies, she is hyper aware of us though," Grace answered.

Gabriel moved forward to look more closely. "She traverses dimensions quite easily, but we are observing her having difficulty transiting back to the 3rd density when she astral travels. Though she returns physically she is still viewing into the fourth dimension. It is confusing to her. The biological parents have moved her into a house where there is a low soul that won't vacate; a suicide victim, a young mother. The disembodied spirit is very drawn to protect her, given the other contracts the incarnate carries.

However, its vibration is read as fearful to the girl. The fear is making access to the dimensions of sleep more difficult, it's forcing her into the lower levels of the astral, and she is pursued there. When she wakes up, she is still seeing inter-dimensionally and she has a hard time grounding in her reality. It's making her skittish with both dream state and conscious contact attempts."

Gabriel flashed a second hologram showing the little girl standing in the hallway in the dark of night screaming bloody murder. Her biological mother shaking her, yelling, "Lisa, Lisa, wake up it's Mommy!"

Noting the look of horror on Lisa's little face Ariel asked, "What is she seeing?"

Gabriel adjusted the setting on the hologram, and they now could see through the same perception filter as the child. It was a horrible black beast, with glowing red eyes and razor sharp teeth; a nightmarish thought-form that followed her from the lower astral plane.

Returning her attention to the current hologram Ariel announced, "No wonder she is terrified of us. Okay that's enough for tonight, no more."

Gabriel shut off the hologram and with it the frequency modulator.

"You think you could alter her perception of the frequency by bringing her up instead of lowering us down?" Ariel ventured.

It was an interesting suggestion. The Little One was already adept at travel. Gabriel was stoic for a while as he considered the image of the little girl cowering in bed. "Are you going down there?"

"Seeing how scared she is, I was thinking of asking Aleah."

Gabriel nodded in agreement, "We can try to bring her into 6th from the dream state."

A few nights later, after the third read through of 'Where is the Bear?' a drink of water and an extra trip to the toilet, Lisa finally settled into bed. Her father tucked her in and kissed her forehead, "There you are, snug as a bug in a rug." After checking for the under-the-bed monster and the closet monster, he turned out the light and closed the door. A little while later she fell into a deep state of sleep.

Lisa heard her name being called by a sweet voice that sounded like it was coming from very far away. She opened her eyes slowly to find that she wasn't in her room. She knew this place but couldn't remember why or when she had been there. Looking down at her bare feet, she could see the floor was made of clouds and light. The ceiling was a swirl of blue that looked like it went on forever. Lisa heard her name again, this time the voice was very close. From between a pair of white marble columns a beautiful woman who looked very much like Lisa's own Mommy appeared.

She was tall and slim, wearing a white dress that was tied at the waist like the women she saw in her illustrated children's Bible. She was beautiful with gold skin and long curly hair. She smiled, Lisa smiled back. She reached out her hand to Lisa. Slowly, Lisa stepped forward and placed her small hand inside the woman's golden one.

"Come Little One, there is much I want to show you."

Suddenly they were surrounded by gold light, and Lisa could feel ripples and tingles in her body. It felt like being on her Daddy's motorcycle, it was fast and the vibration made her head feel like it was buzzing and her teeth chattered. It was shaking her so much that she thought she could fall right out of her own body. She closed her eyes tightly and squeezed the woman's hand.

When the buzzing and tingles stopped, Lisa opened her eyes again. Everything she could see looked like it was made of gold. She watched energy patterns scrambling through the golden light, like when she turned the TV dial to a channel that her Daddy said was snowy and they played with the antenna to see if they could make the picture appear. She gripped the woman's hand tightly and buried her face in the woman's robes. Lisa peeked up at her, she was smiling still and said sweetly, "They don't have shapes here Little One, their bodies are pure light." Lisa didn't understand what that meant. Aleah sat her down on a puffy chair that appeared from nowhere. They watched together. After a few moments, the beings had slowed their vibrations enough to pull themselves into matter and projected themselves to be seated in rows and balconies. Lisa realized the snowy picture was coming into focus. Now she could see them, and they looked like the audience in the rows of seats at the opening song of the Muppet Show.

These people didn't look like people; Lisa thought they looked like cartoon people, like they had been drawn with glow in the dark paint on black paper. Aleah whispered to Lisa, that these 'Angels' could move through all of space and time and take many shapes and forms, just like the Angels in her Bible and stories.

Lisa was too afraid to ask why they didn't have faces when suddenly the light people became clearer to her. They looked like the woman now, golden and beautiful.

They showed Lisa a book of gold with pages made of light. Aleah recognized the Akashic Records of the Universes, "This is the book of God, Little One." Lisa smiled excitedly. Her children's Bible was her favorite book. It had pages that were pink, yellow, orange, green and blue. The blue one was her favorite because it was about Jesus, and she talked to him almost every day. She was happy that they were going to read to her, she loved to hear stories.

Holding Lisa's little hand, Aleah took her out of the council room and for a walk through the town. The roads were dusty like the dirt road to her Grandma's summer cabin by the river. On either side there were white stucco cottages.

It was warm and the sun felt good. The sky was a blue color that Lisa's crayon box did not have. Aleah laughed as Lisa chased after the fluffy chickens strutting by flapping about and pecking the ground. The villagers were all beautiful and friendly, and Lisa loved being there. She felt loved, safe and at home.

The contact had been successful.

Night after night, Aleah came for Lisa. And soon Lisa called her, 'Other Mother', and loved her just as much.

One night, Aleah gave Lisa a small gift, a coin, and took her up the steps to the top of the village, they looked out at the stars together. It was like being at the top of the mountain at Grandma's cabin, the sky was so dark and the stars were so bright, they looked like huge glowing balls in the sky. Aleah covered her in a dome of light, Lisa thought she was like the Little Prince's rose, she didn't know it was to shield her from the frequency. After a little while, she closed her eyes; when she opened them again she was back in her room, snuggled under the pink ruffled canopy with a coin clutched tightly in her hand.

Chapter 7

Dark Night

Alison's bedroom was typical for a 13-year-old girl in England in the early 1970s. A turntable record player sat on the bedside table, posters of Pete Dual and Ben Murphy from 'Alias Smith and Jones' lined the walls, colorful beads and plastic bangles hung from the mirror on her dressing table, and peacock feathers were artistically arranged in a vase on unpainted, pine shelving. Her favorite possessions were a plastic orange lampshade and a matching orange shaggy-nylon rug by her bed. She thought she might like to be a 'hippy' as she got older, which amused Grace as she observed her, because the child seemed to have no awareness at all of the Light. But she did love the clothes.

Alison's experiences on Earth growing up in a non-spiritual, agnostic, military family, combined with her sensitivity as an empath and compounded by four years in a post war British boarding school, had left her isolated, damaged and institutionalized. For her, life was something that had to be survived and nothing more. The girl, whose middle name was Joy, did not know the meaning of the word.

The house her father had moved the family into when he retired from the Royal Air Force was as deep in the countryside as he could find, hedged with farmers fields and rolling landscapes. There he would reunite his family and find peace and tranquility. But for his young teenage daughter the nights without a moon were very dark, not even a neighbor's house to give depth to the ancient Wiltshire backdrop.

Carved into the hillside behind their new home, and visible from Alison's bedroom, was an ancient chalk horse of giant proportions. This was a traditional Wiltshire landmark for sites of historic importance and scenes of violent skirmishes; such as was seen between the Roundheads and the Cavaliers in the 1700s, and before that the Saxons and the Roman invaders. Buried deep beneath the horse were the ruins of the Roman encampment of Oldbury Down.

Oldbury House, as it had been named, soaked up the atmosphere of its surroundings. Alison could feel the presence of so many ghosts from throughout the land's colorful history crossing in and out of the astral. It fed her darkest imaginings. Almost immediately after they had moved in, she began having night terrors. Waking up with the feeling that someone was sitting astride her and pinning the blankets so she couldn't move. It felt like something was sitting on her chest and sucking the air out of her lungs. Her body would be lifted up, as if a hand had grabbed the front of her nightgown and physically pulled her into a sitting position. She couldn't breathe, shout or cry out. But she knew that in some non-physical way she could fight it. She often succeeded in breaking its hold on her and it would stop as suddenly as it started. This night was no exception.

They observed her from the deck of the ship. "Every time we try to tractor her up she wakes and she fights it," Grace said. They watched the hologram in silence as the fearful girl scrambled out of the bed and hurtled towards the door in total darkness, smacking her knee painfully on the bedside table and crunching underfoot the collection of vinyl 45 records she had scattered all over the floor.

"Stop her!" Grace ordered, as she reached the door. The brass knob wouldn't move. Through gritted teeth the frightened girl rattled and twisted, and all the time seemed unable to summon the breath to scream out.

Raffé noted the spiking in her physiological responses. "The readings are all over the place." He said to Grace. "She is petrified. Do you want to bring her up in sleep?"

"No." Grace instructed after a moment, "Let her see me."

Raffé shook his head. "I don't think she can, her fear is quite literally blinding." The beginnings of Grace's materialization in the room just increased the sense of rising terror in the girl, who could clearly feel the presence of what she thought was an entity. To her – with no faith, no belief system and no comparison – it could only be something dark, and it was moving slowly, deliberately and inevitably towards her.

"Her blood pressure is too high!" Raffé noted.

"She is clairsentient. She can feel me, but it is as if she judges any sensation as negative," Grace mused.

Alison could see the lights from the hallway under her door, but the darkness in her room was thick as molasses; it felt encroaching and threatening. Moments passed, and when she thought she would just about collapse and die from the pounding in her chest, Grace finally commanded, "Release her!"

The door handle seemed to free itself and once again Alison was flying down the stairs in search of rescue. The door of the sitting room was at the bottom of the staircase and to the right. She exploded through it and into the room where her parents were sitting.

She had become accustomed to sleeping with her senses on full alert. It was like falling asleep and listening with your whole body at the same time, like an animal in the wild that may fall prey at any moment.

Raffé watched. "This is a drain on her immune system. What do you want to do Grace? I think she may be unreachable."

"No," said Grace. "Not unreachable. But she is choosing a much more difficult path than was necessary." They stood down and let her rest.

After Christmas, Alison felt things intensify more than ever. Whenever she looked in a mirror, her image seemed to morph and change and she thought she could hear voices whispering, though she could never quite make out what they were saying. She hated being alone and made sure one of her friends was with her whenever possible, even in the bathroom.

Then one Saturday, Alison was in town with some school friends and bought a bible and a crucifix; she began to sleep with them under her pillow. Alison didn't know if a crucifix would do any good, she wasn't Catholic. The family were lapsed Methodists, but she didn't know what that even meant. She did believe that there was evil in that house. With that knowledge accepted, she knew there had to be something to balance evil on the other end of that scale; a power for good. *'God would do,'* she thought. She was voting for him and made that clear whenever she could. She was choosing to walk in the light!

"Oh, yes, my dear! That's it!" enthused Grace. "The pendulum is beginning to swing."

*   *   *

Grace and Ariel stood side by side as they observed the second child. Gabriel had arrived and said somewhat bemused, "You realize there is 15 Earth years between these two children? Human society offers very small windows of opportunity in the many stages of linear growth of their young. Their society would not encourage two children of these ages to seek each other out. How do you expect they would ever meet? Even geographically there is a huge discrepancy it seems." He was noticing that the children resided on opposite land masses either side of a huge ocean.

"This is understood," Grace affirmed. "Transcendence of the limitations enforced on them by the human paradigm will be a necessary experience for them both. Their ages allow for the spanning of two generations. It breaks the mold, as there is something in human terms called 'The generation GAP'. Geographically, there are several opportunities along the perceived time tracks to have them cross paths. When they do unite, they will bridge two of the most powerful cultures on the face of the planet creating an environment of acceptance, tolerance and peaceful collaboration, at a time of great upheaval."

Ariel and Gabriel sat back in their seats at the console and observed Lisa's downward spiral. Her family had relocated to the southeast coast of America and they were in a newly developing town on the west coast of Florida.

It was decided that the contact with Aleah would cease. They needed to give the child, Lisa, the opportunity to have her experiences as an incarnate in order to complete the karmic lessons that were required of her in this incarnation. She was now left to exercise Free Will.

The disconnect had left her floundering and spiritually rudderless. The Church offered no answers and she walked away from it. She became fierce in defending against what she knew to be wrong but hadn't yet found anything that felt like truth. As she grew older and tried to conform to the social expectations of school, she became inexplicably drawn to whatever could evoke the deepest and most extreme emotion in her. Her parents would tease and say the music she listened to sounded like a funeral dirge. Had it not been for her academics, they would have been much more concerned about the morbid dress, dark humor, and the strange sketches and paintings. The darker the book, the sadder the poem, the scarier the movie, the angrier the cause, the sillier the laughter, the more intense the love; it all fueled her. Though she could mask her frequency to fit in and get along with anyone, she never felt as though she truly belonged. Aleah would no longer come for her each night, but *They* could reach her in the quiet moments when she would sink to the bottom of the pool and hold her breath, or submerge in the tub with only her nose and mouth breaking the surface of the water. There were those moments of solitude when she was still theirs.

Since the death of her father, the misguided anger she had for the Prime Creator had been intensifying rapidly. She had begged God to intercede and save him from the cancer, but he did nothing and Lisa's dad died the day after Christmas – just two weeks after her 18th birthday. As far as she was concerned she had no use for God or his Angels. She was lost and faithless, and from that state, she would not call out or reach up for help. They would not be able to intercede with her Free Will. Lisa was careening dangerously off course.

"How much has she taken?" Ariel asked.

"Enough," Gabriel answered.

Ariel watched her, standing on the Bridge of Lions at 2 a.m., eyes wide and dilated looking down into the dark waters of the Matanzas Bay below. She wondered if she would survive the drop. Reading the frequency of her thought patterns, Ariel understood it wasn't an act of fear or desperation, it was an act of rebellion; she was pissed and no longer wanted to play the game, she didn't see the point of it. Gabriel pulsed a beat cop two blocks away to turn left onto A1A. He arrived just in time to see Lisa holding herself up on the railing, about to swing her leg over. Seeing the squad car in her peripheral vision, she lowered herself back to the pavement and

:ing at an even pace in the direction of the historic town square.
wed down, but kept going.

Lisa arrived at the old market, she ducked under an archway and pressed up against the side of the building. She suddenly had the feeling that from where she stood, she was invisible to everyone outside the archway. She perceived everything differently from under the archway; the sounds, the smells, the temperature were all changed. She stepped out of the archway, and suddenly everything was loud and in full color again. She ducked back and it was all muted.

Ariel observed her intently. This was getting interesting. The hallucinogen had triggered her already sensitive pineal and Lisa was remembering and playing with inter-dimensional experience. They needed to intervene or they were going to lose her. The problem when an incarnate is set on a path of self-destruction and has turned their back on faith and on God, is finding a way to help them raise their vibration high enough that they can be reached. And do it without breaching their Free Will.

Lisa made her way back to the college dormitory, climbed the four flights of stairs to her room and crept in without waking her roommates. She locked herself in the bathroom and studied her face in the mirror.

"If you're going to, do it now," Gabriel urged Ariel. She nodded and he placed a crystal sheet into the holographic generator. They were going to bend a few rules together.

As Lisa looked into the eyes of her reflection, she watched them change slightly, the pupils became diamond shaped and her deep brown irises glowed with flecks of red and gold. She blinked and rubbed her eyes, it had to be the drugs. Her reflection shifted again and the face looking back was hers, but not her.

Ariel leant forward and boomed, "What are you doing? You get a grip and do it now! You're better than this." It jarred Lisa like a bucket of cold water being dumped over her head.

The next day Lisa sat quietly in an ancient oak on the college campus, semi regretting her antics the night before and nursing the crunchy hangover feeling she had in her body. Writing in her journal, and desperately missing her Dad, she asked no one in particular why she was so alone. She was in a beautiful city, attending a great school, with lots of people that seemed to care for her. Yet she couldn't connect to form a healthy relationship with any of them; she still felt like an outsider.

She did however, love that oak; it was her one place of peace. She admired the way its huge limbs touched the ground around it, the way the Spanish moss made it look like a great-great-grandfather. She loved that it made her feel safe in a way she hadn't felt since her father's diagnosis. Perhaps this was her one true friend. "So what shall I call you?" Lisa jokingly whispered to the tree.

After several quiet minutes, a masculine voice whispered in Lisa's ear, "Gabriel."

Chapter 8

Galadriel's Mirror

2012

The rhythm of the wipers as they swept moonlit rain from the oily windscreen was mesmerizing. Shelley was so tired, and the glare of red and yellow lights from the traffic jam up ahead stung her eyes. But to her relief, in the distance she could just make out the sign for Manhattan.

Just then, an old pickup truck coming up too fast in the inside lane overcompensated on the greasy blacktop, its brakes screeched as they dug in and the truck slid to a stop beside her. *'That was close'*, she thought. The driver looked as though he thought the same thing as he glanced across at her from under his baseball cap. Then they both turned their attention back at the road.

"Where are we supposed to go now?" She mumbled to herself under her breath. She knew if they were diverted, she would be totally lost.

"Can you see what's going on?" Alison asked.

"Roadworks, or something... They must be fixing the bridge. I think there's been an accident too. I don't know why else we would be stuck here so long?" Shelley could see the trail of traffic lights stretching out across the entire bridge. Cars were impatiently beginning to turn around and use the slip road to double back.

"Whoa! Whoa!" she suddenly cried out, "What are you doing?"

"What's going on?" Alison asked, edging forward in her seat.

"The car in front is rolling backwards", Shelley blurted. She brought her hand down hard on the horn, which still hadn't been fixed and made a pathetic 'beeping' sound. But the car just kept coming. "He's gonna hit us!" she cried. Struggling with the wheel she shifted the vehicle into reverse and checked over her right shoulder to see if the lane behind her was clear. Sam was still asleep in the passenger seat, exhausted from the day's events. They were returning home to her father's house from burying him in his childhood hometown, in Connecticut. With no one left she now had sole care and responsibility for her 16-year-old brother, and had left a job in Nashville, as a singer in a small trio, to come home and take care of him.

As she began to back up, a motorbike suddenly appeared out of nowhere in the middle of road behind her; her foot searched frantically for the break. She brought her left hand down on the wheel and tried to swerve around him, but as the tires rumbled over the slick, unfinished road surface, the steering wheel was wrenched out of her hand.

"NO! NO!" She cried fighting to regain control. Searching for the break her foot hit the accelerator. The car shot back, slewing across the road and all she could see coming up in the rearview mirror was an industrial construction lamp dangling from the temporary guardrail. They smashed through it. "We're going over!" she screamed, reaching across her sleeping brother with one arm, and fighting with the wheel with the other.

"Over what?" Alison's voice was distant. This is what she had been waiting for. Everything hung on this moment.

"The bridge! I am going off the bridge!" The car plummeted towards the murky waters below.

Alison began to instruct Shelley, calmly but firmly, **"Shelley, remember you can take a step out of your body and view as an observer, you don't have to remain in your body, or in the car."**

After a momentary silence, Shelley whispered from the recliner in Alison's office, *"Observer..."*

"Good," Alison said, reaching for the voice recorder and moving it a little closer. **"Tell me what you are observing."**

In a state of heightened anxiety, Shelley began describing the events as they unfolded. *"The guard rail doesn't stop me we are going over! We're falling… and falling."*

Concerned for the level of distress in her client's voice, Alison prepared to use the pre-arranged anchor they had established before the session that would 'snap' Shelley back to a fully awakened state. Alison knew that even though Shelley felt removed from the event itself, her body was remembering. She continued to show signs of physiological distress, her breathing was already elevated and her heart racing, as adrenaline pumped through her.

A few seconds later Shelley screamed, *"We are hitting the water!"* Flinching, she brought her arms up to protect her face then lurched forward on impact and fell back again on the recliner, limp and silent.

After a brief pause Alison spoke to her again, **"Shelley, can you hear me? What's happening, what can you see?"**

Shelley's breathing was fast and irregular, *"I can't see, the head lights have gone out, it's pitch black… we are sinking… down and down."*

Alison sat for a moment wondering how she should approach this. At what point should she pull her out? She decided to encourage her to keep talking through the experience. Alison continued to monitor her, but Shelley didn't respond.

Alison reached forward ready to engage the anchor and bring the session to an end. Suddenly, in a small voice, Shelley answered, *"I think I blacked out… The window came in and the car is filling with water… it's freezing!"*

Relieved, Alison continued to direct, **"Can you get out of the car?"**

"Yes, I released my belt. I could swim out through the windscreen, but I can't undo Sam's, it's stuck! I can't get him free…he's panicking!" Shelley's hands were in the air as she fumbled with something invisible, her face contorted with effort and fear.

Alison watched and waited. After a few moments she asked, **"Can you breathe?"**

"It's getting harder and harder…" Shelley answered, her voice weakening.

"Is there anyone there to help you?"

"I can see the lights of the bridge through the surface of the water… I'm still trying to help my brother; I can sort of hear sirens in the distance…" There was

a pause, then she spoke again her voice resigned. *"It's all just darkness - my brother's not here anymore...?"*

Trying not to let her own voice break with emotion, Alison began to guide Shelley through the death transition.

"The fighting is over now, Shelley, it's all done. I want you to go forward to just after the point of your own death. You are now released from your body and rising up in Ascension... What do you see? How do you feel?"

Lying still in the recliner, with a peaceful expression, Shelley said, simply, *"Relaxed."*

Alison loved this part of the session, she found it so comforting. She began to finish up the hour with the usual questions.

"Can you see anything at all?"

"I see only white light...I'm not sad anymore."

"What does it feel like to leave your body?"

"It just feels just like I'm floating."

"Is there anything that you have learned from this life that you can bring forward to the present?"

"I don't have to be afraid of bridges!"

Alison smiled with relief. Shelley's mother had arranged the hypnosis appointment because of her daughter's irrational and crippling fear of crossing bridges over water. By revisiting the lifetime where she had experienced the trauma of falling from a bridge into a river, the charge would be dispelled. She could now release herself from attachment to that past life experience.

Shelley was emerging from the experience with renewed understanding, *"I didn't have to die that way. It was my choice to stay in the car. I was being a good sister..."*

"Yes, you were a good sister. You made the greatest sacrifice of all." Alison's voice quivered. **"Allow yourself to continue to rise up. As you begin to level off who do you see, is there anybody else there?"**

At first Shelley couldn't see anyone, which made Alison feel despondent. Everyone was met by someone; a loved one, a family member, a friend or a guide...

"No... Wait!" said Shelley, "Yes!! There's an old woman here!"

"Do you know her?"

"I feel like I do, but…? Yes! She's has her hand out to me"

"How does it feel to be with her?"

"It feels peaceful. I'm not afraid to just follow her, I trust her."

Alison leaned back in her chair and reached for a glass of water, which she sipped quietly, before speaking.

"That life is done now, Shelley, and you can honor it. You did a great thing, but now you can let it go. Release all thoughts, feelings and associations with that experience as I bring you back up."

Shelley was silent for a moment before she replied, *"Yes."*

Alison took a deep breath, before counting Shelley back up in this space and time. She often felt that past life hypnosis sessions took more out of her than they did out of her clients. She pushed her chair backwards and away from Shelley's recliner, so she could stretch out her legs.

'Sam dies again?' she mused in disbelief. This kid must be a very advanced soul. Lifetime after lifetime he sacrifices himself in his role as 'brother' to serve the dynamic between these two girls. It was an intriguing case; the same soul group reincarnating together throughout time, playing out roles and scenarios for each other, always with the same brother, 'Sam'. But in every lifetime, Sam dies at 16, in tragic circumstances allowing the two sisters to work out their karma in the dynamic created between them by their brother's death. Thing was, they had the same brother this lifetime too, also called 'Sam', who was just coming up on his 16th Birthday.

Alison found it quite fascinating.

*　　*　　*

Her next client that same afternoon had the most uneventful past life she had ever encountered, bar one – in which the woman had been a lone goat herder in a past life somewhere in the Italian mountains in the 1930s. One day *he* – the goat herder – actually lay down on a small wooden bed until he died, because he was so bored.

Alison sympathized. This young man's past life was shaping up in a similar vein. He had been a milkman. He was married, with a child and yet absolutely nothing happened to him, at all, *ever*! He got up, had breakfast, went to work, delivered milk and went home. Though, after the drama of the morning session with Shelley, Alison was quite thankful to take a back seat for the rest of the afternoon.

As was usual towards the end of a past life session, Alison guided the boy through the death transition (he had also died in his sleep) and he rose up out of the physical body and began his journey back into the Spirit Realm where it was usual that he would be met by a Spirit Guide.

On being received into the Spirit world, most people go through orientation with their Guides first, then meet their Soul Group members – mums and dads, loved ones that have already passed on – before experiencing a life review in front of a council where their most recent incarnation is assessed. As a result of the sum of their experiences in that incarnation, they may graduate into a higher spiral of spiritual evolution.

Before the next incarnation is discussed, the newly deceased spend time acclimating as they continue to pass through various stages of reintegration into the Spirit world. They rest and recuperate undergoing healing, and then for some there are periods of re-education before preparing to return to Earth in another incarnated expression of Spirit.

Finally, they enter the screening room where they see a range of potential bodies in action on floor to ceiling screens showing their upcoming life's plan. According to the plan and therefore the incarnate's requirements, they select their new body, or 'vehicle', from four or five versions that have been deemed suitable for the task. These stages rarely varied from client to client.

However, in this case the young man was not met by a regular Spirit Guide, but instead described being met by Archangel Gabriel. As far as Alison knew, Archangels did not usually involve themselves in the affairs of men. Gabriel appeared to intercept the boy and instead of taking him through the usual gateways into the Spirit Realm, led him directly to a healing chamber, where he stayed for quite some time while his subtle bodies were realigned.

Every time Alison tried to question him, the boy simply said, *"I'm not ready."*

After a while, she asked him again, **"Are you still in the chamber?"** The clock was ticking, time was passing, and soon she would need to charge him for lying in the recliner and not much else.

Finally, he replied. *"Okay, I'm ready now."*

From the chamber, he was led by Gabriel to his own *ship*, which he compared to a kind of studio apartment in space. It was equipped with everything he needed, including his own portal, which could be used to deposit him back on his home planet of Orly. He described Orly in a matter of fact tone. It was close to the Central Sun, which, he said as if he were an expert, was where most life in the Universe exists. It is situated about half way between Earth and the other side of this Universe. But he said it was higher than the 'disc' of our system – meaning *the spiral galaxy.*

He described the planet as being mechanical right down to the planetary core, and made of pure gold. It was comprised of intricate machinery that morphed in size and shape to suit their purpose at any given moment. At this point in time, Orly was contracted to integrate the dimensions. When Alison asked what he meant, he said, *"We make sure everything in each dimension is synchronized exactly so that everything happens as and when it is meant to happen."*

He went on to explain that with the coming Shift in human consciousness on Earth, and because it was not possible for the machines of Orly to be replicated and assigned one to each individual person, there needed to be volunteers on the ground, Lightworkers, who could co-ordinate events from down here on Earth.

"Are you a Lightworker?" Alison asked.

"Yes. So are you."

Alison was taken by surprise. She hadn't seen herself that way.

He continued to explain that he was from the 12th Dimension. She asked if all Lightworkers were from the 12th, he said he didn't know. He had never discussed it with them. That made her smile. He told her he had no Karma left to work out here. That his lives on Earth were done and that he was close to knowing it all.

Now he was being given the choice to either stay in Spirit for a while, or return to Source and let Source (God, Prime Creator) choose his next experience. If he did that he would begin again as a 'new soul'. Then he corrected himself, *"That's not really an accurate description, I would start life on another thread in another universe, under a new set of universal laws."* Lastly, he could also choose to return to Earth as a Lightworker.

"What is Orly's involvement with Earth?" Alison thought it prudent to ask.

"There are five or more planets in your system about to ascend into higher dimensions. When the doom and gloom, *that the 'negativity' has planned for Earth, has begun, Orly will shoot a beam into the center of Earth and lift the planet closer to the Central Sun,"* he said.

Familiar with the esoteric teachings around the end of days and Ascension into higher frequencies, dimensions and states of being, Alison pushed him. **"What dimension will be we in then?"**

"The 5ᵗʰ," he answered calmly.

Alison sat in stunned silence by his reply. Then she continued, **"What do you choose?"**

"I choose to come back to Earth as a Lightworker, a volunteer to assist humanity's evolution."

This was intriguing. **"What will your role be?"**

Without hesitation he told her, *"To create new musical tones and harmonies. Music here will change dramatically. When a human hears a harmonic tone, it promotes a feeling that is relative, it is best that one positive uplifting note is followed by another positive harmonic and not a dissonant one."*

Alison didn't know what to say, so she sat quietly for a moment and considered. Anyway, the boy seemed to be pre-occupied.

After a long pause she picked up again where she left off, **"Where are you now?"**

"I am seated at a large round table before the Council."

"What Council?"

"It's not a grand council, just members of the Galactic Federation, what you would consider a local council of beings, all representatives of different planets. Some are amphibian, with luminous skin. All are beautiful". Then as if aside to himself, he said, *"Although if I had seen them on Earth first I may not have thought so."*

"Is Gabriel still with you?"

With his eyes still closed, he physically turned his head to his right as if trying to locate Gabriel's position and nodded affirmatively.

"What do the Council want from you?"

"I have been here several times before," he answered. *'The last time was about 2,000 years ago — before Jesus came.* He paused as though he was pondering something then said, *"People on Earth needed guidance then... just as they do now."*

Alison couldn't resist asking the 6-million-dollar question, **"Who was Jesus?"**

He turned his head slowly back to the right and appeared to be looking someone up and down.

"Looks like Gabriel", he said, "…but it isn't Gabriel. From Gabriel's realm though."

Alison had recently read somewhere in Judaic Christian teachings that there is a theory about Jesus having been seeded from the essences of several others, including Archangel Michael. So she flat out asked, **"Was it Michael?"** and waited to be struck dumb by a bolt of lightning.

There was a momentary pause, as though he were reviewing data of some kind, until he said definitively. *'Yes.'*

Several minutes passed, then he said he was being asked to go and see the body they had chosen for him. Alison was surprised. **"You mean you don't get to choose your body this time?"**

"No. They have chosen a body for me." He stated. "I have to be born in a specific location on the planet at a specific moment in time, and this body will suit me best. Human bodies are only calibrated for 96 years of life. This body is susceptible to the process of being triggered from the 2 strand to the 12 strand structure."

He was led into a room where he could view the holographic body/vehicle laying on a table. After another long pause, Alison again asked him what was happening? He said they were talking to him about his DNA.

"When will the 12 strand be triggered?" Alison asked.

"Now. It will happen gradually… Yours has already begun. We will start to receive our gifts; psychic ability, telepathy, teleportation, levitation - over time."

"WE?" Alison reiterated.

The timber of the boy's voice changed, *"You don't know who you are, do you?"*

The energy in the room shifted, Alison could feel the prickly tell-tale sensation of energy spreading over her back and shoulders. A little unnerved she demanded to know, **"Who *is* this?"**

"I AM Galadriel," said the voice, coming from the boy.

"Who are you? Where are you from?"

"I am Arcturan. I come from a small healing planet in the Bootes system."

Alison didn't answer. What was there to say?

The voice broke in, *"You are an elder, Alison, one of us. Do you understand?"*

Still nothing.

Galadriel continued, *"Listen to your heart, Alison. Your heart tells you the truth. You know many things but you deny them sometimes in your being. You doubt yourself and the existence of the strength, the core of the power of who you are and who you are meant to be. This is your initiation to Elderhood, Alison. Do you understand?"*

Spluttering, Alison managed to blurt out, **"Not really... an Elder of what? An Arcturan Elder?"**

"You have an incarnation as an Arcturan, yes. But it matters not if you are Arcturan, Pleiadian, Sirian, or another. Of course these things have relevance at this time, but you have been all of these things through your expression of Source over numerous lifetimes. We are talking beyond that.

"The Elders are the ones who know the 'truth'. They are drawn from all traditions, from all over the universe. There are many walking amongst you at this time on Earth. The Wisdom Keepers, men and women of the 'Cross'. Those of the 'Cross' are the ancient teachers of Jesus and the apostles and the mysteries of all traditions that carry the pole of truth in their hearts.

"The Cross is your symbol, Alison. Remember this."

She continued, *"You are an Elder, grandmother Alison. You carry the wisdom of the truth of the ages in your heart. People look to you for wisdom and guidance; sharing from their hearts and seeking understanding of the gifts and abilities that are awakening in them, from a deep, soulful, spiritual place. Look to them for guidance the way they look to you and you will understand, Alison.*

"You are the mystic master of the tribe, the one that sits on the Earth in front of the people and propels them forward on the journey of their lives."

Then she boomed a warning, *"But... KNOW who IS of your tribe... and who IS NOT! It is important for you to know and understand. Let them come to you as they will, and you will know they are family of your tribe when they arrive at your doorstep and sit at your feet, but remember Alison, to sit at their feet and heed no other but the word of God.*

"Many people will come to you in the near future and you must be ready, more ready than you are now."

Alison was getting very hot and kicked off her shoes. Galadriel seemed to know this.

"Yes, feel your feet, Alison. How long these feet have walked the planet, how many lifetimes? How many teachers? How many students? How many experiences? The ancient ones gave you these feet; you are at one with the ancient ones. Feel the energy all the way up your legs like the tree trunk, feel the grounded-ness. Believe, have no doubt have no fear."

The tone shifted as Galadriel continued.

"There is much fear manifested in this place, understand this is not karma to be cleared for yourself, do you understand? The karma is not yours to bear; you are like a soldier that goes into battle, to war. You have been chosen for a mission and a station by God. Understand this, it will help you to relax your mind and fall into your body, your Elderhood. Trust the slaying of the old bones. You do not need to hold on anymore to ideas of the past that belittle your experience or the vastness of who you are and who you are deemed by God to be."

There was quiet for a moment as Alison tried to process the information. Puzzled, her mind was filled with thoughts of being unworthy. Galadriel seemed to know her thoughts. *"You think karma is something that has to be worked through, to overcome; you think it means something negative needs to be addressed. So many others are limited by this belief. True karma is the karma of love, only love, Grandmother Alison.*

"You must act quickly; time is of the essence the river is running fast. Gather the women, there will be many, many, many of them. They will shed tears with their hearts breaking open and they will come to you and they will love you like you have never known love before on this planet."

Tears were welling up in Alison's eyes, the words were touching her somewhere very deep inside, as if turning over pebbles and stones laid there a long time ago. She felt Galadriel's energy begin to withdraw.

"We will be back, Alison. There are many, many others who want to sit around this table with you. It is a holy table - a sacred vessel. Do you understand this old, wise grandmother? Are you ready?"

"Yes," Alison mumbled. "Thank you." The energy receded and she took a few deep breaths. *'What the hell just happened?'* she thought to herself, grabbing a tissue from a box on the table she kept for her clients. She pulled herself together aware that the boy was still in trance.

As Alison counted him back up out of hypnosis and into this space and time, he opened his large, soulful brown eyes and looked up at her in silence, waiting for her to speak, as though he had heard everything that was said, and was gauging her reaction. Who was this boy? He was no average kid. He was ethereal to look at. Alison saw him once as he was walking in the street. She was reminded of a monk, it was as though his feet barely touched the ground. His shyness made him uncomfortable in his own skin and from what she knew of him, he lived alone and kept himself to himself. By all accounts he was a talented, alternative musician. He seemed a little socially awkward, but there was nothing about him to indicate to her that he was unusually imaginative, fanciful, or attention seeking – in fact, quite the opposite.

However, the likelihood was, this was merely the product of the fertile imagination of a lonely, misunderstood, attention-seeking boy. It made a great story and she applauded him for that! But any right-minded thinker would have to assume that late night gaming and the sci-fi channel may have played a big part in the creation of it. *'A psychotherapist could probably have a field day with this,'* she thought.

She was new to the concept of 'off worlders', but since becoming a hypnotherapist she had heard enough to know that there was much more to this world than she could see, and she understood there was a much greater purpose for our being here than most of us were aware of. It had led her to study esoteric writers like Blavatsky, Annie Besant and Ledbetter; The Ancient Wisdom, The Secret Doctrines, and now there were many aspects of metaphysics that she felt comfortable with. She believed it was important for personal development to retain an open mind. After all, she hadn't always believed in Angels, but now she couldn't deny them. They had taught her how to heal and assisted her in her work for the past two years. She didn't feel it would be right to say, *'Okay, I believe in Angels, but I don't believe in Aliens.'* What was the basis for that? She may not have experienced them yet… but she wasn't going to deny the possibility that they may exist.

Until fairly recently, her life had been dedicated to the more serious minded pursuit of happiness through the avaricious accrual of material belongings, which would of course eventually result in the illusions of success, and therefore equate to 'happiness'. But this belief system had been seriously challenged over recent years. Through her clients she had seen a different reality; a Spiritual realm of unconditional love and acceptance. Maybe it was her age, but this paradigm resonated more with her these days.

* * *

It was several weeks before her next Past Life session. This time with a girl who was unhappy following the break-up of her young marriage. Everything about the procedure was textbook. She went under hypnosis easily and began to recount a life in the 18th century, where she was forced to live on the outskirts of her village accused of being a 'witch'. The townspeople left her alone in the main, as she had a sister with family and children who lived among them. Sometimes she was called on as an herbalist, to heal a fever, or to be a midwife. She was very proud of how she had built her house into a mound of earth and moss. It was almost hidden from sight. It was excavated by hand and she had crafted utensils from clay, and the furniture had all been made from reclaimed wood from the forest where she foraged daily for berries, nuts and herbs. In this reality, the girl was very similar. She yearned for simplicity of life style that she was being steered away from by family and her new husband. She found the onslaught of modern day too overpowering. In the past life, she was trekking through undergrowth looking for a specific type of healing plant, when she stumbled and was impaled on an old branch. She bled out where she lay.

Instead of being met by a Guide, as was typical, this young woman went straight back to her space ship.

What can only be described as a benevolent ET, or Galactic Guide, entered the room where she lay in a healing chamber. When she came out he talked to her at length about her life.

Before the session ended, other voices began to break through and speak forcing an impromptu interview by Alison with a group describing themselves as 'highly advanced beings.' They claimed they had been trying to connect with humans who would be able to perceive them and receive their messages warning about the future of planet Earth.

Alison asked them to wait, while she struggled with the voice recorder and to her surprise, they agreed! When she was ready, she immediately asked, **"Are you Arcturan?"** Remembering the last words Galadriel had said, *'We will be back.'*

A calm measured voice began to speak very slowly at first, *"Today the information is coming from a Pleiadian source, but this connection is strong and you can easily speak with Arcturans or any other that you wish."*

Alison didn't say anything, she waited for them to finish.

"We are here to assist you. We come from many different places, worlds, and realms. Our future is linked to that of Earth and to all other planets in this system that are coming to Light."

"Are you here for this girl?" Alison enquired.

"No. Interest has been shown in you by outer circle beings, but you are under the full protection of all agreements and treaties of the Galactic Federation and you are gently handled."

Chapter 9

Hybrids

As a guest at the Pleiadian Round Table, Raffé Elohim observed Alison from the forward deck of the Second Tower Ship, somewhere in Earth's atmosphere.

The Council of Light had assembled and was communicating telepathically through an elected spokesman to an array of Galactic, and Celestial representatives, ET observers and affiliates of the Galactic Federation.

Raffé stood to address them. "As you can see," he said pointing briefly towards the holographic insert, "both of the Hybrid/humanoid incarnates are being moved into position.

"From the moment of their arrival in the Earth Matrix, each of them had been assimilating activated strands of DNA and memory implants in preparation to receive the knowledge of who they are, and take charge of their mission.

"The Pleiadians are in the process of recalibrating Hybrid I." He gestured to the holographic image of Alison's office. "The incarnate is being prepared to channel radio frequencies from the infrared system of space, for the creation of a new energy healing modality, called Marconics.

Marconics will act as the transducer for Ascension codes and upgrades to the body of the Human 2.0.'

"Hybrid II is being instructed by the Angelics on the conversion of geometric light frequencies for the expansion of the body's multi-dimensional holographic structure. Each of the Hybrids has garnered relevant experiences within the 3rd dimension during their human lifespan. These experiences will help them deliver this new healing modality on Earth in a way that can be received and accepted, within the traditions of this rather dense and historically hostile planet.

"Together, the two will assist us on the planet surface as we move forward with plans to intercept the evolutionary paths of other preprogramed Hybrid-Humans, or what they call, 'Lightworkers'."

"Earth Angels," chimed the Pleiadian spokesman, enamored of the romantic interpretations of humans.

Raffé smiled, "A simplified view, but, yes! Angelic humans. Blended essences incarnated in waves of time to be ready when called. They will impact Earth's reality matrix with enhanced fluid intelligence, to be able to traverse the dimensions and to create and support more benevolent timelines of probability for the future of this planet. They will also assist others eligible for Ascension who would otherwise be caught in timelines we are in the process of collapsing with the aim of steering the Earth ship away from ultimate catastrophe."

The spokesman interjected, "Are they already within acceptable ranges of vibration?" He was referring to the 'Earth Angels'.

Raffé continued. "Those with higher vibrations are still few. Lightworkers have long memories of persecution, torture and execution and remain predominantly in isolated communities. They are spread thinly across the planet and hidden in small pockets of higher frequencies in which they have either been born, or felt called to. This may explain why even after careful incubation and nurturing, the Light has not spread throughout the human collective as was hoped.

"The religions, though designed to be unifying, have created great separation. Love has filtered down into compartmentalized family units, in which humans place so much importance. The Light has not spread through the formal structures and institutions that govern and control.

The manipulation of humans by earlier invasion forces has been subtle and is total. The collective is immersed in the matrix of fear."

"Then, how do you propose to make a difference at this late stage in the game?" channeled the spokesman.

"With dispensation to relax the Free Will Zone that has limited inter-dimensional communication and intervention with humans to this point in their evolution. The Free Will Zone was implemented for the project's protection, but now it simply impedes our ability to assist. Re-classification of the Free Will Zone will, however, increase the need for expediency of the Closure and Reclamation Project as the planet will now be unprotected, and accessible to those outside the Federations, with less than benign agendas."

"You are looking for our protection?" asked the spokesman, prompted by the Ambassador for the Guardian Alliance."

Raffé turned his attention to the GA Delegate. "We will of course require and therefore respectfully request protection and Guardianship for the final phases, yes."

"This was anticipated and is confirmed," the chairman said with authority. Raffé nodded in gratitude to the GA Council and then continued.

"A healing modality has been fashioned and styled in a way that is familiar, appealing and acceptable to the human Lightworker lineages. They have evolved through local Earth traditions as healers and planetary custodians, deriving most of their knowledge from early ritualistic tribal and spiritual conceptual teachings." He drew up the holographic representation to view Alison more closely.

"Although Hybrid I receives information in a subtle manner and requires constant reassurance, she is quick to act on what she receives. She is demonstrating trust, though she waivers sometimes in her belief of her own abilities. Guidance teams are working with her to help shift her belief system. It is paced and the information is tempered to prevent her from rejecting us.

"Grace Elohim has been data streaming instructions to Hybrid I, for a protocol promoting the development of the Human 3.0 template. The incarnate is responding well to receiving and assimilating the upgrades to her own physical and subtle bodies, which are required to be able to anchor these higher frequencies on to the planet.

"We communicate with her by pulsing imagery, geometry, color and sound waves which evoke cell memory, promotes thought, and eventually feelings that she translates into action. The protocol Hybrid I is devising is invasive to the human energy field. It will release the human from the construct of earlier fear based programing with surgical precision. As Karmic debris is physically and etherically extracted, the being will be liberated from the density accrued in their energetic systems over numerous, consecutive lifetimes of abuse, pain and suffering.

"Through the system she is devising, Hybrid I will teach others to draw down Light encodings from the Adamik and Evik consciousness light streams, that we project to her. These will enable the remote triggering of upgrades that were originally pre-programmed into the Human 2.0 template."

The Council interjected, "You are jumping ahead with this rather ambitious plan, Raffé. You are assuming you can relinquish the old programs without destruction of the 2.0 vehicle."

Raffé leaned forward placing his hands on the table and began to speak with gravitas. "Much has been done in preparation for this time. For generations now, we have found ways to bypass the electromagnetic fields of the Free Will Zone. We funnel information and communications through established channels such as religion, science, psychology and spirituality to slowly awaken memory in the 'sleepers', and to activate 'the knowledge'. We have, over time, been introducing and enhancing technologies that will support humans in their evolution. We have even infiltrated a variety of pre-existing cultural avenues, such as art, literature, music and film over decades of linear time.

"The human mind has been prepared through exposure to the psychological concept of 'synchronicity', to be able to perceive messages and have them confirmed as a means of early communication with us. Once the Earth grid can be made fully operational and the first human energy fields are recalibrated, we will be able to establish direct forms of communication."

The Pleiadian spokesman voiced some of the concerns of those in attendance. "The wisdom must also be integrated by the incarnate before it can be allowed higher access and freedom to roam the multiverse. And this can only be achieved through authentic spiritual evolution. You are not suggesting we by-pass this stage of their development?"

Raffé's response was emphatic, "No." He paused and stood upright. "This requirement is understood. Knowledge can be accessed simply by opening a book, or watching a film, or from a teacher. Wisdom requires transformation of the human spirit. This will not be possible to imitate. The human incarnate must actively choose evolution and seek higher wisdom. Creation teams will pulse this information to those who have attained sufficient light quotients to understand the concept.

"Success in this area will only really be known once we have overcome certain constraints and aspects of their early human programming. It will eventually become more apparent if they are choosing light over dark.

"Once they begin integrations of Higher Soul energies, they will have to find balance on the scale between all aspects of their personalities. Through this process, matter particles and anti-matter particles will begin to emerge from the original karmic seeds which were planted thousands of years ago. If they cannot clear these old patterns they could fall either way on the path. They must choose to be allegiant.

"The true test will come at the earliest point of activation in the Human 2.0 template. Through that awakening, they will either implement their own genuine spiritual evolution or initiate their own destruction."

There was a pause, as all present seemed to consider Raffé's statement. How could it be that a singular human decision could have ramifications that could impact the entire multiverse?

Finally, the chairman asked, "So, what is the current status?"

Raffé moved towards the console. "Grace and Ariel will manipulate the timeline for the purpose of establishing a meeting between Hybrid I and Hybrid II, ensuring that they do not miss each other on the preferred time track." He inserted a small disc into the console and an interactive holographic image of Grace appeared.

She apologized for being unable to attend in person, and acknowledged all those present, before drawing their attention to a future nexus point, further along the Earth's time track.

"It seems that this timeline has been selected by Hybrid I." She announced. "We can see that by this point Hybrid I is already evangelizing and emitting a frequency that is calling to others programed to respond to this new and tailored energy – Marconics. She has managed to hone a protocol that is sufficient to be able to raise a sustainable vibration among the Lightworker populations who answer the call, and who receive the human upgrade.

"On this time track, Hybrid II is currently receiving downloaded packets of information regarding the structure for higher harmonic geometry in the post recalibration body. Unfortunately, the incarnate is currently unstable and is moving between two timelines, one of which will result in the inevitable termination of her current human expression. However, we are working to present options to her and it is hoped that she will settle on a timeline of compliance. It is believed that she can respond fully to the frequency of Marconics and that these two will choose to move forward together."

"If this is not the case?" inquired the spokesman.

Grace paused, "If Hybrid II chooses to exit the material plane then she will work from here, or from the Hyson ship, and we will prepare a human vessel to be an adequate channel for her, she can continue to work in partnership with Hybrid I."

Grace continued, "The next phase will involve the integration and merger of higher soul energies, into the prepared physical human vehicles. Each one assimilated from a higher harmonic bandwidth, and each introducing increased vibrations into the new template.

"Portals to other realities and moments in time will become accessible through the chakra system of the new 3.0 template connecting the human incarnate forward and backward through time to the memories and experiences of the Higher Self. This will cause 'nexus points' in the time space continuum – simultaneous 'Now' moments – that we can use as a bridge to deliver the upgrades inter-dimensionally within the holographic body.

"As the spin within the human 3.0 chakra system increases in speed, the biological vehicle will be raised up in entrainment to higher harmonic vibrations. This new configuration will enable the human body to naturally draw in and assimilate higher light frequencies emanating from the cosmos. Finally, they will evolve to be able to assimilate 5th dimensional electro-tonal frequencies from the lost portions of the Taran grid itself. Then they can re-assemble it within their DNA in readiness to move with the planet as the quantum separation of the 3rd and 5th Dimension is finally realized."

Chapter 10

Descent

Emotionally and physically drained, Alison threw back the covers and fell face down on her bed. Everything ached and she felt completely overwhelmed. She rolled on her back, stuck her feet up on the headboard and gazed up at the ceiling. She brought her hands up to her face and hid behind them, restfully. Then she began rubbing her tired eyes as if trying to relieve the intense pressure she felt building up behind them.

"If I stopped doing this right now, who would I really be letting down?' she thought as she got under the covers to sleep.

She had been receiving messages from the Pleiadians through clients under hypnosis, for months. The Human collective, they had told her, had already awakened to a new 5th Dimensional planet, on December 22, 2012. Humans now had the potential to Ascend into a full state of Consciousness. They had warned her back then that it marked the beginning of the real work towards personal Ascension and eventually the evolution of all humanity. It would be up to each individual to make the decision to ascend into higher vibrational states of being through the attainment of Spiritual mastery.

But Grace Elohim - architect of Project Earth, overseer of Marconics, and the designer of the Human Soul Carrier, was telling her that in most cases even the attainment of Spiritual Mastery wouldn't be enough.

Grace had explained to Alison in numerous channelings how this final attempt to take Earth to Light in a Grand Portal style Ascension, with everyone on board, would fail because of limitations existing within the physical body. The Human 2.0 Template had been so corrupted over time by digressive alien programming that it was now virtually impossible for DNA activations to occur organically. Many on Earth could not assimilate increasing waves of intensifying energies arriving on the planet to assist the Shift. Or, would simply be unable to transmute negative frequency and release themselves from being phase-locked within the 3rd dimension, to achieve true transfiguration. *The passage required by every species returning to the God state.*

Alison was being asked to accept her mission to develop a protocol that would release the human biological vehicle from the bonds of the Earth matrix. Her assignment carried implications far beyond her understanding.

As she dozed off a piece of lined notepaper, inclusive of a red margin, was thrust in her face. Written on it were the words:

1. *You don't have to do anything you don't want to do.*
2. *There are some things you may not need to know.*

Alison had spent most of the evening pressing Grace for answers, until finally she'd said, "It is not surprising that you have so many questions given who your Oversoul is..."

Alison had jumped in, "Who is it?" Grace shook her head from side to side and closed a book marked 'Secrets', as though Alison was not ready to hear the answer. But now, she was being asked to demonstrate the true measure of her faith, and 'commit' to her life's purpose. She worried that she had no idea what that actually meant.

"It is not our intention that you should translate the vibrations of love and encouragement that are being pulsed to you, as *anxiety*. Worry forces down your vibration and takes you further from us, not closer," soothed Grace.

"You cannot be forced to do anything you would not wish to do.

Neither are you judged or held responsible if you decide you must renegotiate your contract.

"We have laid before you several options. Which of them you ultimately choose to take up as your Sword of Truth, is still your choice to make. Whether you grasp the reigns and take control of your direction with more vigor and determination, or uncover a different destiny is up to you.

"We ask you to follow your heart and not to worry."

Alison felt herself relax momentarily. And then it came.

"But, if you do this, and it is seen along the time track that you will do this, it would not be possible for you to 'let us down'. We view the potentials of any timeline and we see what is optimal, but we understand that we must work with 'what is'. That is the gift of Free Will.

"Your commitment merely helps us to know how we can help you go forward in your soul's purpose and deliver Marconics to the wider world. We would not want you to feel uncomfortable in any way with our suggestions for you. We would rather that you define the rules yourself, according to what best serves you in the provision of Marconics. This is why we ask about commitment.

"We will help you move in any direction you choose, but it must be in a direction *you* choose from your *heart* and not from a place of fear. We urge you to trust yourself now, and stand fully in the power of who you came here to be."

Alison awoke slowly the next morning, with a song playing over and over in her head. She hummed it until she reached the chorus and remembered the lyrics. *'Give me reason, but don't give me choice… coz I'll just make the same mistake again.'* By James Blunt. She repeated it over and over.

Knowing they had meaning for her, she spoke the words aloud. "Give me *reason*."

Grace answered immediately, "The reason is that Humanity depends on the contributions made by the Lightworkers that will find their way to you."

Alison felt resigned more than committed. She sighed.

Grace continued, "Planetary alignments are necessary for success and will not be in place for long.

"We would prefer that people were not led to believe they had all the time in the world for this, as it would most certainly prevent them from making immediate effort. But the truth is, everything becomes so retrospectively. It is already done! Every timeline is played out. It matters only which timeline you align with as others are shut down. Does that make sense to you?"

Alison nodded, assuming Grace could see her. She felt pressure, though not pressured. It sounded like a lonely road and she felt as though it had always been so for her, over many, many previous lifetimes.

Grace could feel her sadness. She said softly, "Someone is being prepared for you, Alison. You asked for someone to be your companion and witness this journey.

"We understand how hard it has been for you, struggling with the demands of the 3rd Dimension in terms of how you have negotiated your way through the turbulent waters of commerce and industry in your world. You have learned that you need to protect yourself as well as the work, and as custodian of Marconics you cannot surrender the reigns. You have been chosen because of your experience and talents both here and in other worlds and because of your ability to traverse the dimensions.

"You can bring gravity to the mission that others cannot. You can see the wolf in the trees; you can prepare, and you can protect. Others will not see the pitfalls; your more pragmatic Elohim nature will allow you to see a myriad of colors that are invisible to them.

"Marconics goes forward in your vision, in your name. You *are* Marconics on this plane.

"To ease the path, we have prepared a companion for you; a friend and an ally. She is waiting. And she will come forward, if invited, to provide the love and support that you have so lacked in this lifetime. She has the ability to share your vision with a lightness of ego and she will follow you with commitment and loyalty.

"You must be the mason, the builder; pour the foundations and construct the temple. She will help you fill the temple with light. Without the temple, the Light could not be contained; it could not be focused and would only be defuse and formless.

"You throw the clay and mold the pot. She will fill the pot with water."

Alison knew exactly whom Grace was referring to. Lisa was a Level III practitioner, Alison's student. The two women had hit it off immediately and Alison did not generally enjoy the company of women. But there was honesty and integrity in Lisa that Alison valued. Recent experiences had taught her not to trust anyone. But Lisa was the only other person Alison had met who even spoke the language. They shared the same brand of humor and she could make Alison laugh! She wanted to trust her. Anyway, she was getting the distinct feeling that she was going to have to trust someone soon. Grace was right. She would need someone by her side.

Grace changed the subject. "We urge you to employ balance in your life, Alison, and we know that you have felt lately that you have lacked this in some way. Do what makes you happy. It is a long enough road and there is no need to make it seem any longer."

Like so many Lightworkers, the material realm had lost its attraction for Alison. The Pleiadians had called this feeling of neutrality a necessary by-product of Ascension preparation. She felt done with her experiences here. Yet she sensed she was just about to accept a lengthy assignment on outpost Earth.

She understood that the Marconics healing protocol she had received from Grace would not only free the Human 2.0 from its enforced limitations, it would upgrade the human body allowing it to evolve into a new type of Being altogether; one that could thrive in the challenging frequencies of the Higher Realms. Human 3.0 would be a Hybrid species, a blend of the best of the human experience with Higher Soul aspects of Divinity.

Marconics protocols had been purposed to recalibrate the human body, which, like a finely tuned precision instrument, must be re-tasked to be able to perform and thrive in conditions beyond its original design.

The protocols were beautiful and harmonious, she loved performing them and her clients were experiencing immediate results. Practitioner training classes were also gathering momentum as the modality was beginning to expand rapidly. But Alison felt there was so much more she needed to know and understand.

"Can you tell me more about Marconics?" she asked, as though about to close a deal on a Buick.

Grace said, "Understanding the intricacies of Marconics at this stage is not necessary as it is highly complex and would be almost impossible to explain to you fully. As you are becoming aware, it is multi-layered.

Marconics ripples through the time space continuum, it does not simply occur in your space but also forward and backward through time, and down through the lineage of your own DNA. We can see the story of Marconics as it reaches into the future and it is vast. It would be difficult, if not impossible, for your linear mind to conceive of this. Feel it! That is the only way you will be able to understand the higher concepts of which we speak at this time.

"Listen now, take what you can and leave the rest for another time.

"You are in the process of creating an advanced race of beings, those who will forge the road ahead for *all* others. Not just in this matrix, but throughout the multiverse. This is not to be taken lightly. The truth is not as many imagine, and it will soon be necessary to make it more widely known.

"You must prepare the Lightworkers to step up to provide the knowledge and assist in promoting what is 'truth' in an atmosphere of turmoil and mistrust. These new and advanced beings are already presenting themselves to you as individuals who can quickly discern simply by feeling what is true and what is deceiving. This is a talent which we will say in time will be necessary for the survival of humanity."

* * *

That night, Alison's hands were hot and itchy and raw from her persistent scratching. They flared up whenever she data streamed Grace, and now her inflamed palms were peppered in a raised, angry, rash.

No matter how long she immersed them in bowls of iced water they continued to burn. First the skin would peel off and her fingerprints would disappear. Then fresh new skin would form, but like fine raw silk it would tear whenever she touched anything. She was plastered in lotions and wore cotton gloves to sleep in, so the cream would have a chance to salve the skin. She knew she shouldn't, but there was some guilty pleasure in the moments of scratching at the insatiable itch.

It was still dark outside and Alison was tired. She had to be up at 6:00am to be sure of getting in the shower first, and class was due to begin at 9:00am. She still had no idea of the theme of the lecture. They rarely told her in advance these days. Maybe because she sometimes overruled them, refusing to say some of the things they had urged her to say, in front of a class of beginners. Now, it was as if they just pushed her out on stage and surprised her as much as they did everyone else. Maybe it was better this way, she thought. It relieved her of the responsibility she felt sometimes, as it meant she had little or no control over whether she upset anyone. She had come to trust that whatever was said – whether she or anyone else judged it as extreme – had in that moment needed to be heard by someone.

The itching was driving her mad. The skin was so broken now and her hands visibly swollen, yet she still couldn't stop scratching! When she looked at the clock it was 4:30am. *'Another broken night,'* she thought. She lifted herself out of bed and plopped down on the chair nearby. Her face crumpled as she let her body slump forward in the seat, her shoulders hunched. She felt pathetic.

"I can't do this anymore," she mumbled, as the tears welled up in her eyes. "Can you hear me?" She said lifting her face to look at the ceiling, though for what purpose she didn't quite know. "Hey! Did you hear me? I said I can't do this anymore!"

A blinking light appeared on the dashboard of the console and Gabriel motioned to Raffé. He pulled up the hologram and they watched as Hybrid I sat sobbing in the dimly lit room staring up at the ceiling. "What is she doing?" Raffé asked in puzzlement.

"Why have you left me like this?" she whined pitifully. She imagined that someone, somewhere was at least monitoring her condition. Where were they now? She imagined them huddled around a water cooler talking about the latest reality T.V. show, and grumbling about what a pain in the ass she was. Holding her hands up as if she was being viewed through an invisible camera, she shouted, "You can't just walk away and leave me like this! Look at these!! I know you can do something. I demand that you do something!" Then she gave in to self-pity and sobbed some more.

"Why is she talking to the ceiling?" Raffé asked confused.

"When humans think of us, they assume we must be... 'up'," Gabriel stifled a chuckle.

She finally stumbled back into bed and got a little more sleep. As she surfaced the next morning, an image was forming behind her eyes. It looked like a schematic showing the outline of what looked like an elongated 'laser gun', with a beam of energy shooting out of the muzzle. Underneath it were written the words, 'Resuming Frequency Modulation'. Not sure what it meant she looked up the definition of in the dictionary. It seemed they had split the beam.

Alison felt immense relief, although everyone else in the house was now scratching and burning. She knew it was only a temporary cessation, but she felt happy because they had heard her and they had acted to ease her discomfort.

* * *

Grace watched in silence. Raffé waited for her to speak. He knew what she was thinking and he thought it was too soon.

She waved a luminous hand and the hologram turned 30 degrees, with another hand she drew in a closer image of the incarnate. Beside it, binary code ran like water down an invisible screen. "We are unable to stabilize." she concluded. Grace pre-empted the assembled Council's verdict by stating first, "There will be no withdrawal. She is the only one remotely ready. We follow this one to its conclusion."

"You are too fond of her," Raffé said. Then he whispered, "Why is that? Because she is least like you?" He was trying to rile her.

She whispered back, "Because she is most like I used to be."

She observed the holographic record and summarized her assessment. "Her access is high. She is pulling down the energy, but is not isolating it, not grounding it. She's taking in too much radiation. If we don't do something she will simply 'fry'."

"You have seven others prepared-" began the Sirian delegate.

Grace cut him off, "They are not my incarnate; they are vessels. If we are forced to use vessels we have missed the purpose of this mission."

Raffé stepped forward and began to offer an alternative solution. "We could still-"

"We would be trampling their free will. I won't do it!" She snapped. She had raised her voice at a round table gathering. She stood up and began to pace. "Anyway," she said slowly, "the incarnate has agreed."

The delegation sat silently as Hybrid I curled up on the chair in a room, in a rented house, miles from her own home and began to sob.

"She is certainly dedicated," noted the Pleiadian chairman.

"But she is not yet fully committed," asserted Raffé.

"Grace, you must not consider a merger when the incarnate could still choose not to pursue this any further. You know what you risk."

Grace looked directly at him and he could see she was already decided. The Council agreed unanimously and took their leave. As Grace left the great hall, Raffé followed her through the obsidian halls of her ship.

"Grace, you are exposing yourself." He gestured to one of the Seraphiam Guards, "Find Ariel!" Then he stepped directly into Grace's path and halted her procession. "You need her, Grace. You will need Seraphiam protection." Grace laid her hand gently on the Sirian leather breastplate of her most trusted Adjutant General and with her finger she traced the outline of her own insignia embossed there. The energy of her touch in that moment was poignant for them both. It spoke of many missions and reaffirmed the allegiance between them, a trust that could never be broken.

Softly conceding she said, "Yes, I do need her down there."

Then she drew herself to full height so he would be in no doubt of where she stood. "However, I will go in alone and if I am successful in stabilizing my incarnate then maybe Ariel can do something to prevent further deterioration in the biological vehicle of the other one. There is no point in risking Ariel if I cannot repair the damage here."

Raffé pressed his hand into hers and they melded together. Looking into her eyes, so that she would hear him, he said, "You know that if you do this and she alters her position, I cannot retrieve you without terminating her?"

Grace allowed herself to be held by his gaze for a tender moment, before acknowledging him with a nod.

* * *

Alison felt her eyelids grow heavy, she needed to close them. She could feel the leadenness of her physical body as she moved across the room towards her bedroom. She knew the intensifying pitch in her left ear was frequency, a precursor to communications she would need to be 'put down' to receive.

It was 2pm in the afternoon but there was nothing demanding of her time, so she lay on her bed. It was no sooner had her head touched the pillow when she could see Grace's face. It was as if she was looking through the mirror in the large marble-tiled bathroom she had enjoyed during their recent trip to Florida. She was standing on one-side of the mirror looking in, but instead of seeing her own reflection in it she saw Grace; tall and athletic, with large, beautiful pale blue eyes, and thick, long, blond hair falling around her shoulders. It had a wave in it that would have made Alison's grandmother proud. Grace seemed to be everything Alison was not.

As if picking up on the thoughts of her incarnate, Grace smiled and said, "Then that would make you everything that I am not."

"We are concerned for you, Alison. Your hands, your body... We must stabilize your vehicle before it burns out."

Alison held her hands out and turned them over. Her fingers were like overstuffed sausages, fit to burst, they began to split open as she watched.

Grace continued. "It is early, we had not planned to do this yet, but I will have to come in."

"In?" said Alison, a little alarmed by the phrase. *"What do you mean, 'in'? In where...in me?"*

"Yes."

Alison voice rose a little higher. *"Like a walk-in"?*

Grace seemed puzzled. "No, Alison, not a 'walk-in'. A 'walk-in' happens only when a host body is used by another energy, in a contracted takeover of the vehicle. An exchange, where the original occupant vacates and returns to Spirit. Though it can also be used to describe the invasion of the body by another entity, but that would cause damage to the DNA in both the host, and the 'walk-in'. This is NOT *that.* You are ME! I am you! There is no discrepancy in the frequency between us."

"But you would take over from me?" Alison needed clarification

"No, I would exist alongside you, a deposit of my energy will stay with you.

"Well where will you be?

"I am everywhere... just like you. Alison, I need to come in so I can begin to balance the energy in your body."

'Oh, no, this didn't sound good,' Alison thought, all her fears rushing forward at once. Was Grace finally revealing herself? Was she being

manipulated to comply with some sort of body snatching agenda? It had always been at the back of Alison's mind. She had often asked herself, *'What if...?'* What if she had been so gullible as to swallow everything she had been told by an avaricious alien race, because her ego was so desperate for love and acceptance and the need to believe that there was something more? What if she had been sold a bill of goods only to find she had in fact ransomed humanity? Was this the beginning of a silent invasion that she had held the gate wide open for?

All she could think of to say was, *"Will it hurt?"*

Grace appeared to bristle. There was a pause before she responded, "Do you know what an honor this is?"

Alison thought about it. How could she know? *"No, not really..."* she replied.

Grace chose not to expand on the concept in that moment and said only, "There are others that were prepared for this time. I have chosen you instead of taking a vessel, a being of close vibration that would agree to hold my energy. This integration of you and I would be preferable. I will come in and we will take Marconics forward together."

Alison didn't answer.

After a few moments, Grace asked, "Would you like to be able to improve your vision?"

"Oh, resorting to bribery now, like I'm a child or something," Alison pouted. Then laughing at herself, she said, "Yes, please."

"Can I lose weight too?"

Grace smiled and shook her head, "No."

'What a ridiculous conversation to be having with a reflection in a mirror while you're sleeping,' Alison thought and was immediately struck by how unusual it was to be lucid in a dream and aware that she was asleep at the same time! Examining her hands, she mused over whether she really had a choice? Of course, she could say, 'No.' Then what? If she turned her back on it all could she really go back to being the person she was? Does that ever work?

Grace spoke like a salesman closing a deal. "You have been heard, Alison. We will make the integration as gentle as possible."

"When?"

"It will be within the next few weeks".

"How will I know when you are in?"
Grace smiled, "Your hands will be healed." She said.

*   *   *

One afternoon, a couple of weeks later, Alison felt her self being put down. She could feel the energy of the Galactic Federation heavy, with an almost audible rushing sensation, like white water rapids carving a path through her head and body. She was flashed a brief image of Grace, decked out in the kind of gear you would expect a news correspondent to wear entering a war zone; a khaki vest, with lots of pockets, over desert battle fatigues and a pair of heavy looking lace-up boots standing with a Desert Storm style backpack at her feet. Alison looked into a mirror and saw Grace's reflection, as she braided her long, thick, blond colored hair like she meant business.

In the next moment, Grace's energy began to enter Alison's body starting at the crown of her head. Warm and fluid it began to pour in filling every part of her as it spiraled down towards her feet. When it reached her legs, she felt them lift and rise, as if Grace were putting her on like a pair of tight jeans. Grace's energy circled around her, light and frothy!

"Grace, is that you?" Alison whispered. The energy seemed to increase like a wind blowing through the trees in confirmation. "Happy Birthday, Grace!" Alison greeted, excitedly. "Are you comfortable?" The energy rose and fell again, like breath in her.

She wanted to stay in the moment and at first didn't want to open her eyes to peek. Eventually she tried to rouse herself as she thought she heard footsteps enter the house and walk directly into her room. She found she couldn't move.

"Chris? Is that you?" she called to her husband, but the sound escaped her lips like a whisper. Chris didn't respond. "You have to tell me if it's you, I can't see!" She murmured. Still he didn't answer and she so wanted to tell him Grace had arrived!

Alison fell into a deep sleep and traveled. She spent time in a house that wasn't her own. The furnishings were dated, very seventies, with lots of gold, floral fabrics. There was even a gold candlewick bedspread on the bed. *'Grace loves gold,'* she thought, remembering Grace had said they had been together in other lifetimes, was this one? It felt so real. She picked things up and felt them in her hands, determined to remember she had been there.

Alison suddenly became aware of *being* Grace, and knowing they had done this before. She remembered instructing others on how to integrate and anchor themselves safely in a humanoid body, after transit and on the planet surface. How to access and modify the DNA from within, adjust and recalibrate the energy bodies and entrain them vibrationally with the incoming frequency, so as not to destroy them.

The scene shifted and she saw herself at Grace's desk opening and closing files. She felt a deep sense of hope as though success was imminent. The files she was viewing were dispatches from the ground crews newly arrived on the planet's surface. They contained status updates informing her of the locations of military style installations and mobile units. All units were safe and fully operational, all carrying her orders, all were eager to complete them and come home. These were 'the boots on the ground', but this was not Earth.

The scene switched again, and from a vantage point across a vast desert landscape, she saw the panoramic view of a beautiful, thriving city suddenly be obscured by a huge explosion, and the 'shimmer' of atomic collapse. It startled her.

"For I AM" came the words,

> *"So do not fear for I am with you, do not be dismayed,*
> *I will strengthen you and uphold you with my righteous hand.*
>
> *Grace... Also existing in you as a virtue."*

Alison watched as a white peace dove carrying a wreath flew in, landed, and placed it down in front of her. It nudged it towards her and stepped away... She fell deeply asleep.

When she began to surface again the sun had already gone down. She lay for a moment in the dimly lit room, wondering if what she thought had just happened really had. The energy in the room shifted again and a woman's voice said, "Do not move."

Alison replied in a quiet voice, "I won't."

She felt hands move under her body, which rolled her onto one side, almost tipping her out of bed. Then she was rolled back to the other side and was held in suspension for a moment. After rolling on to her back, her knees were brought up to her chest and she was rocked back and forth repeatedly. She knew that whatever they were doing was helping her assimilate Grace's energy, and she felt loved and cherished, and even heard herself laughing with them.

They showed her an MRI type, scanned image of her body. There was a highlighted patch on her left hip, which flashed in red several times to indicate there was some kind of problem. The rocking motion seemed to solve it. Next, she focused in on her right shoulder blade, where there was a computer graphic of an upload panel, which she observed as the installation bar went from 0% to 90%.

"Breathe," she heard, and she took a long deep breath in.

"Blow out," the voice instructed, so she blew out until she could see multiple download panels, in different colors, all moving like stages in an installation package, until they all recorded 100% complete.

She waited for a moment before drawing their attention to her immediate discomfort. "I am experiencing some strange vibrations in my feet and legs and some pain in my mid-back."

Hearing a voice as if it were her own, it said, *"It is simply an upgrade of you own universal matrix. You have invited another level of recalibration, which is undergoing at this time. I need time to integrate fully into your biological system. It will seem sometimes to have recognizable traits of earlier systemic damage that you have experienced in the past, but it is simply that the same pathways have been used to upgrade as have been routes to damage and illness in the past."*

"What is the vibration in my feet?"

"It is a current of energy that is going to ground. It is delivering the frequency that is required to initiate targeted healing."

"It's in my spine, too."

"Yes, it is to enable the correct configuration of DNA in an area that was damaged through injury and compounded by poor healing."

"Will it go on for long?"

"Not long, no longer than is necessary."

After a short pause, Alison asked, "Am I okay?"

"Yes, Alison, we are fine. Sleep now."

Chapter 11

State of Grace

G race's State Rooms were minimalistic. Alison liked to be surrounded by 'stuff', so she was surprised to find them quite comfortable.

She had first viewed them in meditation, as if she was looking at them through the end of a long spyglass. She felt a strange rushing sensation and it seemed she had been delivered into the room itself. Grace had seemed as excited as Alison was.

"So, yes, exciting adventures for you!" she said. "You can be sure you are not just 'sleeping' any more. You are busy, busy, busy! As you become more conscious of your multi-dimensional nature you will be having multiple, simultaneous experiences. You will be everywhere at once!"

Seeing Alison's eyebrows raise as she smiled and nodded, and said 'Right' in a 'too high' voice, Grace realized this may be a little too much for the human brain to decipher in density. "You may find that you will remember fewer of your dreams," she gently warned.

"You will travel very far and you must pay greater attention to grounding back into your body on your return. Make notes of all the experiences you can while you remember them. It won't be long before you are able to fully shift into conscious multidimensional travel at will."

That sounding appealing to Alison and she tried to take in every minute detail as she looked around. It seemed there were no boundaries, no walls, although everything was within her field of vision. Along one side of what she could only describe as a living area, there were shelves of stunning crystals, artifacts and minerals. Grace pulsed, *'One from each planet in this sub-sector.'*

She described them with affection, like one might speak about their dog or cat. They were all planetary record keepers and each one of them contained within them the story of an entire species – their anthropological, natural and sociological history – the DNA of their planet of origin. Grace could entrain her frequency to the individual vibration of each crystal, and her consciousness could enter the crystalline matrix where she could access the records, and the crystals would share their stories with her. To Alison it seemed rather like having a library of talking reference books, like DVDs. 'The Natural World', by the BBC, Alison thought.

She followed Grace as they passed through a fluid membrane, or partition of some sort, and entered into another area, which by contrast was more clinical. Grace asked if Alison was hungry. Even though she wasn't, she really wanted to see what passed for food up there.

Once, she had successfully managed to place her consciousness up on the Second Tower Pleiadian Ship that she had been connecting to through hypnosis. Since then they had teased her about her persistent search for the canteen, a good cuppa and some cake.

Grace placed her slender, luminous hand over a round disc-shaped plate, and moments later something that looked sort of like a chocolate chip cookie appeared. Not sure she actually wanted to eat it, Alison distracted Grace with a question about the gadget, "What does it do?"

Without speaking, Grace planted in Alison's mind the knowledge of it, as though she had always used one. *'This is a replicator.'* It could copy anything organic or recreate a psychic impression of an experience held in her mind. It replicated vegetables by using the nutrients from the soil of the planet and entirely by-passed the growing process. Grace could hold the image of food she had sampled anywhere in the Galaxy, keeping in mind the memory of its taste and flavor, and the experience could be replicated.

Grace didn't need food, though when she was in a matter body – it was better to sustain it with nutrients this way, and she enjoyed it. Collecting food was like a hobby. Alison smiled, she could get behind a hobby like that.

Grace led Alison deeper into the ship, which opened up into a large rotunda. It was very bright and Alison struggled to see. Above them seemed to hang a strange configuration of dangling metallic looking discs of various sizes; some flattened on one side and others with convex surfaces. All appeared to be coated to reflect small amounts of rainbow light. Grace pulsed that she could program these to project a holographic representation of any place in space or time that she chose. By entering the hologram, she could place herself in the physical experience, as if it were reality. Grace purposed it to help her acclimatize to certain environmental conditions she might expect to encounter on a new world.

"A holographic deck!?!" Alison shrieked, excitedly

"Yes."

"Like the library?" Alison had experienced one before on the Pleiadian ship.

"Would you like to see the library?" Grace asked her. They were immediately transported to a huge, open atrium and appeared to be floating up through the middle of it; higher and higher, passing floor after floor of endless shelving spinning off from the center like layered spokes from the hub of a wheel. She could see beings that appeared to be at workstations in balconies that hung suspended over the atrium on each floor. Then as if with the flick of a switch, they were back in Grace's rooms.

Grace didn't sleep, but she would recharge her energy field and repair cellular damage in her current vehicle while suspended in a conductive liquid crystalline substance she called 'Bioplasma.' She described it as 'the Source of all life'. When submerged in it she could tap into and meld with universal consciousness. In that connected state, she could also bio-relocate at will, leave the ship and arrive anywhere that had the technology to receive her, instantaneously. While in a denser, more matter based, physical soul carrier, she required a Matter Transfer Terminal which would quite literally transfer the biological vehicle like a file, by breaking it down into bytes and reassembling it in another location.

The ability to access the Universal Akasha from her State Rooms, rather than from the master deck, gave her more privacy. She could view any point in time like a movie and enter it via the hologram for the experience. Though under Universal Law she must not intervene without pre-agreement, but there was much that could be learned by viewing an event as it unfolded before her as an unseen observer. If there was something that could be adjusted on the time track, which would avert a less than benevolent outcome, without unraveling the timeline itself, permission could be sought to intercept the timeline at a point on the continuum just prior to the event and change the outcome. The original timeline would always exist, that was the law. But an alternative timeline and even dimension could be created for a more benevolent experience.

Grace would scan through the Akashic Records like one might flick through the pages of a magazine. During one of these 'scrubbing' sessions, she stumbled across the evacuation of Thoth from Tara. He escaped the devastation, stepping through the Falcon Star Gate in Halls of Amenti. She tracked him as he entered Earth's local galactic sector. The Star Gate misfired, causing him to overshoot the time coordinates missing the arrival of the Egyptian Pantheon and army of volunteers who had settled the new civilization.

She had fast-forwarded along the timeline until finally, before the recall of the Pantheon, she had watched him bury something deep beneath the construction of the Sphinx.

*   *   *

At the end of Alison's tour Grace asked, "Would you like to meet Ashtar?" Alison grinned. A moment later they appeared as one being, on the deck of the Hyson ship, a coalition laboratory defended by the Ashtar Command fleet.

It was a heavier density on board than Grace remembered. She took a moment to re-particulate, taking advantage of the lower vibrations provided by the ship's gravitational field. She merged with Alison's consciousness and Alison continued to observe through Grace's eyes.

Ariel and Commander Sheran where waiting to greet them both. They were smiling as though they had just shared an amusing story. Ashtar himself was a hybrid, created from the blended essences of selected Angelics, along with DNA contributions from humans who had succeeded in achieving mastery over their own physicality; similar to the man called Jesus, who had ascended beyond the Earth matrix and into the 5th Dimension with his physical body. Ashtar was a prototype of the new Human 3.0 and was designed to be pleasing to the human eye. In the event of First Contact, he would be the intermediary with Earth, the liaison between Humans and the Galactic Federations.

Ariel felt that he represented Grace's finest work. She was very enamored of his sparkling blue eyes, dirty, blonde shoulder length hair and chiseled jawline. He had certainly developed a more pleasing arrangement of features than some of the other hybrids Grace had created.

Ashtar was keen to draw Grace's attention to the new DNA delivery system he had been working on, and gestured with his hand in the direction of an annex to the main lab. On Grace's instruction he had developed a method of achieving DNA upgrades in even the most digressive and damaged of human systems, which he described as 'Symbiotic Grafting.'

Swimming in a large crystal tank, filled with bio-plasmic fluid, were hundreds of what looked like little bioluminescent creatures. Each measured about an inch-and-a half long; they were thin, with rows of short tentacles running along the shaft of their cylindrical bodies. They reminded her of a sea anemone. Alison flinched, and Ashtar pulsed her that these were benign symbiotes designed specifically for the enhancement of Human DNA.

The 'feelers' moved independently of one another like probing fingers, searching until one tendril found the corresponding one, in another, before sealing to form what looked like a multi-dimensional representation of a double helix configuration. They were conscious and Grace could hear them communicating.

Grace shared her memory with Alison of a time early in the history of Free Will Universe One, during the Lyran Wars. The Anahazi were blending and creating strains to counteract the darkness that was prevailing. Grace's incarnate, a young officer of the fleet, had been instructed to destroy banks of blended essences that were seen along the time tracks to have developed in less than benevolent ways and would be the cause of great suffering. The conscious essences were stored in small cubes that had a consistency similar to that of soap. She had felt their distress as she crushed just one between her hands. After that, she refused to continue and in doing so she went against Divine directive.

Alison knew that this would be like becoming a conscientious objector. Even though there is no punishment for making that choice, stepping out of alignment with Divine Will, is how a *Being* becomes 'Fallen'.

Ariel stood at Ashtar's shoulder while he lifted several active strains out of the tank and handed them to her. They held them gently in the palms of their hands while he explained how these creatures would be the carriers of genetic information.

When introduced into the blood stream of a biological entity they would swim through the vascular system undetected, until reaching the base of the brain stem, where they could affix themselves using 'feelers' or tendrils, which would wrap around the delicate nerves of the spinal synapsis, creating a ganglion. The symbiotes would slowly release deoxyribonucleic acid, which would be absorbed into the intricate structure of arteries and nerves over time, and then begin to replicate, designing new protein coding sequences within existing DNA.

"How do you propose to administer these?" Grace asked, taking one from him as gently as if she was handling a piece of spun class.

New rules had deferred all visits to the planet surface since an unfortunate episode involving a species of Grey. An E.T. who had, while collecting soil samples on Earth, happened upon a party of campers in the Russian mountains with catastrophic results and the untimely death of every member of the party through exposure to radiation. The news of this close encounter had echoed around the world thanks to the upgrade in communications, and had been the cause of much renewed fear among the human population.

Ashtar placed the creatures back in the tank. "Initial activations have begun in the human ground crew," he explained. "The Lightworker volunteers; healers, psychics and mediums, who are carrying the necessary encodings within them, are already accessing higher dimensions of sleep. We are able to intercept them there, and work with them to prepare them as intermediaries for us in the Astral Realms. But until the gravitational speed of the planet can be increased through the activations of the Crystalline Grid, even they will not be able to access the 5th Dimensional eletro-tonal frequencies. They will still need further intervention to draw up and assimilate new DNA strands themselves."

Alison was already imagining one of these things crawling in her spine and felt herself start to 'flicker' in and out. The Commander was still talking.

"As these Lightworkers master higher frequencies and upgrades within the biological vehicle, they will be able to function as a bridge between the dimensions that separate us and enable us to reach the wider population. With their agreement, we can access those who can maintain higher vibrations for intervention using the field of manifestation that lies between the Morphogenetic Field and the matter realm."

'Is that the Partiki Grid?' Alison thought.

Though Grace seemed pleased with the simplicity of the system, Alison's thoughts became distracting as she began to question how many other times the Galactics had intervened in this way to enhance the DNA of a species. Grace told her this wasn't even the first time they had intervened on Earth. She was shocked but was coming to understand that this was nothing new; it had always been this way.

The Pleiadians had told her that many had been on a hospital ship at some time or another to receive upgrades. For some reason it made her think of the 'tooth fairy' and Father Christmas; the two times when children shouldn't mind who appeared in their bedrooms.

Grace felt the spike in Alison's brain activity break their psychic connection, and Alison began to surface from sleep back home in her bed. *'Is this why some people carry such suppressed memories of alien abduction?'* she kept thinking. *'Didn't they know that the fact that it was suppressed is what made the surfacing memory so traumatic? Couldn't they just come clean with humans and tell them the truth?'*

Grace and Alison had discussed this subject before. Grace had tried to explain why it was necessary to keep the truth about Human origins a secret from the Humans. She would say, "You wouldn't let your child watch an adult movie, because you would never expose them to something that wasn't age appropriate. When viewed through the prism of expanded consciousness, Humans are not ready to know the truth of who they are or how they came to be. So higher truth is carefully hidden until they have advanced enough to be able to hold the knowledge. It has been embedded in esoteric mysteries and secular scriptures, or labeled as 'myth' or 'fantasy', or locked in the vaults of the Vatican, or protected by Secret Societies. All of which Humans, in their child like way of fearing anything they don't understand, have also demonized."

Grace gave another analogy knowing how much Alison enjoyed them. "Imagine trying to explain to a fish that above him, though out of his element, in another dimension and therefore state of being - but still occupying the same space - lived tall, multi-colored, bipedal giants, with large skeletons covered in flesh, dry skin and hair, that walk on land and communicate through speech. Then explain that what sustains these alien beings is the very thing that is most poisonous to the fish. Oxygen. Oh, yes, that and a diet of fresh fish!

"What purpose would it serve? The fish has enough to contend with just surviving in water polluted by this alien species, and trying to avoid being caught in the mouth of a larger fish. How would he be able to fully focus on the experience of being a fish, with this knowledge? Until he sprouts legs, and climbs up on the muddy bank, no purpose is served by explaining what awaits him in the higher dimensions.

"The same may be said for humans. It may do more good for you to focus on what is going on in your own dimension. There may be something you can do about that. We could predict that the markets will crash, that war will be declared, that the particle collider in Cern may cause a rip in the fabric of time, or that the Pope's visit to the US heralds the fall of humanity.

"You have read and have heard that all of these predictions are possible, even probable. They all exist. They have in fact already happened, which is why it is possible to make the prediction in the first place.

"We know you struggle with being able to visualize how you will ascend out of the 3rd dimension into the 5th. Will you raise your vibration until you disappear from the room? Will the planet be rent in two in some splendid quantum division with the New Age dawning on one while the 3rd dimension spirals downward into the abyss on the other? Will ships appear in the skies while catastrophic seismic movements scorch the Earth? They are all potentials, but the fact is you can't survive any one of these outcomes without raising vibrations for a dimensional shift. Most of you cannot sustain your vibrational frequencies throughout the span of a single day. How can you keep it high enough for long enough to sustain a SHIFT. You need assistance and we are here to provide it.

"Your Ascension and therefore your survival, is inextricably linked to ours as the entire universe is affected by the outcome of this Shift. That is the truth of it."

"Okay, lets focus on the issues we face in this dimension then. I have heard of a form of New World Order. What will that look like?" Alison asked.

"Socialism. Trans-humanism, Martial Law. Nobody knows at this point. It is one of several potential agendas of interested parties who are bidding for control at this time.

"It is hoped that it would begin with rudimentary new systems of politics, commerce, education, health and monetary systems. Each nation addressing the issues that are specific to them in nature, while all building towards a more centralized system or organization; more inter-connected, less complicated in structure, less restrictive.

"It will take time. Health will be a first concern, making sure that proper care is available to the elderly and all sections of society across the Globe. Food and water distribution will be addressed. New power sources, free energy, and fewer pollutants will be introduced. New technologies, once we are assured that they won't be used for more sinister activities, will be made available."

"By whom?"

"Those that would claim ownership of the planet."

"And you are saying you can prevent that?"

"No. We are saying you can step out of the way of that oncoming train! Remove yourself from that timeline and align with something more creative. We can't save anyone. We can only assist you to save yourselves."

"And we have that power?"

"Yes. You are the creators of your reality. The energy of thought is projected onto particle waves of infinite potentials and if enough of you believe something to be true, it will be manifest in the material realm. This is a double-edged sword. It is an ideal mechanism when vibrations are high and the collective can create their perceived reality from a loving and positive mindset. But, if they still hold fearful imagery in their minds about what could happen in the future, that energy will eventually impact on the field of potentials and determine the reality for the collective.

"Do you see? We don't tell the children grown up stories, incase it gives them nightmares."

Chapter 12

Debut

Alison stood in the wings of the stage at the National Dowser Association conference, looking out at an auditorium of over 300 people.

She felt dizzy and nauseous. She had always been a nervous public speaker, but this was bad. Her heart was leaping out of her chest, her vision blurred and when she tried to stand up she swayed unsteadily. The chairman that year, a nice woman, had seen her stumble on the staircase as she waited in line with other presenters and brought her back stage to sit for a moment and gather herself out of sight. Each presenter had one minute on stage to announce their workshop and schedules for the weekend.

Alison had planned to say what was expected, "I am Alison David Bird, Originator of Marconics, The Human Upgrade – Marconics is the Evolution of Energy Healing for the 5th Dimensional Body Template. For a sample of the energy, or to book a Marconics Recalibration, please visit us at our booth. Come to the dark side, we have cookies!" But the energy was ramping up. She had never felt quite like this. The tones in her ears were like striking tubular bells. The drumming noise in her head and the flush of heat rising and falling in her body told her Grace had something more to say.

"Twenty seconds" said the kind woman with compassionate eyes, as she handed her a paper cup filled with water. Alison sipped it and tried to breathe and overcome the desire to take flight and leg it out through the back door.

"You'll be fine," said the woman, who smiled at her sympathetically and took the cup back.

Lisa, camera ready, was seated with the team in the audience waiting with wild anticipation and support for Alison. The atmosphere was charged. Alison could feel Grace's energy rising up in her body and prayed that she wouldn't be reduced to a puddle in front of an entire audience. As she walked towards her mark at the front of the stage, she made eye contact with one of the girls, who seeing she was challenged by the energy prepared to climb on stage and stand behind her, ready to catch her if it became too much. This was the first time Grace had been so forward since she came in.

'Command the body,' she heard her own voice say, and Alison set her intention to align fully with Grace. The connection was immediate, like a tug on the top of her crown, drawing her upward. She felt taller, became centered and a strange sense of peace moved across her shoulders like a velvet cloak. Aware of the other presenters impatient for their turn, Alison glanced at two women in the front row, who were supposed to time her. One held up a sign saying '60 seconds', and the other was nursing a stopwatch. She looked out at the packed auditorium and felt her feet anchor as she took a long steadying breath.

Lisa watched as Alison's tiny form filled the stage. She opened her mouth and Grace Elohim began to speak.

"I am the Avatar Grace Elohim of the Galactic Federations, the Interstellar Alliance and the Alliance of Worlds. I am here to speak to those who can *hear* me. I know your names…" She paused and you could have heard a pin drop. Most of the audience seemed bemused, some looked on dubiously, but others caught their breath, their mouths fell open, their eyes widened as they listened intently to what was to come next. *'There they are…'* Alison thought.

"You are the architects of the New World." She continued strong and confident as never before. Lisa fumbled with the camera as her hands shook and she struggled to breathe from the frequency that Grace was pushing through Alison's body.

It didn't matter anymore if they hated her, Alison thought, if they booed her off stage or even threw rotten tomatoes, she was bolstered by the knowledge that she was not alone. She could feel the energies of an army standing on stage behind her and they were applauding!

"Did you know this is the seventh attempt to take your planet to Light?" Grace continued, "Six previous attempts have failed, because Lightworkers still can't discern the difference between Light and lack of Light." The sixty-second timer was way overdue. The two women were frantically waving her off stage. *Grace wasn't finished.*

"Do you think that maybe you have all the time in the world, because time does not exist? Or, that you can focus on saving humanity at weekends, but in the week other more pressing matters need your attention? Is this what you truly believe? Ask your selves that question, right now! What is more important? What will truly count against the evolution of your soul in the end?

"The Spiritual Hierarchy has been very gentle in its attempts to encourage you out of your stables but the race is on and you are already lagging behind.

"Much of what you have been led to believe about Spirituality in your Dimension was devised for the Earth school. The truth is more pragmatic. There is a dirty, muddy war waging and we are sorry to wake you from your slumber, but the enemy is at the gate.

"This is your Clarion Call. We are waiting for you and you must make your choice now, and you will be supported in any decision that you make. Please know that you are loved."

She stepped back from the mic and left the stage in a misty fog.

Alison couldn't wait to get out of there, as she heard the next announcer step up and say, '*Hi my name is Mary and I am going to lecture about divining rods, please come to my talk at 1pm.*'

She looked at Lisa, her eyes wide with concern, "How do you think they received it? Did it look like I was grandstanding?"

"You were amazing," Lisa assured her, "the vibration coming off you was incredible. I could barely breathe."

"Yes, you were fantastic," Robin agreed, "They don't know what hit them."

Alison had reason to be concerned, the old school dowsers were cliquish and judge-y.

"No, you were AH Mazing," Lisa beamed at her.

*   *   *

Grace found the experience entirely 'satisfactory', and said so at a meeting of the Council, which had been called to review the situation with Hybrid II, who, it seemed might finally be aligning with the timeline they had foreseen for partnership of the two incarnates. Hybrid II was requesting a contract renegotiation.

Ariel stood in the doorway and winked at Raffé. They both observed Grace's good humor as she took her seat at the round table. The excitement in the room was tangible. After several millennia, the timeline for the retrieval of the Taran crystals was at hand and there was everything to play for. Grace motioned for Ariel to address The Council. Instead of speaking, Ariel waved her hand and a holographic image projected from the center of the table.

"Can you hear me?" Lisa's earnest voice began. They could see her laying in the dark quiet of a strange bedroom in a rented house in Vermont. "I was so touched by Alison tonight, by her bravery to stand there in front of everyone and claim her I AM... I want to speak to my Galactic family."

Ariel and Grace locked eyes. The frequency coming from Lisa was pure and the longing was heartfelt.

"I wish to be reconnected with you, to know who you are, to know your names and to speak with you. I wish to be of service." Lisa sighed deeply. Clearly she was waiting for some kind of response.

Gabriel cast a look at Raffé and smiled, Hybrid II was staring at the ceiling.

After a few moments Raffé observed, "She could still go either way."

"I know, but she heard you tonight, Grace... she felt it!" Ariel countered.

Grace was concerned, "Yes, but she doesn't know, she doesn't understand and there is the potential for her still to come *up*." She was referring to Lisa's original contract to be a guide from the other side.

"Yes, but now she's asking." Ariel pressed on, "In preparation for her death transition she has been lifting the veils. If she chooses to stay in the material realm after all, that level of access would be such a benefit. The two of them together would make a formidable team."

From the hologram, they watched as Lisa began to twitch and move in response to the frequency of the energy being poured down on her. Then they heard her whisper to the darkness, "I just want to put it out there that if it is in alignment with the greater good, if it will support Marconics, if it is supposed to happen, I would welcome the integration with my higher self."

Ariel stepped forward. This is what they had hoped for.

"It's density in a way that we hadn't really anticipated." Grace warned Ariel, speaking from her own experience. She had merged with Alison in the physical realm three months earlier and had begun the process of departiculation and reformation with her incarnated expression. "It's ... heavy and murky. And when she experiences distress, it's very uncomfortable... like being in an open boat on the high seas..." Grace didn't have to finish the thought. Ariel knew that she was going.

The commitment wasn't just on the part of their incarnates. It was a commitment for them as well. They were depositing a portion of themselves in density, in true density and they would be locked there until the incarnate ascended or died.

Ariel felt Uriel's presence beside her. She rested her head on his shoulder. It wouldn't be too much longer before he was deployed. She looked around the table at Grace, Ashtar, Gabriel, Aleah, Lu, and Raffé; all beings that loved her and loved her incarnate.

Ariel turned to Gabriel, "What are your thoughts?"

Gabriel had been the one to make contact with Lisa when she was a teenager and had maintained the connection with her. Of all the 'Angelics', Gabriel was the one Lisa spoke to and trusted the most. He said only, "She's resilient, she'll adapt."

"She's open to it and she trusts Alison," chimed Aleah, Lisa's childhood guide.

"She's a lot like you, only disconnected and even more stubborn," Raffé noted.

Ariel turned to Lu, "Do you want to play Devil's advocate?"

"She's as much yours as she is mine," Lu quipped.

Grace was unsure, knowing they couldn't fully understand, "And if she doesn't commit and surrender fully, Ariel is trapped in an incarnate who is going to die from pancreatic cancer."

Ariel studied the hologram expecting to see her incarnate on the bed; it was empty. She turned and saw Lisa standing behind her, on the deck of the ship, looking equally surprised to be there.

"Uh...? Can she see us?" Gabriel whispered through gritted teeth.

Ariel pulsed a wave of energy at Lisa and broke the connection. Lisa thudded back into bed, feeling like a little kid who had been pushed from the room where the adults were talking. She had only been getting every third or fourth word, but she could see beings at a table and had seen a male and female figure from behind; the female leaning against his shoulder.

Ariel turned to Grace and smiled knowingly. As if to punctuate this, Lisa reappeared in the hologram. "Please," she whispered, "I just want to work with you... to know you. I am here and if it's for the higher good, I surrender myself."

Grace finally conceded. Ariel picked a message she knew Lisa would 'get' and sent it through the hologram. The frequency poured down. In her mind's eye, Lisa translated it through her internal programming as the Disney version of The Little Mermaid. As Ariel and Eric were floating in the row boat, he lamented that he didn't know her name. *'Ariel, her name is Ariel,'* the character Sebastian whispered in his ear.

They watched Lisa sit up in bed. Ariel smiled and poured down more frequency. Now Lisa was seeing flashes of images from Atlantis, from her childhood, the dreams and all those times Lisa had made invocations to Ariel at the start of healing sessions. She got it.

"Tomorrow then," Ariel affirmed with the Council. They would have an opportunity with her during the class.

*　*　*

Lisa sat bolt upright in bed, breathing heavily and grateful for the mattress beneath her. Her eyes trained on the clock. 5:55 a.m.

The dream had been recurring since she was sixteen. It haunted her to the point of inspiring several sketches and oil paintings. They were always the same; a blue woman who looked like her, but was not her, appearing out of rough seas with tsunami waves crashing against the rocks beneath a boiling sky, and in the distance five funnel clouds touching down in the ocean. The dream was becoming more intense, more vivid in its detail and emotion. She woke up soaked with sweat; the stress and adrenaline in the dream had been felt in her body. She got up for a sip of water and tried to go back to sleep.

In the dream, she stood on a balcony high on the bluffs, overlooking the white-capped waves below. The sea reflected the color of the sky; now turbulent with churning clouds it had turned the color of midnight. The wind was electrifying, charged with the mix of ions from the impending storm. She could feel dampness setting in, soaking the fabric of her long cloak.

She turned, re-entering the octagonal-shaped room behind her. It was a magnificent room, completely empty; no obvious doors, no furniture, nothing except long gossamer white curtains that had all been pulled in at the seams of the quartz octagon. The walls were made of sheets of highly polished quartz, with slight imperfections and inclusions.

The atmosphere outside was equally matched by the agitation and sense of urgency indoors. Loud sirens, flickering lights, shouting, coupled with quick, heavy footsteps falling against stone floors, all told her that there was bedlam in the halls. Inside the room, she watched as the quartz walls came alive with shimmering iridescent images and symbols. She began moving her fingers across their surface, resembling the swiftness and precision of a conductor directing an orchestra. Files began downloading into books with strange pages that appeared to be triangular sheets of metallic crystal, laying on the translucent desk that materialized beside her.

Her pace quickened as adrenaline began to surge through her body. A male form appeared in the room beside her, seemingly drawn out of particles of smoke and light pulled from the air itself. He was battle weary, dressed in leather armor, boots and a cloak, identical to her own. She nodded toward him as he began loading books into satchels, and disappeared back through the wall. Another materialized and took more books and exited just like the first... then another... and another. They were coming at such speed, yet the crystal pages of the books continued to download faster than they were being taken.

From deep within the foundation of the building came the rumbling of an earthquake; it grew louder and closer. She felt the floor begin to tilt and roll and the walls vibrate. One after another the armor clad men filed through the room, disappearing into the halls beyond the crystal walls.

Suddenly a voice called to her, from deep inside her own head. It was urging her to leave, evacuate, NOW!

She wouldn't; the work wasn't done. She needed more time; the books were still downloading. The rumbling became more intense and the vibrations more violent. Looking back out to sea through the crystal walls, she counted five fully formed funnel clouds advancing on the bluffs from the sea to the east. There were two more in the far distance.

The voice urged her again, 'GO NOW!' The floor buckled and heaved. The rock groaned heavily as it began to shear away from the cliff face, tipping the room forward, its transparent walls hanging suspended over the surface of the tumultuous waters far below.

'I hope we saved enough,' she thought as the quartz shattered around her and the Octagon tore away from the building. She watched as the beautiful, cold, midnight color rushed up to meet her as she plummeted towards the rocks beneath. Before it all went black, she felt herself begin to de-particulate.

* * *

It was their largest class yet, and the second largest turnout the Dowsers had seen at the conference that year. It was a packed agenda as they were only given a day to teach what normally took two and a half. Alison stood in the center of the stage.

This would be the beginning of a new chapter for Marconics. Alison began to tell the amazing story behind the new protocol that had been experienced for the first time at an event only a month prior.

It had actually begun filtering down in Florida two months prior, when Alison had been woken up in the early hours of the morning with a new move. She had sketched it out but had no understanding of what it was for.

"You know," they had said to her.

"No, I don't, what is it for?"

"YOU KNOW," they kept repeating.

Alison asked why they always had to be so cryptic and enigmatic. "Wouldn't it save time if you just told me these things?" she asked.

They had responded by saying, "This is your design. Imagine the thrill you receive every time you make these connections yourself, like when you were a reporter uncovering leads in a story. You asked not to be bored. You asked Michael to lay out a trail of clues, like breadcrumbs to lead you through the maze."

Lisa said later, "Well next time you make sure they give you a frigging GPS!"

As she was preparing teaching materials for the Provincetown class something very odd happened. She was printing head vectors, which they used to illustrate 'points' and 'holds' over portions of the face. Somehow, her archaic printer and 9-year-old laptop managed to superimpose the ink outline of the top-half of a body vector directly over the space between the hairline and the eye brows on the head vector. The body had been so skillfully placed, that the heart chakra lined up perfectly over the third eye on the head vector. Immediately she knew. "Higher Self Integration!" she shouted. And Grace confirmed with a burst of tingling, frothy energy.

So this became the vector for The Crowning portion of the protocol that Alison was about to demonstrate for only the second time.

"So, now we are ready for 'The Crowning'," Alison began. "This is really exciting for us, because this is a new evolution in Marconics.

"From the teachings and prophecies about this period we understand that there is a component to our Spiritual growth that involves us aligning and integrating our Higher Self, as well as male and female energies..." She looked at the students faces for some acknowledgement that would show her they understood what she was talking about. Several of them were nodding. "Well, we just came from a class where we had the opportunity to *experience* what this actually means."

She had their full attention. "I began to demonstrate this move for the first time at a recent class, using a volunteer student who was laying on the massage bed.

"When I stepped into her field, the energy shifted dramatically, and I felt Grace push forward in my body. I heard myself say aloud, 'We must take a moment to acknowledge that we are standing in the presences of this person's Higher Self'. Then frequency began to pour down on me with an intensity I had not experienced before. My breathing synced up with the girl on the table, and our bodies began to rise and fall together. I could feel a powerful energy enter into my body through my crown as though filling me up like a vessel. The energy took a moment in my heart Chakra as though it was connecting with Grace, and then it began to pass out through my heart chakra into her crown. By this time, we were both laboring to breathe, we began choking and coughing and tears streamed down our red faces as we struggled to contain this immense energy. As her body heaved and arched, her face became contorted and I thought, *'this woman is going to die right here on my table in front of twenty witnesses and I haven't even touched her'*." The class broke out in laughter.

"I was hearing in my mind the whole time *'don't break, don't break,'* and I trusted that I was not supposed to break the energetic connection with her. After a few moments, I could feel that the energy had passed fully through me and into her. I heard Grace say, 'This is the birth of the Avatar Race'."

Alison continued, "There wasn't a dry eye in the house, everyone could feel the higher frequency, and the room was silent. Finally, another student stepped forward and asked, 'Can I get a hug from God.' And she embraced the student on the table."

She explained that they had known that she and the student had contracted to be a part of something truly momentous, as a teaching moment. "Grace addressed the class the next day and explained that the same Deliverer beings that are present whenever a baby is born are present at the delivery of every soul into this plane, curving the dimensions to allow the safe passage of a spirit into this world."

Alison told them that afterwards, the student had felt different from the moment she sat up, saying she could see the connectedness of everything and everyone in the room. "It was the beginning of her journey towards becoming a fully integrated Avatar – a blend of the best of who she is combined with all aspects of her own Divinity, which had now descended to Earth."

Alison said, "This is the true definition of the phrase we use in Spirituality about this time of Heaven coming to Earth, and is symbolically represented in the interlocking pyramid configuration of the Star of David.

"The Crowning would create an opening to merge with higher aspects of Divinity, that which has always been theirs. For some this will be the culmination of much work, for others another stepping stone in their personal evolution." She added.

"Grace had said, *Those who are not ready to merge with what you would perceive to be loftier aspects of themselves, might experience a 'handshake' if you will, with the Mighty I AM PRESENCE. There will be an acknowledgement, a moment between them that will serve as a portal allowing for even greater expansion with the I AM and the incarnate being'.*

"Practitioners could be taught to facilitate the Ascent of the being through the Descent of the Higher Self aspects, to merge as one in the physical body and co-create a completely new vibration of pure creative impulses, allowing new and unseen paradigms to occur."

The class was looking particularly overwhelmed; they were going to have to do this?

Alison assured them that as practitioners they would become 'midwives,' by simply facilitating.

The Higher Self would judge whether the conditions were right for integration. "It will all be by agreement. Some will maintain a connection with their Higher Self without integration. In some cases, according to the being's soul purpose and contracts, integration would not be required or necessary.

"It is almost like leaving the garage door ready to drive the car in, but whether the car enters the garage, or remains in the driveway is moot. Both are accessible to the driver. It is simply a matter of balance whether the Higher Self can be of more service remaining in its own vibrational density or whether it can better serve you by joining with the Avatar. It still acts as the guardian and the overseer, conveying guidance and directional information," said Alison.

She also stressed that it was unlikely it would occur in their own practices back home, that the collective vibration of the Provincetown class had created a safe space and raised the vibration in the room so high, that the Deliverers could curve the dimensions.

Alison was careful not to set expectations that day for integrations. Truly, the team didn't know what to expect. They weren't sure if it had been a one off teaching moment and special contract between Alison and that one student, or if they should expect to see more integrations as they moved forward.

Earlier that morning Lisa had confided in Alison what had occurred the night before. Alison, now looking for a body to demonstrate 'The Crowning' on, turned to her and said, "Are you ready?"

Lisa responded by climbing up onto the massage bed and closed her eyes.

*   *   *

Ariel traveled down the beam of light through the dimensions and connected to the portion of Grace contained within Alison's vehicle. Ariel and Grace stayed together for a moment; Alison could feel the acknowledgement between their two energies.

"You can go still go back," Grace told her.

Ariel proceeded to pour herself in through Lisa's crown and began to spread herself out, navigating through the pathways in the physical body, the etheric templates, funneling through Lisa's meridians and axi-a-tonals like liquid gold filling a long forgotten aqueduct.

Lisa felt the euphoria as Ariel's energy mingled with her own. Once she was spread out, Lisa sat up. Alison looked at her and smiled.

"Okay then?" Alison whispered.

Ariel immediately twisted Lisa's bra strap, *'Why are we wearing this foul thing?'*

"Oh yeah," Lisa smiled, "We're great."

Chapter 13

The Proposal

Alison glanced up at the clock. They had run way over time, the venue manager would be knocking on the door at any moment, which, she had joked with the students earlier, was locked and bolted with no hope of escape. She indicated to an older woman in the second row, a Reiki Master, with her hand up. "Yes, one more question."

"So, we can't have Reiki run on us anymore?"

Alison's left eyebrow arched a little higher, *'Was she hoping the answer had changed since the last time she asked?'* she thought. Fending off the sound of fatigue in her voice, she repeated, "You can do as you like, it's your choice." She took another stab. "Try to look at it this way... If you had become a strict vegan, eating only organic foods and felt healthy and happy doing so, would you then order a fast food burger with fries, next time you passed a drive thru? It would probably make you sick to your stomach, and the toxins would seep into the soft tissue of your body, causing inflammation in your joints and muscle pain, making you feel bloated and heavy with the density.

"You are evolving into a new being. You are raising your vibration and are becoming consciously aware of what works for your developing 5th

Dimensional body template. Why would you consider allowing someone of a lower vibration, who is still working with a three-dimensional energy healing modality, to run a subset of energy on your newly recalibrated Lightbody?"

The woman looked dismayed. Alison had seen it repeatedly... people were reluctant, afraid to move away from what they knew. Particularly healers, who were concerned they would lose clients and consequently their livelihoods.

This is what the Pleiadians had meant about 'enslavement through fear.' It was subtle, but real and so limiting.

Lisa stepped to the front of the room, "We're going to call it a night, thank you everyone. Those of you having the first half of your Recalibration this evening, please see your practitioner to find your time slot. We will begin again tomorrow morning at 9 am, in this room."

While people fumbled under their chairs for bags and water bottles, Lisa and Alison made a beeline for the door before they could be cornered for the next hour with one-to-one questions about whether or not they could still eat fries... It had been a long day.

Back at the rental the team gathered in the kitchen to connect and talk about the evening's presentation, and snatch a quick bite before circling back to start the Recalibrations.

Lisa needed to call home. Alison had made her a proposition: continue to work as a member of the team of practitioners, or join her as partner. Alison had been clear that Lisa's commitment must be total. It was a tough decision. Lisa already had a business partner and a separate healing business. She had hoped to be able to manage both. Alison was making it clear that while Lisa's intentions were good, there was not room for anything that would distract from the mission; they were running out of time.

"No, I totally get it," Lisa began trying to choke back some tears. "How can I expect you to view me as a partner if I can't commit myself 100%?" She was quiet for a moment, and looked up to meet Alison's empathetic expression, "I thought I could do it all, it's just not working." The realization that Lisa was not in fact 'superwoman' was surprising news to her ego.

On the drive back to the venue she thought about the turn of events and really, how surreal it all was... It had only been a short linear time since she and Alison had met in the line for the ladies' loo at an annual holistic healing expo, only to discover that their booths were directly across the aisle from each other. The next thing she knew it was January. She had traveled with her family to Martha's Vineyard, on the East coast, to take a week-long class in a healing modality she knew nothing about but had convinced her husband it was worth uprooting himself and their two small boys to live in a hotel for a week so she could attend.

She fell in love over those 6 days, with her Galactic heritage, family and memories, the energy... and with Alison. She thought to herself, *'Someday, I am going to teach this, I am going to be a part of it.'* She didn't know why or how, and now she was being offered her dream.

The Pleiadians advised that one to one healing sessions and hypnotherapy clients were not going to be the route to critical mass for Alison. She had a larger contract to fulfill. They wanted her teaching and speaking to large groups, spreading the message and the light far and wide. It sounded lovely, but Alison remembered when Galadriel had instructed her to gather the women, thinking, *'What women??? Where were they?'* She had no idea how she'd do it, and yet in less than a year, here they were – this weekend producing another class of newly trained Lightworker practitioners.

The team had all felt *called*, without really understanding why, now they were inextricably connected and they fit together like the pieces of a puzzle.

Mary Pat had first heard Alison speaking during a radio interview 6 months earlier... an interview that Alison insisted had not *actually* taken place. Robin found herself there because her fiancé had discovered Marconics while surfing the web, before the website even went live, Alison attested. Gina stumbled upon the Marconics booth at an expo.

They had all been students together in class that first January, on Martha's Vineyard. Now they were essential to the core team, performing Recalibrations and coaching students at massage tables. They were all strong and powerful women in their own right. Mary Pat, a fiery redhead, always positive and cheerful; one couldn't help but be uplifted in her presence. Alison relied on Mary Pat's ebullient and honest nature. "She had the purity of a child," Alison had said. Gina was like a little flower that had thirsted for the sun on her face and had blossomed in her own special brand of quiet power. Lisa had told her once, not everyone needs to stand at the front and command a classroom, some lead quietly from the sideline. This was Gina's gift. She had a calm energy that radiated patience, kindness and compassion and was possessed of the finesse that only the gentle can manage. Robin and Lisa had bonded in that first class the year prior. Skeptical, cynical... fiercely loyal and protective of Alison and Lisa both, Robin constantly pushed herself out of her comfort zone, reaching ever higher. She was choosing the path and walking it steadfastly.

None of them had ever been in a group of women like this before. They had been called together by Grace, their bonds forged in love. Alison had emerged as the leader they had enlisted to follow, and they were each devoted to her. Now, Lisa was concerned that things would change, as she would be stepping up at Alison's right hand.

She quieted her mind for the Recalibration session but the thoughts were all there waiting for her when she was done.

Lisa had been asking her guides for a renegotiation of her contract. She could see the various potentials before her and, if she accepted her cancer diagnosis, she was staring down a timeline of sickness and death. She had no intention of participating in that.

She could clearly visualize the analogy Alison had used earlier in class to describe the timelines of potential. Trains parked neatly at the station, all pulling out together and heading in one direction, side by side, on multiple tracks. On having passed the first junction, they begin to diverge. At first their separation is subtle, and you can hop from train to train, or straddle two at a time. Now after the second junction, the divergence widens and soon, the gap between the trains will mean 'hopping' between them will no longer be an option. You will have to choose which train you are on or fall between them.

Lisa's trains were barreling locomotives, and she could no longer hold the straddle. How was she going to explain all this to her own clients and students, or, to her partner? There would be no way to make the transition smoothly or gently. It had to be done quickly before Lisa allowed her misplaced compassion to take the form of ego and lead her to believe again that she could do it all. She couldn't go on as too little butter scraped over too much bread. Bouncing back and forth between her Galactic contract and her 3D commitments was tearing her apart.

And now she worried, *'What would her husband think?'* Brendan supported her decision to fully embrace her 'woo woo' rather than return to the world of corporate banking when her severance package ran out. He'd supported her when she opened her practice and began to teach and see clients. He even occasionally sat by the bonfires when she led solstice and equinox celebrations. He could see that she was truly happy and doing something she believed in and loved. Now she was going to turn it all over and walk away, and for what? So she could chase invisible aliens? She always had one foot out the door, either to her own office or on a Marconics trip, which left him with the responsibility of the boys most nights and weekends. She didn't know how he'd perceive this move.

She had pulled off in a shopping center parking lot. It was late, almost closing time. "I miss you Mama, when are you coming home?" her little one had cried into the phone. "I hate when you leave, why do you always leave?" he sobbed, "Can you come home now?"

Lisa choked back her own sobs as she soothed him. What the hell was she doing? Her mortality never scared her until she became a mom. It was a fear of the boys feeling the same loss she did when her own dad died – he was just a few years older than she was now. The thought of the boys growing up without her was crippling at times and now here they were without her and it was by her own hands. Placing the phone on speaker, Brendan's voice filled the car, "She's right you know, babe, you can't do it all. Something's gotta give."

"What do you think I should do?" she asked earnestly.

"It would be better without the constant pull of the office… you are only away over weekends with Marconics – it's the office that makes it all too much. You could work from home for the stuff you and Alison need to do… and then you are just away for the events."

Surprised by his answer, she pushed, "So you think I should leave the business?"

"What do you *want* to do?"

"I want to spend more time with you and the kids and *I want to save the world with Alison*," she blurted through tears.

She knew he pretended not to notice when he'd overheard her *again* on the phone talking to Alison about the Galactics and the ships they'd seen on the road… about the messages channeled in both while conscious and in the dream state… and all the other 'supernatural' experiences they discussed for hours on end.

"Then do it," he said sternly, "and make sure you commit and focus."

She hung up the phone, sat for a moment then broke down. All the fear, doubt, and worry escaping her body through snot and tears. Then the phone rang.

"Where are you?" Robin asked, "You left before us and we beat you home, are you okay?"

"Yes," Lisa lied. It's really hard to lie to an empath, they listen to your feelings and not your words.

"Uh-huh. So, why are you crying?"

"It was a rough call with Gabe." The girls did not know about Alison's offer yet. "I'll be there in a little bit. I just wanted to grab something from the grocery store before coming home." Robin reluctantly hung up.

When Lisa got back to the house she knew she'd have to explain her tardiness; she had a house full of concerned women to answer to. She shared the details of her 'Gabe phone call' with them and they empathized with the emotional pull. After the girls went to bed, Alison could see Lisa was emotionally exhausted. "Why don't you just stop for a moment and sit down?" Alison urged. Alison understood the importance of stillness and connection. Lisa's normal adrenaline rushes caused her to pace like a caged lion, generally resulting with Alison teasing her with the threat of being 'sacked' because she would not sit still – ever. Instead, to Alison's surprise, Lisa flopped on the couch in a heap and closed her swollen eyes.

"Take some deep breaths and allow the tension in your body to melt away." Years of following and then leading guided meditations made Lisa susceptible to Alison's soothing command and she immediately responded. They had never tried hypnosis together, but seeing the opportunity to help ease her, Alison knew she could bring Lisa down and enable her to emerge relaxed and calm. Alison continued to talk her into full relaxation using guided imagery and hypnosis. Her plan was to allow Lisa's subconscious mind to open and enable the overload in her critical mind to disperse.

"Visualize a staircase with a handrail, descending one step at a time from 20 to 19, 19 to 18 … 12, 11… 3, 2, 1

"At the foot of the staircase, you should see a hallway. Can you see the hallway? If you can give me a nod."

"It's not a hallway," Lisa responded aloud.

Alison pulled up a chair and moved closer to the couch. **"What is it?"** she asked.

"It's a wormhole, spiraling counterclockwise. I am at the end of it."

"You're at one end of it? You've come down the staircase and you can see down into the wormhole?" Alison tried to suppress the tingle of excitement... this had potential.

"Yes." Lisa could see the swirling of blue and purple energy opening into space and time.

"Does it feel safe to step into the wormhole?"

"Yes, it's going home."

"You're going home?"

"Yes."

"Then I want you to step into the wormhole, not yet, but when I say so. I will count backwards from 5 to 0 and when I reach 0 you will have arrived at your destination. Do you understand me?"

"Yes."

"Ok get ready to step into the wormhole, 5, 4, 3, 2, 1, 0. You are at your destination. What do you see? ... What do you see?"

"White light, lots of white light." As her eyes adjusted, *"There are rolling, grassy hills. There's a tree at the top of the highest hill. It's a strange looking tree."*

"Describe the tree."

"It's angular ... there are clocks..." Lisa could see a tall black tree standing alone on a hill. It was huge and wide, with twisting angular branches. It looked like a man-made object trying to pose as organic. There was something other-worldly about it.

"Clocks?" quizzed Alison.

"Yes, clocks. They're... On it? In it? The tree is alone on this hill. I can see the roots going down into the hill. There are no leaves. It's slick and black."

"Where are you?"

"It's a place between the places. A world between the worlds."

"Does the tree contain anything living?"

"No..." Lisa could feel herself scanning the tree for life forms. *"No."*

"What does it require you to do here in order for you to move forward?"

"There's a door in the tree."

"Can you walk forward towards the door?"

"Yes."

"I want you to walk forward and reach your hand out for the handle if there is one. Is there a handle?"

Before Lisa could even touch it, it moved. "It's just opened inward."

"Are you ready to step into the tree?"

"Yes."

"Do you remember our anchor?" Alison asked in regard to the prompt they would use to bring Lisa out if things became too stressful.

"Yes."

"Counting backwards from 3 to 0. 3, 2, 1, 0 – step into the tree. Look around you and tell me what you see."

"Mirrors, mirrors… There are torches hanging on the walls. It's very cold." It reminded Lisa of a castle corridor, with roughly hewn, stone walls.

"What is the purpose of this place?"

"To go to the worlds." Lisa could see movement in each of the mirrors, and they were not her reflection. "This is where we go to travel to the worlds. We come back to this place."

"This tree has been depicted before in spiritual symbolism. Do you know which mirror you would need to go through to get to your planet?"

"Yes." One of the mirrors took on a strange shimmer, like a rainbow oil slick over the surface of water.

"Are you ready to step through?"

"Yes."

"When you step through I will count backwards from 5 to 0. When we reach 0 you will have arrived at your destination. Prepare to step through. 5, 4, 3, 2, 1 and 0. What do you see? Where are you now?"

"One half of the planet is blue and the other half is red. I have been here before."

"And whose planet is this?"

"Mine."

"And who are you?"

"ARIEL!"

"How long has it been since you've been here Ariel?"

"2,000 years."

"You haven't been home for 2,000 years?"

"No."

"Do you have loved ones at home?"

"Yes."

"Who did you leave at home?"

"My family."

"Tell me about your family."

"It's all of them. The Seraphiam, they are all mine." Lisa could feel the expansion in her heart as Ariel spoke of them.

"Why did you have to leave your home?"

"I was called to come here."

"Here being...?"

"Earth."

"Do you have to do what you are called to do?"

"It is my job but an honor, my honor."

"Who calls you?"

Lisa Chuckled, *"You do!"*

"And who am I?"

"Grace Elohim."

Chapter 14

The Butcher

Ariel became a frequent visitor from that point on, always happy to chat. Lisa was beginning to build up resistance to hypnosis, which relies on a fight flight response. She could see by the look on Alison's eye that she wanted answers, and her subconscious mind would take up 'warrior stance'. It was unlikely her friend was going to intimidate her enough for Fight or Flight. They laughed about the different ways Alison would redirect the subconscious mind, and create the required response to achieve a deep hypnotic state. She had even used Battlefield hypnosis, which is useful when needing to get someone who is in trauma to disconnect from the body's physiological reaction, such as pain. On several occasions, Alison would creep up on her and give her a sharp slap on the head to bring her down. *'That couldn't go on much longer,'* Alison thought, *'she was going to get her nose broken.'* Lisa wouldn't turn her back to her for fear of getting slapped.

On this occasion, it was late at night, and both women were tired following class, but always tried to make the most of the opportunity to 'run with scissors' when they were alone together.

Alison used a double 'whammy'. Lisa thought she was already in hypnosis, Alison hit her in the forehead again with the flat of her hand, the surprise created the exact conditions Alison was looking for and a deeper state of hypnosis. Both women preferred to get information this way, as it meant that their human filters were suspended, and there was less risk of distortion of the information, though an increased risk for bruises.

Ariel immediately began to push forward in Lisa's body.

"Hello Alison,"

"Hi Ariel, are you well?"

Alison had worked with Ariel under hypnosis who, appeared to have PTSD, following an incident when she was in form. Lisa could still feel the pain from it sometimes, and gradually it was being healed.

Grace had told Alison the mission was to reclaim the Atlanteans. Alison had never really put too much store in the Atlantean stories, it seemed like myth to her. So she asked if Ariel could give them more of the backstory. She began to speak. "Your human story begins millennia before the first humans walked the Earth."

Alison waited for her to continue.

"The human body was designed and created to be a vehicle template for the hybrid races and for Light Beings to have form when desired and appropriate. We wanted to construct a dense vehicle that could contain light and withstand the higher vibrational frequencies while being able to experience the richness of density."

"Grace Elohim was the creator of the winning template..." Alison stated, pulling forward one of Grace's memories. Grace had shown Alison her being ushered into a 'classroom' setting. There was a competition for the human vehicle, and Grace's design had won.

"Yes, and We were tasked with populating these vehicles with souls, with aspects of self," Ariel replied.

"Did someone die for those plans? A being?" Alison ventured.

"There was a great schism among the Angels," Ariel began. "There was a time when we all followed the directive of protecting the humans from the forces of opposition that would use them for their resources."

"What resources?"

"The resources of the planet and the resources of their quantum energy. The incarnate soul fragments are exposed and vulnerable in human form. The human body, or vehicle, was designed with greatness beyond which you can imagine. The powers you would call supernatural or superhuman were natural and human."

"Is this where the split between the Elohim and Elohei occurred? The Elohim were cautious against the fully operating human light bodies?" Alison pressed.

"Yes," Ariel answered, "in light you are beautiful and capable of great compassion and great love. In the density of the 3rd Dimension, you are equally capable of great horrors and atrocities stemming from fear."

"Am I correct in understanding that, as humans, we were sequestered here to experience Free Will, on a protected world?"

"Yes, here you would have the opportunity to gather the wealth of emotion created by the human experience with the soul programming to act in accordance with Divine will."

"Heaven on Earth," Alison remarked.

"Heaven on Earth," Ariel confirmed. "Grace's design was the prototype before bringing the body vehicle to the higher dimensions."

They sat for a moment in silence.

"Your collective consciousness records your human fall from Grace, your fall from the garden," Ariel offered. "The Angelic factions were split into groups."

"Why?" Alison wondered aloud, "Weren't the Angelics in service to Divine Will?"

"Free Will has always been one of the big dividing issues." Ariel continued, "The images humans hold of us with wings and halos is lovely but not entirely accurate. You could liken us to your military. Orders are followed, we serve with honor and devotion."

"Do you not have any freedom of choice?" Alison asked.

"We do not experience Free Will like humanity does. We must do what has to be done. There is little tolerance when orders are not followed," Ariel stated matter-of-factly.

"That sounds like a police state," Alison said, feeling a bit sorry for her Angelic friend.

Ariel affirmed proudly, "We are the one and the many. We can have an individual experience and then we can experience the Collective. You have to understand, there is a deep interconnectedness in our being."

She continued, "There is true honor and loyalty in our service to one another, unlike what you have experienced on Earth. It is our honor to serve."

"Some think the fallen Angelics are jealous of Free Will and are angry with humans. What is your take on that?" Alison asked.

"Sadly, the human mind cannot comprehend the peace, compassion, and love that is available in light. Free Will is a gift, we respect the power of that gift too much to want to interfere," Ariel answered quietly.

"We've been told that Angelics see us like children. That they love us and they want to protect us-"

"Mainly from yourselves," Ariel interrupted.

Alison laughed in agreement and then after a moment inquired, "Can we talk about Mars?"

"The early humans, what you could call Human Version 1.0., as progeny of the Elohim and protected by the Seraphiam, were being developed and delivered to 3D Earth around the same time that the planet Mars was made uninhabitable."

"Were the beings from Mars also being delivered to 5D Earth?"

"Yes some…" Ariel thought of a wartime analogy Alison would like, "Some of the beings from Mars were delivered to 5D Earth, we call her Tara, with the intention that their knowledge could be translated and used for advancement in human evolution. Think of this like Nazi scientists being rescued from wartime Germany and brought to America for their knowledge and expertise. At some point in time, the Allies thought it would be a good idea to play with atoms and particulates, and while we have harnessed an awesome power of creation – nuclear fusion; we have also created an immense source of destruction – nuclear weaponry, the atom bomb."

"I get that," Alison stated, "my understanding is that the original human body had a much larger brain and that this was the beginning of the split."

"Yes," Ariel explained, "By enlarging the brain capacity, the human vehicle could incorporate fully functional pineal and pituitary glands. This would mean a brand new species of Beings would be unleashed in the density and duality of 3rd Dimensional reality with limitless access to universal knowledge, advanced capabilities for technology and healing, and the potential for agelessness. They were not immortal but would not atrophy, and they would be free to create or destroy reality without limitations."

Alison sucked in a breath, "Good God." Then added sarcastically, "I can't imagine *that* was a popular idea among the Elohim!"

"True, many argued that this was a dangerous road," Ariel agreed.

"Earth was meant to be an experiment, an example of how Free Will and enlightenment could work with a mix of races and diverse genetics. Isn't that right?" Alison asked.

"The microcosm would expand outward to the macrocosm," Ariel confirmed. "We wanted to know, could a denser body vehicle with the ability to have individuality survive the trappings of ego and be truly magnificent? The majority of the creation team wanted to let nature ride its course with very little interference outside of protection. The minority was concerned that giving so much power and intelligence to one species without an evolutionary history could prove to be dangerous. The duality of the 3rd Dimension is loaded with the traps of the ego mind. Fear creates an opportunity for all species to act in a way that is out of alignment with Divine Will and direction."

"So ultimately the factions that wanted to turn humanity loose and see how we would do being the custodians of the Earth won out?" Alison asked, knowing the answer already.

"Yes. For a time, there was what you would call Heaven on Earth. The human race cared for the Earth and for one another."

"This would be in alignment with our stories of Eden or Atlantis," Alison noted.

"Yes, for a time, like very smart and very obedient children, humanity lived in the grace and under the guidance of the Creators."

Alison thought for a moment about Atlantean lore and Lightworker memories. They have a common thread of advanced healing abilities and an innate knowledge of crystals and herbs.

As though reading Alison's thoughts on the access she knew humanity once had, Ariel confirmed, "You could heal with the power of thought to define and control your DNA. You also had access to technology and mathematical understanding that were the results of millions of years of development by your founding races."

"That was truly what we as humans would consider a Golden Age," Alison commented. "So why was there a schism?"

"There were others that wanted to educate and further enhance the abilities of the human potential. The Elohim and Seraphiam did not agree with this agenda. The continued enhancements without an evolutionary process were risky in the dimension of your reality."

"It is my understanding that our evolutionary process was devised," Alison pressed with an eyebrow raised. Grace had taught Alison about the multidimensional lightbody of the early humans. Humans were magnificent beings that volunteered to experience density and in doing so agreed to being 'dumbed down.' The truth they knew was that they volunteered to have their chakras clipped, like a bird's wings, because they were trapped in density. This was done close to the spine and changed the chakras from spherical and multisensory to conical and covered with a cap. In addition, they were sealed with a biomatrix substance to ensure the experience of true density. The human pituitary and pineal were decreased in size and functionality and the energy fields were reduced to be egg shaped and about 4-6 feet in diameter.

"We watched as the humanoids of Mars destroyed themselves with war and experiments that threatened the fabric of this Universe. The benefits of transplanting the survivors of Mars to 5th Dimensional Earth were twofold. We had hoped that the younger 'children' would learn from the older ones and not repeat the same mistakes. We hoped the older ones could atone and clear karma by helping the younger ones..."

"So the survivors of Mars were deposited in Atlantis..." Alison finished Ariel's thought, "and they kept on doing what they were doing..."

"We could not allow the misuse of energy to continue," Ariel said with a heaviness in Lisa's voice. "Not only were they threatening life on 5D Earth, but in destroying the planet with the use of Dark Matter and Dark Energy - a ripple effect would have echoed through the galaxy, and then the Universe, and then the multiverse. You have the saying 'as above so below' and you know the reverse to be true."

"We are the anchor," Alison stated quietly, "As we destroy ourselves, we are also destroying you."

"We could not allow the unraveling of Dark Matter in your world to begin to unravel the fabric of this universe," Ariel said sadly.

"Who gave the order to evacuate and destroy?" Alison asked.

Ariel dodged the question and allowed Lisa forward.

"I was being shown black smoke attached to them, a poison, a toxin, it was a suffocating substance, thick and oily but moved like smoke and it was shutting them down," Lisa described a vision to Alison. "The black smoke wanted their knowledge, their essence, but it was not planning on using them for good."

Both understood the Atlanteans did not deliberately misuse their knowledge of healing, crystals, harmonics and physics; it was that others wanted to use Atlantean powers for destruction.

"I have more questions for Ariel," Alison waited for Ariel to come forward again.

"Ariel, who gave the orders to evacuate and destroy?"

"We assumed forms in density and arrived in the citadel of Atlantis to save the knowledge that was stored there," Ariel replied.

Alison already knew that many records of the Atlanteans and their culture had been evacuated on ships. Some were taken by others through the Star Gate and traveled to different locations.

Grace was showing Alison the Fall through a hologram they observed as newly deployed troops arriving in the desert. There was a feeling of optimism that ran through the Atlantean outpost.

By midnight, everything had changed. To their shock, confusion, and disbelief, intelligence informed them that it was already too late to affect a rescue. Through Grace's eyes, Alison watched as in the distance a vast section of the 5D earth grid collapsed sucking the terra firma above it into an abyss. Where this beautiful 5th Dimensional Society had once lived and thrived, there now hung a devastating, fiery mushroom cloud.

Ariel simultaneously took Lisa to the Octagonal room overlooking the bluffs on the coast where Grace and others were evacuating the records to be protected. The room had huge floor to ceiling windows that were made of highly polished and thinly cut slabs of quartz, just as in Lisa's recurring dream. The midnight sky was as turbulent as the sea itself. Lisa watched through Ariel's eyes, as Grace left with Alison. Grace ran through the corridors, up several flights of crumbling stone steps until she reached an extraction point and was pulled upward in a beam of light to a ship of morphing gold.

Back in the records room with Ariel, Lisa could feel the sense of urgency and rising tension as hurried people rushed to and fro in the halls outside. It was as though she had consciously entered the dream but realized she was reliving Ariel's memory. There was a loud 'cracking' sound followed by a rumbling which echoed in vibration beneath their feet, and the floor began to buckle and roll. The Octagonal room suddenly sheared away from the face of the cliff, throwing them to the ground, and as it slid slowly down onto the rocks below they saw the crashing waves rise up to meet them. The crystal walls splintered from the pressure and the water rushed in to take them. *Did we die here?' Lisa wondered.*

"Ariel, who gave the orders?" Alison asked again.

"This is where the Angelics fractured," Ariel replied.

"Who gave the orders?" Alison asked again with more urgency in her tone.

"The Martian survivors expanded on their experiments and began tampering with chemical DNA. They had released something primeval from the core of the 5th dimensional Earth. They created an abomination, something we call the Vilkriss. It is soulless, unable to activate, with no spiritual DNA of its own."

"Ariel, who ordered it?"

Ariel said nothing.

"Ariel, I want to know. Who gave the order?"

"Grace did."

The silence was deafening.

"You have to realize, the thing they created would consume everything... and so Grace had no choice but to order destruction."

She continued, "There were those who had helped bring light to the humans, who were tasked with protecting them, with loving them. And to destroy them was perceived as a terrible act of betrayal by many. There were among the Angelics those who refused to follow orders and they were cast out. Dropped into density and tied to the fate of the Earth. As Earth returns to light, so they might too. If Earth is lost and so they will too be lost."

"Ariel, are you classed as 'Fallen'?" Alison asked gently.

"The Angelics of the side realms, those closer to the humans felt betrayed with what they were asked to do. They completed their task and stepped out of the Councils and Federations because they would not interfere again where Free Will was concerned. You would consider this an 'honorable discharge.'"

"And what about you Ariel, would I consider you to be a fallen angel?"

Ariel shook her head. "There is much that is not understood about that term," Ariel said firmly. "There are times in history when a great Angel of Death, an Angelic Destroyer travels through density and eliminates life."

"Was that you? Ariel, did you carry out Grace's orders?"

"A large weapon was planted under Atlantis."

"What kind of weapon? What did it do?"

"It was a weapon of cataclysmic creation. As it was detonated great vibrations traveled below the surface of the planet and it began to break and shatter – ravaged by earthquakes and tidal waves."

Alison asked again, "Ariel, are you the one who carried out the orders?"

After a moment, Alison noticed tears running down Lisa's cheeks. Ariel sighed and said only, "The Butcher of Atlantis."

Surprised at the term and observing Lisa's distress Alison knew she would need to bring Lisa back up. Alison ventured one last question, "Who is that? Who is the Butcher of Atlantis?"

Ariel hesitated as Lisa began sobbing. Finally pointing at Lisa's body Ariel answered, "Me."

> *"The Seraphiam had been tasked with the protection of the souls. And while the loss of human life was regrettable, it was necessary. Knowing that the soul has the ability to stay on the Karmic wheel and return to Earth, return to its place of celestial/ dimensional origin, or return to infinite light with the Source, it was acceptable to lose the battle if there was a chance the war could be won."*

> *- Ariel*

*　　*　　*

It wasn't the right time to bring Tara to light. The light humans were so pure, so healthy and balanced, but they lacked mastery, or maturity to see the difference between light and lack of light as the Martian masculine energies of war and of power were corrupting their knowledge. Tara's destruction was appropriate.

It struck Lisa then that her role in all of this, Ariel's role, has always been to do what needed to be done; to carry out orders. Ariel is both a *Savior* and a *Destroyer.*

Those that could be saved, those that could save themselves were saved. Many of the light warriors on Earth at this time carry cellular memories of the destruction of Atlantis. A holographic insert placed in the collective memory caused Lightworkers to believe that is was due to their misuse of crystals that their Atlantean home was destroyed. Humans needed to have a healthy fear of the experimentation so as not to repeat the mistakes of the past and a sense of deep remorse for the part they played in the loss.

Chapter 15

Fecking Sedona

E verything about the Sedona trip was off from the moment Alison reached the airport parking lot in Boston. She arrived at airport check-in with e-tickets in hand to hear that her reservation had not been received and that the airline had no seats. Alison's fears were beginning to crystalize.

"I should have just cancelled this thing as soon as Lisa said she couldn't make it," she told Chris, who on this occasion was along for the ride. He knew that she would view these signs as a series of gentle warnings that there was danger ahead. The Galactics had said right at the start of Marconics, "Do not leave the North East."

But that was two years ago,' Alison thought, and they never actually explained why. Was this still the case? Sedona had seemed like such an obvious choice for a class. By the time she remembered their warning, the ink on the contracts was already dry.

They would rarely tell you what you should or shouldn't do, they didn't even respond to the vibration of the word 'should'. To intervene in your decision-making would be an infringement of Free Will. But they would send you subtle road signs, if they observed you heading for a precipice.

Although Lisa had accepted Alison's proposal to join her in partnership, she had already made a prior commitment to a family vacation that same week which she joked would result in divorce if she cancelled on her husband. Sedona would be Alison's final trip alone and she wasn't looking forward to it.

A week earlier Alison had asked, "Will I be under attack in Arizona?" Grace replied, "No more than usual."

Perhaps the answer begged the question. Instead Alison asked, "Do they need us there?"

'Yes.'

Well, someone clearly did not want her there, as now she could feel the frictional energy of resistance. In weaker moments in the run up, she almost cancelled. But she knew she had a responsibility to those who had already registered.

Just before boarding the flight her concerns were validated. She received a text from an online booking agent she often used to find house rentals when the team was on the road. She read it and in disbelief handed the phone off to Chris and watched his eyebrows knit together as he read the message aloud. The accommodation she had booked for the whole team that week did not actually exist.

After spending the first uncomfortable night in a gloomy resort style studio apartment, provided by the booking agency in an emergency, they were relocated to an alternative rental in the valley the next day. It was very modern and minimalistic, decorated in only three colors: red, white and black.

"Don't touch the sculptures," the owner had warned. The plush red daybed on unforgiving aluminum legs looked very uninviting, and the knee-high, glass coffee tables were asking for trouble.

The house was not to Alison's taste, but there they were. It wasn't big enough for the girls as well, so they had to make alternative arrangements with a resort close to the venue. Alison felt they had been Shanghaied.

She slept badly that night, dreaming that she had heard a knocking on the front door of the house, which woke her up. She had opened it only to be met by a pair of black, almond shaped eyes, set in the face of a short, Grey E.T. who pushed his way into the house, followed by several others. She and Chris ran through the house looking for an escape. Finally, as she rounded the kitchen island, one of them wrestled her to the ground and everything went black. The next thing she remembered was pain in her lower abdomen. She could barely stand and was being supported under each arm by beings she couldn't see. They took her weight as she screamed and looking down, watched in horror as something slick and wet slipped from between her legs and splattered on a cold, hard floor.

Eventually, she awoke hot and sweaty in the strange bed in the middle of a desert somewhere in Arizona. She got up and carefully picked her way between the freestanding sculptures and the glass coffee table towards the kitchen. As she was trying to work out the state-of-the-art coffee machine, Chris appeared from the bedroom, pointing to his mouth.

"What the hell is this?" he demanded to know. Angry red pressure marks in a two-prong pattern were visible on his lower lip, around which were small broken veins.

"I-I don't know?" Alison stammered, barely disguising the wide-eyed look of shock that flashed across her face. "Were you pursing your lips too tightly as you slept?" she asked, pitifully. She wasn't going to voice her true concern, which was that it looked as though a metallic instrument hooked over his lower jaw had held his mouth open, after they were captured by several Grey Aliens that broke into the house the night before. He clearly wasn't in the best of moods as it was.

The drive to the venue was little short of magical, though, and Alison took it as a sign that they weren't alone. The clouds took the form of trumpeting Angels; even Chris couldn't miss the significance of the imagery. She was beginning to accept that as usual there was a reason to be there, even though it was the smallest class she had seen in a while, she knew this didn't matter. Any one of those attending, or all of them, could be the entire purpose of the trip.

During the lecture that day, she data streamed St. Germain. He had been sent by Grace to keep her entertained, after Alison had complained that she was never around for a girly chat, like Ariel was for Lisa. Grace was all business. Alison needed some lightness of spirit. So, Grace had asked Germain to step in, and he did!

He wasn't like the version recorded in the famous Discourses. He came to her as his incarnation of the Compte de St Germain, friend and confident of King Louis, Marie Antoinette and Madame de Pompadour.

He wore a foppish, silk damask 'frock coat' with frilled lace sleeves tight at the wrist, finished off with a white powdered wig and he carried a porcelain topped cane. He was an affiliate of Alison's Higher Self lineage, as bearer of the Violet Flame, and had been a guide for Alison in the early days, and she enjoyed his wicked irreverence. He was quick to point out he wasn't actually a Saint at all, but had taken the name from a town in France and apparently enjoyed all things sparkly and feminine.

He showed up right on time and as usual was in his element as he entranced the class for several hours. In the afternoon, Alison prepared to demonstrate the Crowning.

Two young Australian travelers who had first contacted Alison about a year earlier, had traveled a great distance to finally attend a class with her. Skye and Ian were beautiful New Agers, with a strong and obvious soul connection and a keen interest in the work. They felt familiar to Alison and she was inexplicably drawn to them. She enjoyed their passion for the subject and their intelligent questions.

That afternoon, Alison volunteered Skye for the demonstration and began the Crowning. Skye began to register REM about 30 seconds after Alison stepped into the field, and was an active mover on the table. Her fair skin flushed as she appeared to become more agitated and began uttering words and phrases in a language no one recognized. She started snatching at a silver necklace around her throat.

"What is this? What is this… it is burning me. Get it off."

Robin took the necklace off, and an anklet that was also beginning to cause her discomfort. The energy was intense, but eventually subsided as the integration concluded and Skye sat up and swung her legs over the side of the table. Her blue eyes were like saucers, gazing slowly around the room, looking at everyone in turn as if she was seeing them for the first time. She had the expression of the purest child. Then without warning, she shoved her hand unceremoniously between her legs.

"What is *this?*" she asked, surprised and intrigued by the strange configuration. She began to tug at her clothes. "Ugh, these are horrible, they must come off!"

Alison took both her hands in hers and looked her in the eyes, "No Skye, no! You can't take your clothes off here." She affirmed, as the others began to laugh.

Gradually and reluctantly Skye began to settle down. "I am Gold." She kept saying, "I am Golden…I came from a ship made of Gold!"

Alison was familiar with a race of beings that were said to be 'golden'. She had seen them once in a vision. They were the forefathers of the Elohim. "Are you Anahazi?" Alison asked her.

Skye's face lit up! "Yes… Yes!"

The energy between them suddenly became electrified, and engulfed Alison with an overwhelming wave of emotion. They locked eyes as memories of their relationship came flooding forward. Alison felt the tears would choke her if she tried to fight them back. Her breathing quickened and her heart raced until, embarrassed to be taken so off guard in front of a class full of students, she created a distraction by stepping forward to offer Skye's new integration a welcoming hug. But as they embraced something else was initiated.

Alison's body began to convulse as a huge download of energy emptied over her like a bucket of water. Sadness welled up from the deepest part of her soul and exploded into an uncontrollable sob. A bolt of energy shot from Skye's heart space into her own and they held on to each other unable to stand alone, or apart, as their bodies heaved with the racking of emotional release.

Gradually, Alison lifted her head and looked at Skye in total recognition, "What are we doing here?" A new integration was forward.

"Do you remember me now?" Skye asked her.

Alison nodded. "Yes," she sobbed.

"Do you know me now my sister?"

"Yes, *yes.*" They rocked each other back and forth as the class observed in silence.

Eventually, Alison looked across at Ian who was watching intently. She smiled in recognition of him too, which he could not yet see. "It's your turn I think?" She said. He nodded and smiled. Alison composed herself as Ian took up position on the massage table in front of her.

Then Skye said, "I think I am supposed to do this."

"Okay," Alison conceded. This would be a good demonstration for the class to see, one student performing a Crowning on another so soon, she thought.

The integration began to build steadily; it was a massive energy, which could be felt throughout the room. It challenged both Skye and Ian physically to bring the energy through. Ian was beginning to burn up and seeing that he was struggling, Alison stepped in to assist Skye, encouraging the energy to move through his body by connecting with it energetically and coaxing it down. As she reached the foot of the table she grabbed Ian's ankles to help him ground and felt almost blinded by the vision of a huge golden orb… A sun! *'This energy isn't even of this universe,'* Alison thought.

Eventually, the integration settled, Ian got off the table and he and Skye moved to the edge of the room to recuperate as Alison went on with the class. Students began to practice on each other and shortly a second girl began to speak in tongues as though the energy she had integrated was extremely unhappy to have suddenly found itself in the room. While the recipient of another integration twirled around in the middle of the floor like a child, saying, "Well this is the *strangest* workshop I've ever been to."

Alison watched as geometric shapes in shimmering colors lay over the top of a woman's body before the Higher Self slowly descended into it. She did not normally *see* geometry like that. But all the while she could feel a persistent energetic pull from the side of the room. As class drew to a close, she tried to remain focused but her heart was racing, her face was sweating and her hair stuck to her forehead. Eventually she could not avoid the distraction and looked up to see what was going on.

Skye and Ian were standing in the corner disheveled and wide eyed. Both were staring straight at her, they seemed bemused with their heads tilted quizzically, to one side. They looked like…well… a pair of aliens!

Alison burst out laughing, "OH, NO! You guys *cannot* go out looking like that!" She grinned. "Put your clothes on and pull yourselves together!" Everyone laughed, and class was dismissed for the day.

Alison knew that Skye had somehow facilitated a huge integration for her that day. So, that evening she began to state the I Am. "I am… I Am… I AM Horus!" she exclaimed. Horus? How was that possible? She saw the name behind her eyes, as though hurriedly scribbled on a piece of paper. The vision changed and she watched a small Egyptian boy of about 7 years old playing in a courtyard.

"Horus, is that you?" she enquired.

She could feel a deep rumbling sensation emerging from within.

"It is indeed. We have much to do together you and I."

Puzzled, she asked, "Are you an aspect of my higher self?"

"I am an aspect of your Oversoul, as you would see it. It is not so much a direct line, as you have understood."

"Are you integrating with me?" she persisted.

"I am not a full integration at this time."

"Then what is the purpose of your being here?"

"We work together."

"What is the nature of your work?"

"The same as yours..."

Alison was tired and little impatient. "Please explain."

"I am an element of the darkness and a facet of the light. I can bring to bear all aspects of the realities you seek to create. I am in the process of assisting in the emergence of great light on your planet."

She liked his answer. "How will you do this?" she asked more politely.

"By assisting you and others on the path to redemption."

Redemption, she thought, for what? "Why do we need redeeming?"

"You have fallen so far from the source of your sustenance. To bring you back fully into the light takes much negotiation, like a navigator may be forced to negotiate shallow waters with the risk of running aground, so we here must do the same."

It was beginning to sink in that the whole of humanity was considered by the Higher Realms to be *Fallen*. "How do you relate to me exactly?"

"At Source, we are all part of the whole. You are also part of the whole. You have at your disposal any aspect of Source that can best assist you at any time. It is not so much about 'whom' and 'how many'. They can be anyone, or all."

"Can you tell me more?"

"The string of pearls is a wonderful analogy. The necklace is entire unto itself, and yet you can release the pearls and have them roll away and remain separate and exclusive. Each with their own luster and imperfections, every pearl is an individual in and of itself. But when they are strung together in a necklace, they become something more than just the sum of the pearls. More beautiful and more functional for the integral parts that complete it."

"That was beautiful. I don't think I could have put that so well?"

"Ah, but you just did!"

"This is still a difficult concept for us to understand. How do we go from being only human to becoming our own source of wisdom? We are used to looking up to our teachers, and authority figures make our decisions and tell us how to be, how to think and what to do. It isn't easy to trust that we have all the answers."

He chuckled. "Do you even have all the questions?"

"Probably not." She answered, thoughtfully.

"And yet, even knowing that, it may surprise you to know that the answers are all at hand.

"How can that be?"

"Every life you have ever lived, and will ever live, is stored within the vibrating fields of energy surrounding your physical body, waiting to be accessed in the way a computer can pull down a byte of information. This is the beauty of the 'Now' moment. There is nothing really to be discovered that has not already been discovered. There are no new questions, only you returning to a page holder you left for yourself to find."

Alison thought she was beginning to understand. So, why was he here? "How can you help us going forward?"

"I have memories of the Egyptian, Sumerian and African history that will enlighten you to the truth of the beginnings of this civilization. It will help you understand what needs to be done. How you can assist the Earth in her procession. The memories will help you accept why it has to be you!"

Alison felt a knock on her heart when he said that. *'What did he mean by it?'* she thought, "Why *does* it have to be me?"

"You already have some understanding of this, I think. It will come to you and it must be revealed by you, to you."

"Did I do something wrong back then?"

"You know better than that. You know that nothing is wrong in the scheme of things. Unwise... perhaps? Poorly judged, ill advised? There are many words to describe the reasons for why some things happen. The consequences were not known before these events unfurled. You cannot hold yourself responsible for an unforeseeable turn of events, can you?"

"So I *am* responsible?" She shifted uncomfortably in her chair.

"Only because you choose to be."

The next morning, Skye and Ian arrived early and waited to speak with Alison.

Skye had endured a sleepless night. Over the course of it she had come to understand that she was here as Ian's protector in this realm. She had been kept awake all night by etheric 'baboons' that she could see scrambling all over the roof of their RV, and was worried that something was very wrong!

Alison knew that baboons were a symbol of protection in Egyptian lore.

Ian was an extremely connected young man, pure and sensory. He could see frequency, though he couldn't read it. He had no formal metaphysical education and was unpolluted by the teachings, which meant he had no preconceived ideas. Everything was *feeling* based with him, which made him very authentic. He spoke softly as he told Alison he had heard his integration say, "If I cannot find room, I will have to leave and I will have to take you with me."

Alison realized Ian had integrated an Oversoul, not a Higher Self. In that moment she was pulsed by the name, 'Ra'. As she looked at Skye, she knew she was looking at Seth. Lisa had recently integrated Isis. A quick search of Wikipedia would reveal that Isis and Seth were not 'besties', since he carved up his brother Osiris – Isis's husband, and left him scattered along the banks of the Nile Delta. This could be why Lisa could not be present. *Redemption indeed.*

Lisa had been putting the final touches to the I AM Merge protocol that would create the geometric and harmonic infrastructure to house an Oversoul, without burning out the biological vehicle. They had tried the sequence on each other, but not on another student.

Alison invited Skye and Ian to come to the house that evening and moved the priceless glass coffee tables aside to accommodate the massage table. When they arrived she was a little startled by Ian's immediate assessment of the energy in the house, "E.T. has been here," he said as he looked around.

"How do you know" Alison was a little disconcerted.

"I can see the frequency," he replied. At least Chris didn't hear him; he had gone out for the evening. So Alison felt safe to recount the dream experience of the first night they had spent in that house, which still hovered over her like a grey cloud. She had found it quite disturbing.

At the end of her story, she added, "But the weirdest thing is, that I still feel it. I still have stinging pain between my legs."

"Oh! So do I!" Skye jumped in. "I have been so sore down there the last couple of days." They all looked from one to the other, unable to voice what was in their minds. *'Had we been part of some abduction, impregnation experiment?'*

It was late so they got Ian settled on the massage table, and Alison had Skye move to the far corner of the open planned house, so as not to interfere with Ian's energy signature.

Alison had never run the I Am Merge protocol before, and Lisa had emailed the instructions from a beach somewhere in Aruba. She knew that she could call the energy down and that Grace would not allow her to mess up. She had Lisa's notes and followed them to the letter. Several times she felt herself stop in transit as she was guided and reminded where she needed to be.

As she ran the protocol Ian reacted to the positioning of Alison's hands above his body, as though he knew where she was at all times. Even from across the room and with her eyes closed, Skye felt every move and her reactions mirrored Ian's. The energy was electrifying.

At the end of the session, Ian sat bolt upright, and someone else was looking out through his eyes.

Alison addressed the being, "How are you now?"

"There is space… there is space…" answered the being known as Ra.

During the course of that weekend, Ian had integrated his Oversoul, a member of the Ra Confederacy, a collective from Andromeda, and Skye took in the being known as Seth, and had facilitated the integration of the being Horus for Alison.

Something was up, as they say… and Alison did not have a clue what it was.

As they arrived at the airport in Phoenix to begin their journey back to Boston, Alison received a disgruntled phone call from the landlady of the Sedona house. She demanded to know what they had been doing in the house, and accused her of holding wild parties.

"Where you drunk, or something, and you fell into it without knowing?" Alison had no idea what she was talking about.

The cleaner had discovered a vertical floor to ceiling crack in the door of the mirrored wardrobe, in the spare room-. Alison had been in the room just once, on arriving at the house but had not been anywhere near it since. There had been no crack in it then!

After checking in with Grace about it later, she was told it was no accident.

"The mirror was a portal. We had to shut it down." She said.

"Were we under attack?" Alison asked

"You were attacked, yes, but not taken." She assured her.

But Alison had memories of what felt like impregnation, and miscarriage. She had been afraid to think about what might have taken place that night. And frankly didn't know what to do with the thought that they had failed to protect her from it. Why did she have this memory if she was not 'taken'?"

"Those are memories of a different life time, of your previous experiences in Khem, before it became Egypt. They are beginning to return to you now."

Over the ensuing days and nights, memories and concepts surrounding that lifetime began to unfold. The survivors of the Taran cataclysm, who found themselves stranded in the density of the planet Earth, struggled to begin again in their etheric state. She had memories of the North African region known then as Khem; where volunteers would arrive to help construct and rebuild a new society and help establish the cradle of a new civilization.

On the 5th dimensional planet, those who had been preparing for Ascension to Gaia, in 7th Dimension, followed a different evolutionary command. They could not reproduce the way that humans do.

In order to survive trapped in such density, they began to experiment with more physical versions of soul carriers, and they had to find a way to reproduce them without the technologies lost to them; like the animals they found on this planet did. So experimentation began, the splicing of DNA with the species available to them and their reproductive systems. They were creating Chimera.

*   *   *

When Lisa returned she wanted to know all about Sedona. She was sad to have missed this class so soon after becoming a partner. Alison described the events of the week including the arrival of three more of the Egyptian Pantheon, in a phone call.

They knew this meant that there was something more that needed to pass between the four of them. The Egyptians were not amassing for nothing.

Alison recounted a story that Ian had told her. She felt this might be what linked Isis, Horus, Seth and Ra.

Several years earlier, Ian had visited a crystal shop on his way to the Blue Mountains National Park to look for stones he could wire-wrap for jewelry to take to an upcoming healing expo. While he was there, he noticed a basket on the counter of unusual quartz points, with a strange pink hue. He asked how much they were and bought the entire basket. On returning home he turned them out on the floor and began to arrange them. Each one contained a small metallic looking triangular-shaped 'chip'. A clear voice commanded him, "Go and get the others."

Reluctantly, he made the trek back and asked if there were more pink crystals. To his surprise, the owner of the store went into the basement and brought up a large bag of them that she said she had bought some 20 years earlier for a mineral show she never went to, and they had been sitting there ever since. She wanted over $1,000.00 for them. He bought them all and took them home. As he laid them with the others on the floor he heard the voice command again, "Go and get the others."

Wishing he had thought to make sure he had them all, he drive out to the park again, to the crystal store and asked if there were more to be had.

"Only what is on display," said the woman pointing to some additional crystals randomly scattered among the display cases.

At this point Ian felt bad taking them all. Maybe the others were meant for someone else to find. He would leave them for now and come back in a few months. If they were still there then he would buy them.

A year later, he returned to the shop and bought the remaining crystals.

On reuniting them all on the floor of his apartment, he heard once more, "Go and get the others."

Frustrated, he decided to take one more trip to the store. "Are you sure there are not more of these crystals, maybe in the basement?" he asked again. The woman assured him he had all that she had in stock. "Okay," he said, "then as I'm here I'll take a bag of clear quartz points."

The lady brought him up a plastic bag filled with quartz points to make into jewelry. He paid and went home. That night as he emptied the bag on his kitchen table, he found hidden among the clear quartz crystals, more of the pink ones, all with the signature metallic triangle. He laid them all out on the floor in a large grid and discovered he now had 500 of them.

He told Alison earnestly, "I am custodian and protector of these crystals. I know there is work I have to do with them, but I don't know what it is. I know that until it is revealed I must keep them safely hidden."

Chapter 16

On the Swing

"Wow…" Lisa sat in the driver's seat with her mouth hanging open. "I can't believe I missed all that!" Alison had already told her about the events in Sedona over the phone, but Lisa relished the opportunity to hear it all in person.

Lisa loved the sound of Skye and Ian and couldn't wait to meet them when they had planned to come to Martha's Vineyard at the start of the New Year. *Alison was right; something was definitely up,* Lisa thought. She felt Isis prickle the skin along her spine. She hadn't heard anything from Isis other than her name when she first came in and Lisa had claimed the 'I AM' presence earlier that summer.

Now they were returning to Vermont to teach a private advanced class to a small group of practitioners. It was going to be an intimate class and the first time Alison and Lisa would be there without the team.

A Marconics student, Alice, owned a beautiful 5th Dimensional oasis deep in the heart of the Vermont countryside that had become a popular summer venue. She had remodeled a lovely old Dutch barn set on an acre of land against a back drop of vibrant landscaped gardens backing up to a river overlooked by a mountain. Everything had been cultivated by Alice's own 'little pilgrim hands' and vibrationally, the land reciprocated the love it received from its caretaker and guardian.

In the back yard, nestled among the hip-high kale, pear trees, and wildflowers, there was a frog pond, a gazebo and a large fire pit surrounded by 20 or so Adirondack chairs. At the center of it was a portal. Alison and Lisa usually steered away from that in favor of opting for the Gazebo, or to go down by the riverbank to put their feet, and occasionally their whole bodies, in the cool running water.

Over the summer a major storm surge had caused flooding at the back of the property. A large garden beside the river had been badly damaged. Now it resembled ancient ruins, complete with broken pottery, cracked paving stones, and two 15-foot tall, Corinthian style columns that Alice had been able to reclaim and had posted at the entry to the garden. It was Alison's favorite place on the property and she and Lisa would often sneak down there on the breaks during class.

When they arrived Alice was beaming from ear to ear with news of her own to share. Surprisingly, she had been guided to read up on ancient Egyptian mythology and had been receiving communication from Ma'at. "It has to do with the harmonics," Alice shared over tea and her raw organic 'primal' fudge, "It's not Ma'at, it's Maaaaaat," drawing out the 'ah' sound in the goddess's name. "And the same with Nut, it's more like Nuuuuuwt."

Alison recounted her recent experiences in Sedona, the astral attack and the dream of bloody miscarriage, which the team had concluded were memories that related to attempts at early breeding programs after the settlement of Khem.

That evening in their hotel room, Alison admitted to Lisa she had tried to get some 'yes' and 'no' answers about Khem and Egypt, a few days earlier by using a pendulum. It had been some time since Grace had allowed her to use one. Whenever she tried, the pendulum would just swing back and forth as if to say 'no, no, no, no - NO!' But she wanted to know if she had been right about Skye and Ian's integrations. She was sure that Skye had received Seth, and Ian had received Ra. When Seth delivered Horus for Alison, she felt there was a healing, a clearing that occurred between those two beings. It also made sense if there was any truth to the lore why Lisa couldn't be present. Isis and Seth might have had some unfinished karma.

It was all unfolding for Alison, but Skye wasn't claiming Seth. She felt sure she was supposed to receive Hathor.

Skye and Ian had a deep soul connection, they were about to be married and what could be more romantic for them than Ra and Hathor walking down the aisle - soul mates in the higher realms. But Lisa had seen Hathor with Robin weeks before Isis arrived.

Alison wasn't sure if Skye and Ian were allowing their desire to be validated as twin flames get in the way of accepting Seth. If not, then she had been wrong about what went down in Sedona, and with all of this new information coming in; that could throw everything off.

"Well, let me try," Lisa suggested. "We're not asking questions for personal gain, we're not trying to *divine* anything – we're just looking for confirmation."

"What the hell then, let's give it a go."

Alison sat at the table with her questions ready and Lisa stood with the pendulum, which she had constructed from a silver pendant she had removed from around her neck.

"Are we connected to the Galactic Federation of light?" Alison asked.

The pendulum swung back and fore, in a '*Yes*' motion

"Are you lying to me?"

It switched and began to swing side to side, '*No.*'

"Did Skye integrate Seth?"

Yes

"Did Ian integrate Ra?"

Yes

"Did Alison integrate Horus?"

Yes

So far so good, they were pleased with the outcome. The connection seemed clear so they pressed on. They also were asking for clarity around the different types of Higher Soul integrations, now that Isis and Horus had seemingly just strolled in. So Alison tried to establish a base line by asking about Lisa's integration with Ariel first, "Is Ariel Lisa's Oversoul?"

No. They threw each other a look across the table

Alison plowed on. "Is Lisa a vessel for Ariel?"

No

"Is Ariel Lisa's Higher Self?"

No

Alison's face fell in dismay, and as she looked across at Lisa she could see she wore a similar expression.

"Are we still connected to the Galactic Federation of Light?"

Yes

"Are you lying to me?"

Yes

"Crap!" said Lisa. She dropped the pendulum on the table and sat back in her chair.

"Alison," said Lisa.

"Yes," replied Alison.

"A yellow film just descended over you, can you see it?"

"Yes, it's over you too." Alison confirmed.

They stood and facing each other as the vibration suddenly dropped through the floor. There was a presence in the room.

Alison closed her eyes to be able to see inter-dimensionally and watched as something large and dark dropped in behind Lisa.

"Um… Alison…?"

"Yes?" said Alison, slowly, her eyes still closed.

"There's something in this room, isn't there?"

"Yes…"

"It's standing right behind me, isn't it?"

"Yes"

"Damn it!" Lisa cursed. Whatever it was, it was big and it was threatening.

"There are two smaller ones in the room as well," Alison noted calmly. Lisa could see them too. They looked like dark energy silhouettes against the light color of the walls.

Lisa felt for Ariel. She was on alert but didn't seem to be completely freaking out.

Alison called for Galactic support and Lisa called in the Archangels. They both felt the energy in the room shift as the two smaller beings were immediately neutralized. The larger one was still looming over Lisa, and Alison watched wide-eyed as the Archangels beheaded it.

"Alison,"

"Yeeesss,"

"How much trouble do you think we're in?" Lisa asked sheepishly.

"A shitload," Alison confirmed. They knew there would be backlash from Grace and Ariel for this, who had warned them many times about playing with matches.

* * *

That afternoon in class three integrations took place. One woman had remained on the table settling in with her integration. As she was downloading information from her higher self, she decided to share with the group of women.

"She was showing me how we as women used to handle our periods in the olden days," She began. "We used to use cotton and wool. Certain pieces we would keep and others would get thrown away." The student seemed delighted with this information and the sharing got more and more graphic.

Lisa shot Alison *'the look'* and interrupted. "Wow - well, thanks for sharing that."

As class neared the end of the day, Alison looked over to see Lisa was struggling to stand up and had doubled up in pain at the end of the massage table.

"What's going on, are you okay?" Alison asked concerned.

"I don't know. I have a piercing pain going all the way up…" indicating the central column of her body. She excused herself and went into the bathroom. She came out and whispered to Alison, "seriously, what the heck? I just got my period – I'm 10 days early, that *never* happens!"

"Let's go," Alison whispered back, and called the close of class for the day. They'd reconvene in the morning.

As they headed back to the hotel, Lisa downloaded.

"There is something missing with the story of Seth. I think it has to do with blood sacrifices."

"Go on," Alison encouraged.

"Well, here's the thing – the lore says Seth dismembered Osiris. But there was a contract in place. It wasn't a murder in the way we would perceive it."

"I get that," Alison agreed.

"It has to do with the DNA. I think it's a reference to the seedings. It's also Karma - Seth and Osiris were like Jesus and Judas. I don't think Judas was the bad guy."

Alison nodded. She knew where Lisa was going with this and had come to the same conclusions.

"Jesus and Judas had an understanding and an agreement that Judas would turn Jesus in, so that the 'blood' would be on Judas's hands as the betrayer rather than putting a karmic debt on any of the other apostles. I feel that was the same with Osiris and Seth - that there needed to be a blood sacrifice, a volunteering of the DNA, the volunteering to participate in the process of adding density to the new soul carriers they were experimenting with in Khem."

"Yes, that's right. Throughout history the sacrifice of blood was for us to understand the seedings in the DNA. It was just misunderstood, misinterpreted."

"Yes, no need to be throwing virgins into volcanoes and shedding blood that way."

After dinner, Alison thought they might try to get a few answers from Ariel.

Alison decided to lead Lisa to allow for other connections to be made.

"You are at the foot of the staircase, and you are aware that you can hear activity behind a door in the hallway. There is jovial noise. People are talking and laughing. Light is coming from under the door, and you feel yourself being drawn to it. When you approach the door you see there is a beautiful crystal doorknob. You are aware of the laughter and the joy that is coming from this room.

"You want to be on the other side of the door. Place your hand on the doorknob, turn it, and allow the door to open inwards... The light is very bright... almost blinding since you've come from the darkness of the hallway. It's difficult to make out at first who is there. As you step into the room you are aware of the beings that are turning to welcome you.

"As your vision begins to clear and you can make out their faces you'll recognize who they are; every one of these beings has been waiting for you. They've created this safe space here for you where you can join them and be peaceful and calm. Here you are able to address them in your own language and translate their answers through your own systems into a language you can understand.

"You'll notice in the middle of the room there is a large round table. The beings are moving toward the table now. Each one of them is taking a seat around it and one of them is beckoning to you and is indicating the seat next to him is yours. Go take your seat at the table and make yourself comfortable there. This is where you belong. You've been here many, many times before.

"Look around the table and see the faces in the room, see those you recognize and who you remember.

"What can you see?"

Lisa allowed her mind to scan. As the picture came into focus, she began to describe to Alison. *"I can see myself entering into the room. It's constructed of light, yet it's solid."*

"I am at a round table, the Council is here and there is a hologram at the center of the table. They are showing me splitting cells. Cell division... This is to help us understand more of the Atlantean and Egyptian stories, and how it relates to the hybrids."

Alison observed that Lisa was quiet for a few moments, engaged in with the Council. Alison's calm, soothing voice pushed through the silence.

"Is Grace at the table?"

"Yes, she's seated next to Ariel and Ashtar, they are on either side of her. Michael is there."

"Are you in a body?"

"I have an awareness that I'm in a body, it's a different body...The energy system feels different, stronger, more powerful." As the frequency crystallized, she could see the form more clearly. *"Ah,"* she sighed, *"I believe this is a hybrid body... they are allowing me to experience through this perception filter."*

"Who else is seated at the round table?"

"Raffé. The style of clothing is a little different than how I've seen him before." Alison and Lisa both thought Raffé looked like one of the Centurions from Roman antiquity. She noted the odd presentation. It was a translation of the frequency. *"It looks like he is wearing brander's breeches. I don't know where that phrase is coming from, but he is beside Grace. Only he is standing behind her to the left. Other beings are stepping forward now*

and I can see Metatron, represented as lightning and fire. Angelics are also present. Gabriel flashed in as a tree so I would recognize him, and now he is revealing his face to resemble an image I would know. His eyes are blue gray. There's a spark of light coming from his forehead, and his hair is light, long and curly – he is smiling. He is gesturing to me – a hand to his heart, a hand to his forehead and both extend out toward me."

"How do you interpret that gesture?"

Lisa felt the vibration of love coming from that gesture. It was intimate and powerful. *"It's a greeting, a recognition. It means... 'So you know me in your heart.'"*

"What else can you see?"

"There is a Mantis presence. He is revealing himself in humanoid form. I do not know his name but he is one we have worked with in the past. He is showing me his headdress. It looks like something tribal, like a clan chief might have worn in the Middle Ages; A wolf's head or a bear's head to denote his strength and bravery. This is the headdress of a mantis. He is lending me his protection..." Lisa was quiet for a moment, and then conceded, *"There are other vibrations present, but I am not able to see who is there."*

"So Lisa, we are going to ask one of these beings to step forward and act as a chair for the rest. One being is going to funnel the information from the Council and relate the answers back to you... Who is there?"

Lisa responded in a deep, husky voice, *"EEEE set"*

"Who are you?"

"I am, I am an original Being. You call us... the Pantheon."

"Are you an aspect of Lisa's higher self?"

"Yes... Alison," Lisa broke through, *"the Egyptians have shown up at the table."*

"Is this the first time we have spoken to you through Lisa?"

"She has experienced our vibration before, she knows us as Isis."

"Do they need us to do something with the crystals?"

"Yes. We will need to activate them, to listen to them. They are encoded with the original plans for the light bodies, the original plans... for Ascension attempt number six. Where we went wrong, and how to fix it. When we go back to... it will be Tara, but when we go to Gaia, in 7th Dimension, that is where Atlantis is.

"This is the Atlantis that didn't get destroyed?"

"Correct"

"Atlanteans are still living there? When they talk about 'Atlantis rising' is that what they mean?"

"Yes. That's our home… for the hybrids."

"Are Lisa and I hybrids?"

"Yes. That is what we came here to be." Lisa fell silent. The energy in the room changed and Alison could feel the prickling in her skin.

"Why is the Pantheon returning at this time?"

"So that the future will not be subject to the mistakes of the past.

"More of the truth will be revealed through your integration of these higher aspects of yourself. You have been trained, both of you, through your experiences in telepathic travel to the library… to the ships… to Amenti… to the light cities… the work will be done just like this, but you will all travel as a group.

"This is how you will be able to access the knowledge contained within the Atlantean crystals. You will bring them with you and once the connection is forged, no matter where they are, if they are lost, or even destroyed… you would maintain connection to the consciousness stored in them because the information will be activated and placed in the library."

"I thought everything was already stored in the library?"

"No."

"Is that because of the action that Thoth took? Or, is that because of the fall of Atlantis?" Alison ventured, remembering that Thoth the Atlantean had been credited with stealing important records from Atlantis.

"They were… mislaid during the evacuation of Atlantis. Thoth had them in his care, yes. His actions have been misunderstood. He did a great service by protecting them."

"Where is Thoth, will he integrate with one of us?"

"He will not, he remains in Spirit and is accessible as a guide."

"And what about Ra?"

As though looking around in the higher realms, Isis responded, *"I do not see him here."*

"Has he integrated?"

"Yes, but the process is not complete."

"It is not complete?" There was a touch of alarm in Alison's voice as she was immediately concerned that something went wrong with the psychic surgery she had performed on Ian, during the I AM Merge.

Isis explained, "The integration is not complete. It is up to the free will of the incarnate. The structures are in place. You have done nothing wrong."

Alison was relieved, **"Is there a risk with Higher Self integration, can it harm someone, or even result in their death?"** The one thing Alison would not abide was being used to intentionally or unintentionally cause harm.

"You are wondering about the experience you had with Ian, yes? There are not many among you that are carrying such a high level of contract. You know that. Others will not be subjected to such risk; they have not contracted for it. Could their bodies burn out? Yes. Which is why you have been given the protocol."

Alison was quiet for a moment.

"Did Seth integrate with Skye?"

Again it felt to Lisa like Isis was searching the higher realms before answering. *"I do not see him here."*

Wondering about her own Egyptian connection, Alison asked, **"Who do I have?"**

"The Falcon," Isis said with a smile.

"Horus?"

"Yes."

"Who in history did Horus previously incarnate as?"

"He was not incarnated. Humans would have considered him a God King – the majority of the pantheon are coming from 10 and 11."

"Those are Angelic Realms. Is he Angelic?"

"We are all Angelics. The first expression of source in density; Let there be light."

Isis chuckled darkly and said only, *"When that connection with Horus is unleashed, the call will be even stronger to others that are waiting to awaken."*

From the command room, Ariel shot a warning look to Isis. There were some things the incarnates were not yet ready to know. They were allowing a flow of information to be accessed by the women through data streaming, but it needed to be tactical in its delivery and detail.

Perplexed by the cryptic message, Alison fired off several questions before Isis could answer the first one. **"Is Horus a higher energy than**

Grace, a stronger energy than Grace? Is Horus my higher self? Then, who is Grace?"

"We don't understand your question? Grace is an expression of Source. Grace is in charge, tasked with maintaining, managing, directing, orchestrating, the project of Earth, the human Atlantean initiative. She is responsible for this Universe; but belonging to many others."

"Do we need to find more of the Egyptians to be able to take this telepathic journey with the crystals?

"No, what you will require will be provided. Any vibrations that are not present will be able to link to you once you access the Halls of Amenti. You may call them forth and they will respond, telepathically. We are already calling them together to fulfill our contracts to activate the crystals, unlock the knowledge and to create a shift in the timeline. This is the most important thing that will be happening for us all at the start of the new year."

"What timeline do you want us to switch to?"

"Critical mass, critical mass where enough of us can lift off and split"

"We've heard for so long that the shift was going to occur, is that now not true?"

"It is still a possibility. Understand that the shift of this timeline is not a direct result of your action or lack of action. There are other beings working for other agendas, as you know…"

Lisa broke through and whispered to Alison, "She just said 'You win some and lose some.' They are fighting for the timeline."

Lisa was being shown a battle for the timeline being conceded by Arcturans to beings with faces like Reptilians. "The battle was lost, with many casualties. But the war wages on."

Critical mass was a positive in Alison's book; reassurance that Human Collective could make the higher choices and see a more benevolent and seamless Shift.

"Is it significant that the mislaid crystals have finally surfaced? Are they to assist our Ascension? Or, are they just records.?"

Ariel nodded to Isis again. These two women were not going to follow on blind faith alone, but too much knowledge too soon, could put the operation at risk.

Isis reigned herself in, *"They will aid your Ascension in the way that we had discussed before, in awakening others to the story, helping them to resonate with their truth."*

"What is stored in them?"

There was a momentary pause, which told Alison they were not about to reveal that to her. *"Your human story. And the mistakes that were made, as you would see it from a human perspective, how previous attempts to return Earth to light were fought and opposed by avaricious agendas that won out, trapping Atlantean souls within this karmic density.*

"We traveled the portal bridge to merge with the morphogenetic fields of your Earth and become manifest on its surface. Our vibrations were sent down on a far reaching mission to reclaim the souls that were lost when Atlantis fell through the dimensions.

"We deactivated our DNA, in order to reduce and solidify our energetics, so that we could function in density. But when we arrived we did not realize that the portals would not be accessible for our return journey. To survive in such heavy gravity we knew we must find a new way to thrive.

"Our original understanding of souls, of spirit, of vibrational frequencies descending into density from the higher realms was that we would be able to incarnate divinity in this three-dimensional reality. It was not so. We became disconnected from Source. We did not fully understand the implications of this. Consequently, all our attempts to bring this planet to light have been unsuccessful."

Alison could feel the vibration in the room change again as Isis receded. Lisa took a deep breath and exhaled slowly. She was still deep within the hypnotic state. Alison could see that she was serene and decided to push the session further.

"Lisa, can you pull Ariel forward?"

"Yes."

"Hello Alison,"

"Thank you, Ariel"

"Ariel, do you know what Isis meant when she said a while ago 'When the energy of Horus is unleashed,' that was an interesting choice of words... what did that mean?"

Ariel decided that next time she would gag Isis. There was no choice now. They'd have to provide more disclosure without compromising the mission or the women. If asked direct questions they could not pour down the frequency of a 'lie.' It would be detected immediately; they'd know.

"There is tremendous power with Horus and when you allow yourself to connect into that vibration...When you claim that 'I AM', what you know now will pale in comparison to what you will know then."

"I don't understand?"

"What was learned, in what you would call Egypt, was that the spiritual beings placed in the dense vehicles began to fall asleep and forget. They fell victims to the trappings of the three-dimensional matter world.

"The reason that we project down to density is for the richness of the experience that we cannot have in the higher realms. We can see that walking bare foot in the grass may be a wonderful experience, but cannot feel it under our feet the way that you can in your human biological soul carriers.

"This is why the first blend of hybrids was created, and are being contained on ship at this moment. So that they can be the forefathers of this new lineage of beings, able to bring the vibrations of Oneness, of Unity and Enlightenment that we have come to know in the higher realms, down to merge with the human experience, maintaining all of the wonderment of true physical form.

"Our hope is that humanity and the human experience – all of the wonder and joy contained within the human experience – will be blended with these divine essences to create new beings... retaining individuality but instantly and acutely connected to Source, freely operating under Divine Directive."

"That sounds pretty amazing."

"Yes."

"Will this happen on our timeline?"

"hmmm... From our perspective the timelines remain difficult to access because at any given moment there are multiple players affecting, challenging, switching, the outcomes within the Free Will zone."

"And you need us to help you promote and support one timeline over another?"

"You are seeking clarity of the timelines and how they work? They are a web, not just a single time track or linear line. Lisa's suspicion of the timelines involves a combination of the multiverse and collapsing wave theories and this would be accurate. We have moved you, Alison and Lisa, many times from one collapsing timeline onto another, with a different potential outcome.

"As different timelines are observed and made real, and new more positive

ones created through collective consciousness, the requirement is to begin collapsing more negative ones, to eventually align with one, as we move the energy waves forward towards achieving critical mass.

"As far as Marconics is concerned and the role you and your team will play in this Ascension; you will address the more difficult timelines of probability. As one timeline reaches critical mass, we will shift your team onto a less benevolent one, to advance the reclamation and closure of this project."

Suddenly Lisa's physical body began to shake and tremble.

Ariel sensed Alison's concern, *"Guardian presence in this room is extremely palpable. Lisa's physical vehicle is experiencing extreme cold."*

Alison unceremoniously grabbed a huge comforter and threw it over Lisa to stop her shaking. **"Ariel,"** Alison continued, **"Is this is a good way for us to check in with you, and the Council?"**

"Yes, this is a good way for you to speak to us. Lisa is calm and her fears are not at play."

"Can you help her maintain that?"

"We can try. Her concerns of doing something wrong or dangerous or detrimental to you or herself or the mission limit her in that way. She doesn't doubt her abilities. In being concerned about allowing her ego to be in play she allows her ego to be in play. It's what you would call the chicken and the egg. We will plant the seed and so can you. The doubting will eventually subside."

"Is there a way to help her with discernment and doubt?"

"It has been difficult for her to access and decode the telepathic communications that have been sent down to her — it is a matter of learning how to speak a new language."

Claircognizance was uncharted territory for Lisa. She relied on her strong clairvoyant, clairaudient, and clairsentient senses. She couldn't just know something, she had to see it, to hear it, or feel it. She needed proof it wasn't made up in her head. Alison, on the other hand, could 'know' something and once she 'knew' it; she rarely wavered.

"Will her fears be eased moving forward? Or, will they impact her ability to deliver on the mission?"

"Lisa is acutely aware of what she is being called to do. She is committed to this mission alongside you, and to you. She understands that her soul contracts have changed. It is a matter of whether she will be able to step into the levels of multi-dimensionalism that are opening up for her, as per her request."

"Can we talk about the higher self integrations? Why are we seeing so many integrations in the classroom now?

"The 'troops' are being deployed because the timelines are speeding up and the stakes are being raised. We are sending boots to ground to support you. This is why there are so many 'deliveries.' We confirm that without the presence of the Higher Selves and the Oversouls, our project cannot succeed. Incarnate divinity, cannot be achieved on the Earth plane if critical mass cannot be achieved."

"And if you are not successful this time?"

"If it fails this time, those that have raised their vibrations high enough will be taken off world – they will be removed from the Earth."

'Now we're getting somewhere,' Alison thought. **"Removed? Like in a death transition?"**

"To those around them this would be experienced as death, yes. In some cases there will be walk-ins; other souls contracted to stay within the three dimensional matrix that will trade places with those who will exit the body in Ascension.

"It is dependent on timelines and whether we will reach critical mass with the collective of Earth. The most likely and most probable outcome will be an instantaneous transfer of awareness from the physical vibration of the 3rd dimension into a hybrid vehicle within the 5th dimension. It is unlikely that the physical vehicles that exist in the density of the 3rd dimensional Earth will be able to sustain the intensity of the vibrational frequencies within the higher 5th Dimension and beyond.

"Originally as this information was passed down, those that heard it would not have been ready to receive it. In this new paradigm, we would love all of humanity to raise their vibrational signatures high enough to be able to facilitate Earth's return to 5th while the planet is inhabited – however, it is not the most probable outcome.

"The Higher Selves and Oversouls are progressively integrating with their incarnates to support Plan 'B' – Hybridization.

"When the incarnate integrates their Oversoul, the Oversoul enters the hologram of the 3rd dimensional reality in a shared experience. It assimilates all of the memories and experiences the incarnate has had by joining with their physical vehicle. The Oversoul shares the human experience firsthand.

"As the Ascension continues, the human souls will have an opportunity to

rise up with the vibration of the Oversoul. If they have met the requirements and achieved mastery, then they may populate a hybrid vehicle as their own Oversoul.

"Alternatively, they would remain phase-locked in 3D and continue to burn out their quantum energy as it is tied to 3D Earth in this fall system, and be reabsorbed by their Oversoul in a death transition. They will cease to exist as an individual expression."

"That's Plan 'B'?"

"Yes."

"We still have free will then, it's a choice – we can stay or, we can go provided we meet the requirements?"

"When Lisa ascends she will become a blended essence, like Ashtar, or Sananda. She will be mostly Lisa, with a blend of Ariel, Isis, and others according to future choices and alignments.

"She will become a Hybrid, a unique blended essence, with the Galactic Memory of all of those who have contributed to her blend, stored in the hybrid vehicle. Yet she will also be Lisa, retaining the virtue of Lisa's humanity.

"When you were told about the Ascension plan to bring the Human Vehicle to light, the more expansive truth is, that it is your human personality, your human incarnated consciousness that will be brought to a vehicle in light, should you choose it.

"The Human Upgrade is enhancing the human vehicle to be able to experience the higher light frequencies in THIS density... which in turn enables the integration of the Oversoul ... which in turn enables the Ascension of the human incarnate soul to Light Body."

"Thank you."

"Thank you."

"I will check in again and we send our love."

"And we too, we send our love."

*   *   *

Alison began the process to bring Lisa back up from hypnosis. She had been under for a long time.

Lisa's eyes gradually fluttered open, greeted by Alison's smile. "How do you feel? It looked like a struggle to come back up this time."

"It felt like my eyes were super-glued shut!" Lisa agreed.

Alison pulled a face and laughed, "They were literally rolled to the top of your head!" She passed Lisa her cell phone so she could see the video.

"Holy cow!" Lisa marveled.

"Truly, I could see them way up here," Alison pointed to her forehead, "While you were trying to..."

"Open them?"

"Oh no, they were open, they were kind of half open, but the eyeballs would not come down. I could see them flickering, it reminded me of one of those gaming machines in a casino, pull the arm to get three cherries?"

"Oh wow, it really is hard to open them," Lisa was rubbing vigorously.

"They been suckered shut!" Alison teased.

It took time to come down fully from such a high altitude of frequency, they needed time to release and rearrange their confused thoughts.

"So... wow! The whole critical mass timeline thing...?" said Lisa.

"Yeah, I was a little surprised about that too. It was not the answer I was expecting. It sounded as if they were saying, *'Yeah, you know? This whole 'seamless shift', critical mass thing... it's really, probably... not so much going to happen. Just so's ya know...*"

Lisa picked up on Alison's thread, "So, you kids go right ahead and keep on rooting for that, but...."

"Rah, rah, yay, yay!" Alison cheered, then raised an eye-brow and drummed her fingers on her chin. "And so, what if we have to snatch you up...? It means you're gonna pass on that whole astral thing – so that's great!" She joked.

Then pondering, "I'm not even sure critical mass can be the best option from their perspective... After all they have witnessed of humanity? Surely there are far too many people unable to make higher choices here, without setting them loose to run amok in the higher realms." She mused.

Lisa said, "They were showing me that if enough people became aware, the ripple effect will continue to move over the planet and that over time the Earth will become a better place."

"A gradual shift, yes, I get that. But I thought we didn't have time for that now?"

"Well, if they reached critical mass Earth will, eventually, just naturally ascend up seamlessly. It'll just sort of happen."

"But from our perspective that sounds like the least attractive option, doesn't it? *'Watchya mean we gotta be here for another 40 years doing this, and then what? JUST DIE??!'*"

Lisa laughed so hard she snorted. She knew Alison secretly wanted the Ascension with trumpets and fanfare, perhaps a heraldic angel or two? Or, dammit, at least a spaceship landing on the lawn.

Alison back-peddled. "I mean, I'm pleased if everyone is making this nice easy transition, but at the same time it's like – *'oh… great… I'm still here'*."

They both gasped for air between the peals of laughter.

"I think if that happens, we'll see change quicker than we anticipated. It won't be as violent and bloody as being yanked up in cataclysm would be. And I think that if--"

"Yes," Alison interrupted, teasing, "Always nice not to be violent and bloody!"

"Yes! Yes! *Says the Butcher*!" Lisa pointed to herself with both thumbs.

Now it was Alison's turn to snort with laughter as she coughed out, "WE could do with a little less 'violent and bloody'."

"It's all good," said Alison after a moment. "Whichever way it comes down it's all good. But what I'm trying to do, more and more is release any expectations I have around any of it. I just don't want to be instilling expectations in others. We don't want to be talking 'rapture' if there ain't any; that's the only thing that concerns me."

"Well that's the whole thing though - it hasn't been determined yet."

"It's very difficult to tell people to get on the train. *'Well where's it going?'* 'uh, we don't know.' Isn't it?"

"Well I think if we can get enough people awakened, the plan is to bring us up in a very peaceful and gentle way; and eventually we will look around and realize that we have paradise on Earth. Then we will be in the 5th Dimension."

"And strangely, when you look around sometimes, it doesn't seem like that could be very far off. When you hear the way they talk about how the higher dimensions look down onto the grass but are not able to feel it, you start to get a sense of how great we have it here. Also, I'm starting to get a sense that they can't wait to get down here themselves…"

"That's what I think that whole hybridization process is about. Earth would become like one of Ariel's 'worlds between the worlds', that she likes to visit for R&R, when she 'assumes form'."

Alison began tapping her chin again. Her voice took on a conspiratorial tone, "So! The truth is…"

"Uh oh," Lisa couldn't suppress the smirk, "Oh no, uh oh – here we go…"

"Bear with me…" Alison's journalistic mind was pulling the headline together.

"My hands are itchy," Lisa commented. It was a side effect from holding the frequency for so long.

"Just bear with me on this – The truth is that… um, Earth is prime real estate."

"Yes, it is."

"And those in the higher dimensions are looking down at the lovely green grass and thinking – *You know… we should get ourselves some of that*."

"Yes…" They were moving on to Alison's favorite conspiracy theory.

"We should have a holiday home on the waterside, just there," she pretended to pin point a spot on Martha's Vineyard, where she lived.

"Yes…" Lisa was holding the giggles back thinking 'Here it comes…'

"And what would be really cool is… if we could persuade them to smarten themselves up a bit… take better care of those bodies so we can get some second hand mileage out of them!"

The giggling took hold of them both.

Lisa joined in, "That's right! We don't want to live in Harlem, we want to go to the Upper East Side."

"So we're not going to TELL them… actually… we just want to come down and use your bodies for a while. They're not going to be bothered to do the work necessary to raise those vibrations to make their bodies good temples for us anyway… so we're going to tell them that they need to raise their vibrational frequency or THEY DIE - that'll make them do it!"

Both women were crying with laughter.

Lisa howled, "Yes! Yes, and then we can pop down and have some chocolate and run through the grass barefoot!"

Now they were laughing so hard neither one could speak at all.

"That could be it! It could be a takeover! It could be body snatching…

or, it could be a case of *'we let the kids use the holiday house for long enough it's time they went and got their own place. Cause I'm planning to retire down there'.*" Alison went silent for a moment. "I feel that there is..."

"What?"

"I think there is moooore --"

"Of course there is!" Lisa blurted.

"-- to the picture than they're telling us and even if it's a case of *'We've devised a new game. And we think the next level of experience would be fun if we could experience it too. We'd like to experience it there, but you are currently 'there'.*"

"No, they don't want to be here, they don't want to be here in this density."

"No, they want to be on the planet when the planet is in paradise!"

Lisa opened her mouth and then closed it. Then she had to agree, "Yes..."

"Yes." Alison smiled.

"The thing is... that at their level they have the unity, they have the oneness, they have the love and compassion...they have all of those things ... that we talk about hoping to achieve in 5th Density. They have it already. But what they don't have is the earthy, crunchy ability to have sex, eat chocolate and go swimming."

"No! That's right, and they want some of that too." Alison agreed.

"But they want to have it without the entrapment of ego ... and extreme duality. Without having to work a 9-5 job, and preferably without paying taxes..." It did sound like their description of hybridization. The best of humanity blended with divinity."

"So we are a 'fixer-upper' are we?" Alison asked.

"Yes."

"A 'fixer upper' on the beach... that they need to make habitable... for their next experience."

"Right." Lisa agreed.

"And why not...?"

"Well I think that's one of the things about going to light, going to light is wonderful... but after a few hundred millennia..."

Alison's eyes grew wide to match her insane smile, "It must be... really...really...blah." One thing she hated was boredom.

"Here I am," Lisa gestured dramatically, "STILL light.... Woo hoo, thumbs-up!"

They broke out into another fit of giggles.

Lisa shimmied her shoulders, and made 'jazz hands'. "WOO! Look at me over here! I'm a vibrating geometric shape..."

Laughing, Alison chirped, "Busy being a celestial body!"

Lisa exaggerated a heavy, tired, tone, "FOR... THE... LAST... FOUR HUNDRED AND FIFTY BILLION YEARS ... OH MY GOD, CAN WE GET A COOKIE?!?!"

They were peeing themselves.

"Anyone know where Uriel is???" Alison couldn't help herself, no one ever seemed to have the faintest idea of where Uriel was and they laughed even harder!

Seriously!" Lisa roared. Then she held her hands up. "Oh wow!"

"Let me see, are they burning?"

"Yeah, I got little blisters popping up."

Suddenly, Alison became the big sister, and Lisa the little one. Alison patted her leg and sent her off to the bathroom, "Well there you go now. Go run your hands under the cold water. Obviously you've held this vibration for too long."

* * *

It was the last day and as promised, time was made for "The Crownings." Alice had received Higher Self integrations before. They reminded Alison of a hiccough; not the dramatic integrations that could result in snot, tears, contortions, and hysterical laughter. Alice had declared that her integrations were *dignified*, and she was glad for it.

Lisa looked over to see Alice on a massage table turning red as her chest and face flushed. She felt the telltale pressure in her own crown and heart centers, walked across the room to the table and traded places with the student practitioner. This was a contract and Alice's Higher Self was being persnickety.

After a moment of engaging in Alice's field, Lisa felt pushed aside as the integration began. Alice was lost in the moment of emotion and ecstasy that can accompany a deeply spiritual experience – the loud *'oh yeahs'* did not smack of 'dignified.' The energy pouring down on them both was frothy and jubilant. When it was complete, Alice's eyes opened and Ma'at was looking out of them. Isis leant down in Lisa's body and kissed Alice's face on the cheeks. Her deep voice rumbled low in Lisa's throat, "Welcome sister, we've been waiting for you,"

*   *   *

Before leaving town Alison and Lisa met Alice for an early lunch. They realized that they would need to use Ian's crystals and the power of the 'full clan', either on the Vineyard or back at Alice's place. They had been told 'the twelve' would come together; they were already being called.' They realized they did not mean 12 incarnates, simply the 12 first expressions of Source in this density, as represented by the Egyptian Pantheon… and they could each be carrying one or multiples of them.

·   They sketched out on paper –

Alison/Horus

Lisa/Isis

Alice/Ma'at & Nut

Ian/Ra

Skye/Seth

That left six more to come. They suspected Osiris was already here. He came in during the very first Crowning Alison had demonstrated in Provincetown, a few months earlier. He had been the first. That left Hathor & Thoth… the call was out and they knew to have faith.

They decided to take one more stroll through Alison's favorite garden before leaving, as they wouldn't be back in Vermont before the spring. The air was warm and sweet and everything seemed at peace. As they neared the white columns the energy changed.

The portal was in the center of the backyard by the fire pit, this was something different. As if called by a concealed force, Alison was drawn through the columns of the garden that had been destroyed by the storm surge, which now reminded her of Atlantis with its chipped pots and cracked pathways. She climbed on to the huge wooden swinging bench at the very end and sat for a few moments feeling the energy.

Lisa stood by the gate, head cocked listening to the toning wooden chimes hanging from a tall pine. It sounded like voices, like monks singing. "Can you hear that?" she asked Alice.

Just then Alison called down to them, "Come here and sit, there is something going on with the energy. Come down here." Lisa plopped down on Alison's right side, closest to the river. Alice sat on her left. They took their feet off the ground and allowed the swing to move.

The rocking combined with the gentle running water and soft rustling breeze was hypnotic as they sat with their faces pointed towards the warm fall sun. They each began to take themselves down through their own personal individual styles of meditation.

Alison remembered the Pleiadians telling her to open a portal in the third eye to correspond with the portal in the garden to be able to forge a connection and a link to it. For the first time she could see Horus's eye pulsing out gold light which was washing through Alison's energy field. She could hear Alice on one side gasping at some realization or concept that she had now fully grasped.

Alison found she was opening her eyes and could see that the columns were vibrating. She was disappointed that she had allowed herself to break from the meditation and wondered why she had opened her eyes. Lisa had her head bowed and her hands almost clawing in her lap. She was rocking and it was her jerking motions that were causing the swing to move.

Lisa heard Isis calling, "Wind, Wind, WIND!" and the wind began to pick up. She heard Isis call for the wind again and the chimes got louder and the wind whipped through the dry fall leaves overhead. Isis called the water, and the river no longer sounded like a babbling brook but like raging rapids. Finally, Isis called forth the fire. Lisa was struck by heat and the roar of an interdimensional blaze that ignited in Alice's fire pit.

Instinctively Alison knew to place her hand on the sacred heart space on Lisa's back. The instant she made contact with her, Lisa sat bolt upright with her face skyward. She ceased to be Lisa and Alison could see Isis in the proud stance of an Egyptian Queen. Alison heard Germain command her, *'Go my little flying monkey.'*

Alison knew that Lisa had left this dimension and she should not lose the connection with her. She was holding the space for her to return. Lisa was gone.

The chimes were playing a beautiful melody that sounded to Alison like medieval monks toning somewhere out in space. It was as if reality had been suspended, and they were frozen in a moment outside of time and space.

Lisa saw a pair of golden eyes looking right at her; the two eyes of Horus - the left and the right. Suddenly, Lisa felt Isis lurch forward. She began speaking to Lisa in a form of telepathic synchronicity that she had not yet experienced. She was in Isis's body, looking through *her* eyes.

She heard the high pitched cry of a falcon piercing the sky and was downloaded with Isis's memories in a full disclosure of all she had experienced and participated in during her time in Khem; all that she needed to be redeemed for.

Then Lisa felt the full impact of a punch as it thudded hard on the center of her back. She lurched backward in the swing as she crash-landed back into her own physical body with speed and force. Alison barely managed to catch Lisa before she toppled off it, and pulled her in.

"They followed Horus – we did, we followed him through the desert. He led the Atlantean survivors to the new land to begin again," Lisa was crying from the intensity of the experience. "We were trapped; we couldn't go home. Lisa sucked in a deep breath. "I – was – cutting up – a body – it was awful – savage," she was barely comprehensible through the uncontrollable sobbing, "it was alive!"

Alison shushed her and both she and Alice held Lisa until she calmed down. She described to them both in vivid detail everything Isis showed her.

"What made you slap me on the back?" Lisa finally thought to ask Alison.

"I didn't slap you."

"Yes you did, I felt it. That's what pulled me back. I think if I stayed longer, I might not have been able to come back."

"I had my hand on your back the whole time, and that's when you lifted your face. I never moved it." Alison told her what she'd heard St. Germain say, and that she was being guided to maintain a connection with Lisa who had been out of her body for almost two hours.

Alison looked at her, "You're going to be the Oracle in this."

They slowly left the garden and stood in the sloping green yard for moment. Somehow it was 2 o'clock. It had remained eerily quiet, not even a car had passed by during the two and half hours they were outside. Sad to leave, they hugged and kissed Alice goodbye and headed out east on the only road out of town. A half-mile down the road a tractor-trailer stacked with logs had overturned, shedding its load and blocking their way. The policeman re-directing traffic sent them back west.

GPS would not give another route and kept recalculating its same path. They had no choice but to head back toward Alice's – without GPS Lisa's navigational skills were non-existent and in the States, Alison's were limited to the Vineyard. It took them over an hour from when they left Alice's to get back to their starting point and on the highway out of town – normally a ten-minute drive.

As they rounded the bend near Alice's barn, hugging the curve of the river, the car suddenly lurched towards the water, as though hit broadside by an unseen force. Lisa compensated, turning the wheel but the unseen hand was forcing the car off the road. Suddenly they hit an invisible barrier bouncing them back on course.

"What the HELL was that?" Alison demanded.

"*Something* tried to push us off the road!"

"… and *something else* stopped it."

Chapter 17

The Library

It was a nice treat for Alison; usually she was the one leading the path to relaxation and an open subconscious mind. She relaxed as best she could. The white wicker chairs aligned perfectly with the beach theme of the quiet Cape Cod hotel, but they left little to be desired in terms of comfort.

Lisa followed the hypnosis script she had heard Alison use and helped her to reach a state where she could lower her critical filters.

She guided her through the imagery. "Allow your eyes to adjust to the light. You're now in the corridor that leads to inner chambers of the halls of Amenti. As you focus on the passageway you may be aware of the light source that enables you to go forward. You can walk down the hallway observing what the walls are made of.

"They are limestone..." Alison answered.

"Good," said Lisa, pleased. "Be aware of any sounds that you might be hearing, any smells. And now notice that there is an archway and above the archway there are markings.

"It says... Thoth," Alison whispered.

Lisa was quiet for a moment and continued, "Stepping through the archway, you find yourself in the vast Hall of Amenti. Observe, what do you see around you? Take in the scene."

Alison took a moment to reply. *"I just came through the arch, up a spiral of stone steps, in a huge domed hall, with floor upon floor of arched colonnades. There's a hole in the roof, which seems to look out into space. If you look up through it, you can see stars."*

Lisa was honing in on the frequency of Alison's connection. "What else do you see?"

"Behind me, in the walls, there seem to be open fronted, recessed arches, about body height with two stone foot panels at the base. I think they may be portals. Access to the library, it looks like you are meant to stand in them with your back to the wall and they spin around."

"Okay. Do you want to try one?" Lisa asked. Alison stepped on to the foot panels and turned around to face outward into the domed hall.

She set the intent of where she wanted to go, and affirmed aloud, *"I want to see the librarian."* The stone recess turned 180 degrees and when it stopped, Alison was standing in a huge dusty, old library stacked in tiers and lined with representations of ancient books. *"This must be the way I've chosen to view the library - in book representations. They're morphing and changing as I speak."*

Lisa could see it too. "And there is the librarian," she said. "I've got a telepathic connection with him right now... Are you aware of how you'd like to be able to access the volumes?"

"There's a big book already open in front of me with a page marker in it," answered Alison.

"I'm hearing that we can ask a librarian to come forth and that we should be able to ask some questions and they can read the volumes to us that are appropriate. Alison, they're saying 'We would like to read to you from the Book of Life.'"

"Yes! There's a young boy somewhere here too. Like the librarian's assistant, and I see somebody in robes, like a Plato type figure. He has an Angelic presence."

Lisa took a couple of deep breaths, "My heart is just racing right now and I heard the words 'in the beginning' and they are showing me the creation of the Milky Way Galaxy, conscious projection and particulates are coming together and swirling like one of those gyroscopic children's toys. The spiral shape of the galaxy is being formed and molded and it's just millennia passing by in seconds."

Alison said, *"I can see the planet, but it's like the planet was pre-…"*

"-fabricated?" Interjected Lisa.

"Yeah! And I see it's here, it's hanging suspended in some kind of instrument in readiness. Can that be right?"

"Yes." Lisa could see it now. "I am hearing this quote 'In a single day and night there was creation'. The air feels very slippery like it's hard for me to breathe."

"The air on Earth?" Alison asked.

"I don't know which air I'm breathing, I don't know where I am. It's like I'm breathing in liquid."

"That's the air on Earth - it has a different density. Something's not right with the quality it needs to be adjusted to be fit."

"Fit for what?" Lisa asked.

"For seedings." Alison's voice had changed and Lisa could feel a shift in the energy in the room.

Lisa moved the recorder closer. **"Can you see what they look like?"**

"Fish"

"Are these the fish beings you've seen before?" she asked. **"Do they look like what we would describe as dolphins or whales?"**

"No. They are more land based than that. They've been adopted for land."

"Do you know what time period you are in?"

The speaker continued, *"Following the destruction of the Sirian planet, these creatures needed somewhere to be. It felt right for the humans to make way for the survivors of that system, seeing they were the ones that destroyed it. But the needs are not the same and the conditions are not acceptable for either the humans or the fish people. The human seedings are trying to blend with what you describe as the 'fish people' and it is not appropriate."*

"This is a disturbance within the DNA vibrations, yes? It creates digressive DNA?"

"It's a disturbance within the plan!" spoke the voice.

"Whose plan?"

"The Elohim. We did not plan for a blend of the Taran humans and fish people. We hoped they would be able to accommodate each other's needs.

"Was the planet made ready for the etheric Taran?"

"It was necessary to recalibrate the planet Earth itself. What may have been appropriate conditions to support life for some, like the ratio of oxygen to other gasses, and the quality of the water, gravity on its surface, were not appropriate for others. It was necessary to reset and make adaptations to the planet's DNA and increase the planet's rate of spin to support life."

Lisa ventured, **"Would it be accurate to say that diverse star races would have assimilated into Earth's flora and fauna and that failed attempts to blend would have resulted in other sentient creatures on Earth? – or, not so sentient creatures on Earth - like in the case of insects and reptiles?"**

"Well…that's not strictly true; especially of reptiles. There are some sentient beings among the insects and reptiles. Reptiles have a symbiotic relationship with the planet's own life force, chi, kundalini. The creatures that are closest to the surface of the planet stimulate the planet's own kundalini by a merge of the meridians as you would perceive it. Ants and other insects conduct heat on the planet surface."

Lisa pondered the information, but she was off topic. **"Would you be able to access any of the volumes describing our transition from Tara into the seeding of Khem?"**

"Hmmm… Khem was already seeded. It wasn't the seeding that occurred. It was an evolution – It was a fall through the dimensions that occurred when Tara fell. Tara was not a 3-dimensional place. Khem was."

It made Lisa wonder if the fall of Atlantis and the more widely held belief that is had sunk beneath the sea, had been symbolic for its fall through dimensions of time and space.

"So, when the Taran beings fell through the dimensions and arrived in Khem, they incarnated into what we came to know as the Egyptian pantheon. Is that accurate?" Lisa asked.

The voice paused, *"They manifested into the matrix. Time has been concertinaed, over the centuries events have been combined and timelines misread. They originally began on the 5th dimensional planet, Tara, in another region of time and space…"*

"They?" Lisa interjected.

"Those that became the Lemurians and the Atlanteans, in your perspective.

"The experiment on Tara was seeded by beings from higher harmonic universes. In Harmonic Universe Five the Elohim were created to oversee the

project and for several million years, humanoids existed in harmony on Tara with fully activated 12-strand DNA."

"Just a moment," Lisa interrupted, "What is Harmonic Universe Five? What dimension is that?"

The speaker took a moment. *"As you can understand it, each Harmonic Universe contains three dimensions. Harmonic One contains dimensions one, two and three. Harmonic Two contains four, five and six… Harmonic Five contains thirteen, fourteen and fifteen – this is where your Elohim and Seraphiam Oversouls are accessing you from."*

Lisa felt her head beginning to tick. "um… so… what you're saying is… we're accessing outside of the 12 dimensions of our planet's grid system? Is that right?"

"Yes."

"Okay, thank you. Back to Tara. You said both Lemurians and Atlanteans came from Tara?"

"Over time and through the introduction of digressive DNA by visiting extraterrestrials, genetic mutations occurred within the compromised beings on Tara. This resulted eventually in a schism in the society which broke into two factions that continued on very different evolutionary paths."

"So one society was the Atlanteans… the others, Lemurians?" Lisa asked.

"The forefathers of, as you would see it, yes. One of these groups began manipulating the gravitational fields of the planet's core, which resulted in a catastrophic explosion that ripped a hole in Tara's crystalline grid.

"When the grid collapsed and the planet broke up, gaseous clouds of de-particulates and fragmented soul-substances that were contained within the grid and on the planet surface seeped out into space, and were sucked through a black hole and thrust into what is now your region of the sub-universe. Over millions of years of linear time, those particulates settled in vibration drawing in density of matter and gradually forming the solar system, as you know it."

Lisa realized this is what she and Alison had seen at the start of their journey in the Library.

"Originally there were 12 planets in this system; two were in collision with each other, one became your moon and the other planet broke up and became the asteroid belt. A third was knocked into a wider, elliptical orbit. Each

planet in this system contains within the core, DNA encoding, consciousness and memories of Tara.

"The cataclysm was foreseen and beings from the higher harmonic universal structure used their soul essences to form the morphogenetic fields that created the core of the new, cooling planet Earth. This gradually enabled the capture of these fragmented, dispersed soul particulates and by drawing them in and lowering the vibration, droplets of essences were formed in readiness to begin the first cycles of human incarnations again. This was the beginning of an ambitious plan to rescue the lost souls of Tara."

"How would that even be possible?" Lisa quizzed.

"On planets like Earth the dimensions are pulsed out from the planetary core at the first dimension, and emanate outwards through the second dimension just below the Earth's crust – the Telluric realm, up to the 3rd dimensional matter realm, then into the Astral realm in the 4th Dimension. The soul cycles through the Earth's time space matrix incarnating and returning to the ether, passing through the Spirit world in fourth, also known as heaven or the astral plane. As the soul continues with the re-incarnational process, it spirals upwards again on its evolutionary path shedding dark matter through experiences on the physical plane, until it is ready to cycle out of the density of the lower levels of creation and Ascend out of the planet's matrix.

"It took much longer than you can imagine for the Taran survivors to create the civilization of Egypt out of three-dimensional Khem. They were not matter beings; they were more etheric in form than the local population, which made it very difficult for the survivors to negotiate their way around a denser matter based world. It was necessary to create a race of workers from the locals, who could be their hands and their feet on the ground, who could do the physical construction required to build a new infrastructure, and that took time.

"The blended essences of the Tarans into denser form could only be done through the local indigenous peoples. Early attempts at hybridization were made… almost like your fable of Frankenstein".

"Would these be some of the memories Alison has shared with the attempts to create pregnancies that failed and some of what I've been shown by Isis with the hacking of the bodies?"

"Yes. The population at that time was primitive, not so different from the perspective of a Taran, as any other animal. And so the blending of DNA

and essences of humanoids took place in the hopes we could create a vehicle that could provide the necessary conditions to sustain and hold the higher vibrations."

"So did the Taran survivors create the Egyptian pantheon with these blends?"

"No, the 'Pantheon' as you call them, volunteered to descend to the surface as did many others, for the rescue mission. They manipulated the indigenous populations to evolve the Human 1.0. to Human 2.0 soul carrier, using Grace's design.

"In some cases the vehicles were created and populated with blended essences, some of which were rescued from the Taran culture and stored or preserved. Others were taken from beings that arrived on the dense planet from other places as part of a volunteer force. And interested factions observing what was happening on the surface, saw an opportunity for the transfer of Earth's ownership. And so it was messy for a long time but it was deemed to be worth allowing it to continue to prevent the complete loss of an otherwise advanced civilization."

Lisa said, **"We've understood that some of the survivors found their way to Africa, England, Australia, even the landmass that became the Americas?"**

"Yes, all the early tribal cultures. Earth was unusually diverse and at this time like a Petri dish. There was a time period when it was necessary to stand back and allow all manner of experimentation to see what would emerge that could survive, be resilient and sustainable by the planet herself. It was a dark time for those involved. Many of us seek redemption for this period of Earth's history."

"Are you saying then, that the volunteers and visitors were seeding various expressions of populated humans to see which vehicles would 'fly'?"

"Yes, but only in isolated pockets, not around the globe."

"So is this why we would have in our human folklore and history, pockets of advanced civilizations that suddenly disappeared or no longer remember their origins?" Lisa asked thinking of the ancient Egyptians, the Mayans, the Rapa Nui of Easter Island...

"Many of those civilizations did not so much disappear. Due to changing conditions on the planet surface, they couldn't continue to thrive where they

were, so they relocated. The planet became like a DNA bank where the materials could be protected for projects that would be originating elsewhere. Experimentation may have resulted in the furtherance of other species on your planet. There were occasions for the moving of resources from the planet at that time, like water, energy, minerals, chlorophyll and precious metals – there was a battle for control."

"**You're referencing gold? Where do the Annunaki fit into this? We understand that there was a dumbing down of the human vehicle and we are aware of the chakra 'caps' that were placed on the physical body and our understanding is that this was not completely voluntary. That this was necessary... Was this to create a slave race to mine gold for the Annunaki?**"

"No, it was more to do with the Taran survivors being etheric and unable to function in the density of the three-dimensional planet. They needed to pull in density and matter.

"Enhancements were also introduced within the DNA of the early humans that were not far enough along on their own evolutionary path. They were 'raised up' to level the field with the other seedings arriving on the planet. Adjustments of the vibrations were artificially manipulated to allow to different types of beings at very different levels of their evolution to exist side by side."

"**So is it fair to say that the Taran-Atlantean-Egyptian memories that are being recovered and shared with us at this time are being shared because we need this information in order to help our own evolutionary process as we elevate the vibrations of our current vehicles. We're doing the opposite of the Tarans, instead of falling through the dimensions we're ascending upward?**"

"It's been a long wait for the stranded Atlantean survivors, who have been unable to regain their position on the Ascension path. There are many reasons that these memories are resurfacing. Partly because it will help you release karmic blockages that would otherwise prevent you from rising further. It will also help you release much of the sadness and the guilt that you hold around your experiences of Tara, Lemuria, Atlantis and other places. And it will assist you to understand the true nature of your planet's history so certain things will not be repeated. Uncovering these memories will re-activate certain strands of your DNA. Like a series of electrical impulses, which will loosen and burn

off coatings, the membranes that have been there by way of protection for all of these years."

"Thank you. In order for us to be able to move forward on the most benevolent wave to Ascension are we moving in the right direction by learning what we can about Egypt? Or, is that pushing us in the wrong direction?"

"It's not specifically relevant."

Puzzled, Lisa couldn't help but ask the obvious, **"Alison and I had integrations with Horus and Isis respectively. We've seen others with Nefertari, Ahkenaton, Hathor, Ma'at, Sehkmet, Osiris, Ra, Set, and Nut. If it is irrelevant, then why are they returning en masse?"**

From the control room Grace and Ariel had been watching, pleased with the field exercise; their incarnates had managed to access the library and were negotiating within it while sharing a multidimensional telepathic experience.

In response to Lisa's question, Grace pulsed the Librarian to close the book.

He responded instead with Grace's own elevator speech. *"It is partly reminding you that you are so much more than you've been led to believe over recent periods of your history. It would be very difficult for you to be able to imagine the scale of your abilities if you only saw yourself in terms of the identity of your current incarnation. When you become aware of your previous incarnations, your previous achievements, your previous identities, your previous successes, it enables you to step into alignment with your true power.*

"In that alignment you are able to bring forth the full weight of your creative processes.

"You can't create that which you can't believe you can create.

"There is a certain usefulness in the memories that you will bring forward from those incarnations. They will serve as ignition switches for pathways that your brain and memory will use, almost like portals, to events and occurrences which have happened in the past so that you are not left having to go through the process of reinventing The Wheel."

Chapter 18

Klax

Grace was back in her staterooms. She had just used the bio-MT terminal to transport herself back from Orly, where she had been overseeing the calibration of synchronized parallel dimensions, to secure consecutive nexus points along the projected timelines of Earth.

They had been set for the period of the Gregorian Earth Calendar between the Winter Solstice and the Spring Equinox of the next cycle.

She knew that the events of this period would be pivotal to the reclamation of Atlantean souls. They would require pinpoint accuracy and precision across all timelines if they were to maintain control, and if necessary intervene at crucial junctures.

She needed to be able to access and manipulate holographic projections, make adjustments that would filter down and steer events onto predicted pathways. Orly was online for the *Reset*.

Grace was now preparing herself to receive Comptroller Klax, who had *kindly* agreed to meet her on Free Worlds territory, for her protection. He agreed she would not be welcome on The Belt by certain members of the Council of Orion.

Grace's project was beginning to attract unwanted attention from some of the more unsavory regions of the Galaxy, specifically Quadrant 4. It was rumored that she was interfering with matters that were infringing on sworn agreements with planets under Orion dominion. Delicately balanced negotiations for the custodianship of Quadrant 4 were in play. Orion and The Belt Alliance had particular interest and investment in several planets that were being re-categorized near the Pleiades. The Pleiadian water planet, Earth, would be the jewel in the crown and they intended to have it.

She wasn't taking any chances with this meeting, there was no love lost between Comptroller Klax, the Ra Confederacy, and the Elohim.

The Seraphiam were able to move more freely through the gates of Orion, they knew how to get down and dirty with the Reptilians. *'Must be something in the Warrior Code,'* thought Grace, remembering Ariel trained with and fought alongside Sobek. She had enlisted Raffé to accompany her and asked for Ariel, Uriel, Michael and Aikuso to observe and stand by.

Grace was assuming a different physical form for this negotiation; an ancient tribal model from an earlier incarnation of hers who fought in the Lyran wars. The biological vehicle was adorned with a crest of bone, which protected her crown beneath two layers of thick, black scales. She had four translucent eyelids shielding orange eyes, and intended to have one pair closed at all times to disguise her frequency. She boasted a pair of strong, powerful back legs for kicking and jumping, which made her considerably taller than usual, and long muscular arms, which ended in a set of sharp talons.

Klax would take her a little more seriously than if she looked like 'a snack'. If she needed to throw down, she would be ready.

"I see you have on the little black dress," said Raffé, faintly amused by the vision of loveliness he faced as he materialized on deck.

"Oh, this ole' thing?" Grace replied. "I just threw it on." They felt so 'hip' with their Earth pop culture references.

It made them both laugh. Until Raffé asked, "How did it go?" He knew where Grace had been.

"It went well, I think. We may have a small problem, but nothing that concerns me too much." She replied.

Raffé knew better than that. If it had been just a 'small' problem, Grace would not have shared it. "What?"

Grace sighed, she didn't want to have to explain this now, Klax would require their complete mental focus.

"Grace... What is it?" Raffé pressed.

"There may be a rift in the timeline."

"When?" He knew exactly when... The precise moment they couldn't afford to have one. "You can't stabilize the timeline for the Taran Crystals?"

Grace whispered quickly to him. "There is a rift opening up beneath the location Hybrids I and II have chosen for the venue. It is destabilizing daily. The dimensional slippages will mean they will always be straddling timelines. We can't keep the two incarnates together on the same one, and it's not possible to shift them on to another simultaneously. The timeline would collapse completely."

"But if we don't move them we could lose them both in the *Reset*," Raffé deduced.

"We have virtually no control." Affirmed Grace, "They could end up rolling around like pearls on a marble floor and simply slip through a crack and we will never get them back."

"Oh, Grace..." Raffé sympathized. That was exactly the reaction she had been hoping to avoid. Now he would expect her to pull back.

There was a sudden *shift*... Their eyes locked; Klax was onboard.

Grace looked at Raffé, handsome even in full body armor. "You couldn't find your diner Jacket?' She teased as they linked arms and walked through the halls.

"I think it's, 'dinner' jacket..." he corrected, enthralled by her orange eyes, "You wear one when you eat dinner."

"What's dinner?"

"In your case, probably a large mouse."

Comptroller Klax was not alone. He had brought an escort of several very large Reptilian overlords, from Rigel.

Ariel was bristling at the presence of an elder Zeta Reticuli. Grace wasn't sure about his purpose for being there at all. Had they forged a new alliance between them? She hadn't been informed.

The energy in the council chamber was already thick with a metallic flavor, the reason for her choice of body armor was to help her absorb some of the tougher frequencies the Reptilians were emitting.

She could feel the Zeta as he attempted to probe her thoughts, and she blocked him by holding an image in her mind of a human male and female, in the act of copulation. For some reason this made Zeta very uncomfortable.

They chose their seats at the round table, which was customary and respectful. *'No head higher than another'*, except for hers. She was exceptionally tall in that 'little black dress'.

The Zeta offered to chair the meeting. Since he already knew what everyone else was thinking, it was agreed. Perhaps it would distract him. He poked at Ariel telepathically, only to find she was holding an image in her mind of pulling his innards out with her bare hands.

The chairman communicated telepathically to avoid the need for translation of multiple dialects, and clearly didn't intend to waste time.

"We demand that you cease the Zeta/Reptilian rehabilitation programs."

"It's a little soon to be making demands!" barked Raffé, "Please take note of your surroundings." He said with an edge.

"I'm sure no offense was intended," Grace oozed, "but we might as well dispense with the pleasantries and cut to the chase." The Zeta detected something flash through her mind, but he couldn't dial it in.

Grace began to speak, she directed everything eye to eye with Klax. "You have had millennia to prepare for this Ascension event. You were engaged in this project by the Federation as contractors only. You agreed to provide counter experiences to simulate reality and relativity in the material realm on Earth. You were engaged for the sole purpose of assisting in human evolution, and the eventual Ascension of this planet. Now you are refusing to go home when the job is complete."

Klax waved his hand dismissively. "This has already been discussed at length. We do not intend to walk away from a project that bears our mark with nothing to show for our efforts." He wasn't going to be drawn in by this again. The sanctions imposed by the Federation were ineffective. The Ra Confederacy had made their decision. They were staying and they would fight to defend their right. More than half the population of Earth had Reptilian Oversouls.

The expressionless face of the Zeta pulsed telepathically.

'The Free Worlds Initiative, to 'enlighten' species that align with incarnates protected by Free Will projects, such as on Earth, is something we cannot

condone. The practice of so-called rehabilitating non-participating Oversouls by disconnecting them from their own human expressions on Earth, is in breach of Intergalactic Law.

'This is a Free Will Zone and we are all are entitled to have our rights observed. We demand that these Initiatives be dissolved.'

Raffé spoke loudly, "What rights? Your presence alone in this Quadrant directly contravenes the Covenant of Palaidor." The vibration in the room rolled back in response. He self corrected and changed his demeanor to display greater respect.

"The Council of Orion must be specific. There are many contributors to the various projects you have described here, many alliances and agreements to preserve. You have refused to become an ally of the Federations, or to include yourself in any way in the Ascension of this Galaxy. In spite of repeated directives for you to return to your own planets, you continue to flaunt the law yourselves.

"You do not hold all the cards here; you must be able to lay something on the table."

Klax by-passed the Grey and responded to Raffé directly in a low growl, "We want a piece of the pie we helped to bake," The color of his aura was growing darker by the second. Grace knew they must turn this around.

Ariel could feel the Seraphiam as they connected to one another through the heart to form a protective cordon around Grace and Raffé. They continued to quietly monitor the heightened mood of the room by scanning mentally, physically and energetically; except for Uriel, who Ariel observed was strangely pre-occupied. He had stepped out of formation and was standing very close to Raffé. It was as though they were being attentive to something Ariel couldn't sense. Was Zeta blocking her?

Grace remained stoic and paused while they all caught their breath. Slowly and deliberately she said, "We will not speak the language of war here." She could see by their faces they were relieved to hear it. No one wanted to see another Galactic war. "So let's discuss how we can come to a mutually beneficial agreement."

Ariel heard this as 'stand down' and pulsed the Seraphiam.

"The Reptilians have been custodians of the three dimensional planets for the last 2,000 linear years. We can all agree that the stage you helped to set has been ripe with a full range of experience. You are requesting to be considered as the ongoing future custodians of the planet Earth. Am I correct?"

Klax didn't even bother to acknowledge her with an answer. She knew he would take Earth if he had to, at great cost and human suffering.

She played on, "Custodianship is only granted to participating members of the Galactic Federation."

"We were never invited."

Grace tried to block her thoughts; it seemed Raffé was right after all. This is what they had been after all along.

"Those with the Federations and Alliances are all working towards the Ascension of free worlds."

There was silence.

"However," she continued, "None of us want to see custodianship pass to the Corlian or the Insects for that matter. We may be able to consider special dispensation, if we can arrive at a compromise. We propose a Treaty which will stipulate that you either become contributing members of the Galactic Federation, or you vacate this universe entirely, a directive from on high that will be enforced… In return, you will be granted dominion over all ascending three-dimensional planets in this sector, once the dimensional shift is completed.

Seven planets in the Galactic sector. This had got their attention.

"We will consider this proposal…"

"There's more," Grace interjected. "You will agree to allow Reptilian, Zeta and Insectoid humanoids that have evolved to meet the requirements for Ascension into higher bandwidths and have requested it, to remain as part of the Oversoul Rehabilitation and Enlightenment Programs."

"On Earth only?"

"On all planets. Upon agreement impartial mediation will be sought."

"Mantis." Snapped Klax.

"Agreed."

Chapter 19

Anniversary Waltz

Lisa met Alison at the ferry. "Happy Anniversary," she said with a smile and a huge hug. It had been a year since the very first Recalibration class and they had been preparing for this retreat for months. This second annual intensive marked the start of their 'New Year.' They were going to be teaching together for the first time as partners, a new chapter for both of them.

It had only been a little over a year since meeting each other, and six months really since their partnership began. Alison was surprised at how the team had grown in strength, and how committed they were to the mission. Grace had told Alison early on that individuals would cycle in and out of Marconics. They would be present as witnesses, participants, students and teachers, each contributing their gifts, staying for the proverbial reason, season, or lifetime. Upon the completion of their mission, they would cycle out.

It was wonderful for Alison and Lisa, theirs was a friendship built on trust, mutual respect, and a deep love that neither of them fully understood. This friendship had been seen as an important development. While Grace and Ariel could see that the partnership would make their incarnates more powerful together, it was the developing friendship that would make them unstoppable. The two women complimented each other beautifully. It was a pleasant surprise for Alison to have an American get British humor and Lisa could deliver on sarcasm and match wits; they laughed a lot. They were anchoring for each other, and realizing that they had the opportunity to propel each other further. Together they were unraveling new truths, and exploring new heights.

Alison got into the passenger's side of the car. "Victoria Bradley is coming."

Lisa raised an eyebrow and replied with a snort. She was not a fan of Victoria's. They had found that others were responding to 'The Call' as well, and asking to step up to become part of the team. Alison had achieved building her team in this way. She had hopes that Victoria might be one of the first to anchor a satellite in Europe in the way that she thought Skye and Ian might do in Australia. Vicky was already doing a fair amount of spiritual teaching. She had asked about volunteering with the team as an audition of sorts. Alison wanted to see if she could hold her own teaching advanced spiritual concepts.

Noting the snort Alison ventured, "Can you please give her a chance?" She was smiling and Lisa couldn't resist.

"Fine," she sighed. Lisa knew it was her ego judging Vicky; they had come through the same class together. While she dazzled some of the girls, Lisa found her spiritually arrogant, spoiled, and she behaved with a sense of entitlement that made her want to set her dupatta scarf on fire. Alison saw something in her though, and Lisa supported Alison.

"I know you're not crazy about her, it's not like she'll be on our *Core* team," Alison referenced their group of five.

"No, I know that," Lisa conceded. "I will try, I promise." Lisa put her hand up in a scout's honor gesture. She could see Alison's wisdom in it. Vicky was a logical choice. She was well educated and well versed in spirituality. She had been teaching nutrition, yoga, and meditation at different spiritual centers in London. To teach a protocol is one thing, to be able to converse fluently on spiritual alchemy was another, and this is where Alison hoped Vicky would shine.

Lightworkers were traveling in from all over the country converging on the sleepy Cape Cod town to immerse themselves in the Ascension energy of Marconics. Their expectations were high, yet they really had no idea of what to expect. Under higher guidance, Alison had requested that Skye and Ian bring the crystals. They only knew that there was work to be done with the 'Original Clan', those they had come to know as the Egyptian Pantheon, and that a sampling of the crystals would act as ambassadors for all 500.

Alison and Lisa asked the team to prepare to stay on an extra two days after class to do the work with Ian's crystals. They didn't know what that would entail or how long it would take. Grace and Ariel had been quiet on the matter; Alison half joked that she and Lisa were flying a plane with no instruments through fog on a moonless night, and now the radio was down. It was a lot of pressure to ask the others to stay longer. It meant asking them to take extra days off of work and incur additional travel costs while the women didn't know if they would just be sitting like a bunch of hippies around a crystal grid meditating with jack shit happening...or if there would be 'magic.' They asked anyway.

Skye and Ian - with Seth and Ra - were traveling in from Australia. Alice with Ma'at and Nut was coming down from Vermont. Their team had anchored Osiris, Isis, Horus, Nefertari and Ramses. Although not yet integrated, Hathor and Thoth had been in the team's field along with Sekhmet and Sobek who came to Alison and Lisa both offering his protection. Alison thought Vicky was a strong candidate to receive an Egyptian integration and complete the Pantheon.

*   *   *

The intensive class was split into two parts stretched over 6 days. The first part was a training for Level I & II students to learn the healing protocol and begin their introduction to the concept of Galactic involvement in their Shift. The Level III class was where the higher concepts and The Recalibration was taught. They had decided that this Level III would be the first class to hear what they had learned of their Atlantean origins, the 'truth' of Atlantis as it had been revealed to them.

The Level I & II students were an eclectic group, but they soaked up a lot of information in a short amount of time, and were asking thought provoking questions. Alison, Lisa and the team were each anchoring a point in the room, beaming Marconics frequencies and elevating the space to an otherworldly vibration. The students remarked that they could feel the difference in the vibration between the classroom and the rest of the yoga studio; there was a marked drop down into density when they stepped outside the door.

At the end of the morning lecture, the team filed out to the hallway for a break as the students milled about in search of snacks and caffeine. Skye marched up to Lisa and announced, "There was a spider on you when you were talking, did you know?"

Lisa shuddered; she hated spiders, too many legs, too many eyes. "Is it still there?" she asked patting herself down.

"No, no, it was an etheric spider. It's funny," she mused, her blue eyes boring into Lisa's own, "I had the strangest urge to go over and slap it off you, but I thought it would be a terrible disruption while you were speaking."

"Spiders are spiritual guardians," a passerby offered, eavesdropping on their conversation.

"Yeah, I don't 'do' spiders. Next time Skye, slap it off!" Lisa joked.

* * *

"We can't see anything on her, Ariel," Gabriel affirmed as Raffé replayed the moment in the hologram.

"Are you *sure*?" Ariel was watching intently; she couldn't see anything either. "We need this monitored closely, we know that there is a potential for the timeline to shift in an unfavorable way," her voice was stiff.

They could expect interference to take any form. The presence of an etheric spider was cause for scrutiny.

"It would be wise at this juncture to deploy additional protection," Raffé counseled.

"I agree, additional protection is needed. Who from the Guardian Alliance is on deck?" She asked. It was unspoken between them; their priority was always Grace's protection. They both loved her, they were both loyal to her, they would both lay down their immortality for her.

"We have an Arcturan ship commander on standby; his incarnate could be ready. There are other incarnates who are ready to receive essence downloads," Gabriel announced, looking over the holograms, data flashing rapidly.

Raffé nodded his approval.

"And if that isn't enough?" Ariel ventured.

"Mercenaries. Hyperborean." Gabriel said after a moment of the race of giants, "They can be absorbed by the incarnates as essence downloads as well."

"Good," Ariel wouldn't feel reassured until it was over; they had been this close too many times. "We cannot allow any compromise here, Grace has scoured the Akasha for opportunities, and this is it... we won't get another." Ariel didn't need to elaborate. They all knew what was at stake.

* * *

The team had rented another room in the Yoga studio to act as break room; a place to perform Recalibrations, and for Vicky to use as a classroom. They filed in and sat wherever they could to discuss expectations for the weekend. They were coming up on The Crowning portion of the protocol later that day, and Alison wanted to ensure they were prepared for a full house of Higher Self integrations.

"I loved the analogy you used of the pearls, Alison," Skye commented, referencing Alison's description of the higher selves being like pearls. Each one individual and lustrous in its own right, but when strung together, as a complete necklace, they are collectively more beautiful. Alison described the higher selves lining up, dropping into the incarnate one by one, each enhancing the vibration and raising them up in a 'Jacob's Ladder' style of Ascension.

Skye and Ian were as lovely as Alison described. Lisa noted they were like a spiritual Ken and Barbie; beautiful, free, and perfectly matched. Ian leant forward, "Yes, we have felt the dropping in of the pearls. We are waiting for my beloved to receive Hathor. We can see her waiting to come in." They were totally besotted with each other.

It was a little uncomfortable though, for Alison and Lisa both, how Ian and Skye addressed each other: my beloved, my love, my dearest. The cynic in each of them was triggered. On one hand it was bold and refreshing, on the other hand, it felt like it was lifted from a spiritual romance novel, the cover emblazoned with a busty, corseted beauty languishing in the arms of a rugged muscular angel.

Skye and Ian were still convinced that she would be receiving Hathor, they were the only ones though. Alison felt it best to let them hold that thought until it proved not to be the case.

Skye announced excitedly, "I have four pearls in total that I can see lined up to go. We've been talking to two of our higher selves who are waiting to come in."

"What are they saying when you talk to them?" Alison asked, curiosity piqued.

"Oh it's more of a nodding than language. We ask them 'yes' and 'no' questions. They are black, like a killer whale and kind of shiny and rubbery, chubby faced with elongated heads. We asked them where they were from and we got 'Alcyone'," Skye offered referencing the largest star in the Pleiades. "They shook their heads yes."

'Black... shiny... rubbery... and elongated head' evoked the image of Ridley Scott's Alien in Alison's mind. That did not sound like a positive in her book. The only thing missing was the acidy spit.

Skye began to jerk from receiving a sudden download of energy. She slumped over, resting her elbows on her knees, head hanging as her body twitched and vibrated uncontrollably. Victoria seized the opportunity to take the floor. Since arriving at class she had skirted the responsibilities the rest of the team had taken on, like showing up on time, lugging massage tables, setting up the room, and generally participating. She was, however, keen to place herself center stage and wanted Alison's undivided attention.

As Skye's body lurched and heaved under the frequency of the download, Lisa was worried she was going to knock herself out on the coffee table. "Can we get her to sit on the floor?" she suggested.

"It's fine," Skye replied.

"She gets these a lot," Ian concurred.

"So Alison, as I was saying," Lisa realized Vicky had not let Alison's attention go, "I was reading about the Adam Kadmon... how do you feel your work in Marconics relates to the Adamik and Evik consciousness, because most people don't really understand that."

Lisa tried to suppress the eye roll she could feel coming on, Vicky had Alison all to herself and she was not going to back to down. Alison thought it was strange that Vicky continued on nonplussed about Skye's continued download, which had the rest of the team occupied. Eventually, Skye settled.

With the break over, they returned to the classroom.

As The Crownings began, each of the practitioner 'midwives' noted a strange sensation in the back of their heart spaces. The room had turned ice cold, a signature the team had come to associate with the presence of the Guardian Alliance.

Ten tables all reported feeling the chill and pressure at the back of the heart. Alison was at one table, with a student who was mid integration, Lisa at another. They looked up at each other, both having heard 'Guardians' in their minds.

Alison had a bemused look on her face. "Did we just integrate the Guardian Alliance?"

"Yes!" Lisa confirmed. They knew that this was significant.

*   *   *

The next morning, they funneled into the second half of class. As the team prepared the room, Lisa looked at Alison, "What is that noise? Do you hear that? It is giving me a splitting headache!"

"I don't know. It's killing me too."

A few moments later Skye walked up to them. "Are you ladies okay? I feel sick, like I am going to throw up. Do you hear that noise?"

Robin stepped in, "Gina, Mary Pat and I have headaches too… Victoria is playing a crystal bowl."

Alison and Lisa exchanged a look. They walked to the back of the room where Vicky had been sitting unnoticed by them. A large lavender bowl sat in front of her, the striker in her hand as she rounded the perimeter of the bowl repeatedly making a sound that was bombarding their senses.

Vicky smiled as they approached and closed her eyes, thoroughly enjoying her own melody. "Vicky, please stop with the bowl. It's making everyone sick," Alison instructed.

The smile faltered momentarily. Clearly this was not the response she expected for her impromptu concert.

"We all have headaches," Lisa added.

"Oh, well that can't be because of my bowl," Vicky affirmed, "This is one of the rarest and most valuable bowls on the market. It's infused with gold, it's an *Isis bowl*," she emphasized, as though the name should mean something to them.

"Ahh, right… well, that may be, but the frequency it is emitting is discordant for the entire team," Alison opened her hands in an expansive gesture. Everyone had the 'headache' face on and Skye was hunched over with Ian rubbing her back.

Vicky surveyed the room. "Sometimes people have a hard time with it at first. It's such a high vibration they aren't used to it. But I find if I keep playing, they eventually entrain to it," she made a strange gesture with her head and neck, as though she popped it into alignment, highlighting the entrainment, "… and then it's fine." She smiled again.

Alison surveyed the bowl more closely. Seeing a deep crack in the frosted lavender structure that looked like it had been filled with brownish smoky glass, Alison asked "Has it been repaired?"

"No, no -that's how it was made."

Alison wasn't so sure. "No more with the bowl," she commanded.

As the students piled in, the team noticed that some had begun coughing; a deep hacking cough that sounded like it needed a round of antibiotics and heavy duty cough syrup.

It was time now to share with the Level III students the truth about their Atlantean origins. They were there for healing, to release Atlantean cell memories deep within their DNA codes enabling them to move forward.

Alison began by describing part of the Taran history, "It was an experiment to be able to create experiences for Angelics in a denser form in order that they could have individualized physical experiences. The planet was seeded very successfully for about a million of our years. Then it began to be visited by various other races in the system and these visitors brought about digression in the genetics.

"The Atlanteans had a level of spiritual purity which equated to that of a 12-year-old girl. Off world visitors were bringing different levels of density with them. If they were mating with Atlanteans, then there were further digressive genetic occurrences. This resulted in a division of the Taran population into two separate races; one that later became known as the Atlanteans and the other, Lemurians. This separation was compounded as one culture evolved spiritually, and the other continued to evolve technologically.

"Mars at that time was also evolving as a technological planet. The population was referred to as 'The Laggards' because they lacked spirituality. Within the system of Free Will the humanoids on Mars chose to pursue scientific advancement and began experimenting with Merkaba Lightbodies. They began manipulating Merkaba fields- not only their own individual fields but also larger planetary Merkabas serving as Star Gates. They began harnessing energy from the Core of the planet itself resulting in distortion and 'negative spin'."

The students were nodding, understanding that 'negative spin' referred to the deliberate interference of energetic development and a permanent damning of the individual's Ascension.

Alison continued, "Finally, their experiments resulted in the destruction of the planetary grid and their atmosphere. There were mass evacuations, some escaping using Merkaba technology – but most were lost. The planet was destroyed, which is why in our current reality we perceive it to be a dead planet.

"It was thought by the spiritual hierarchy that the survivors of the Martian planet, who transported themselves to TARA, the 5th Dimensional sister planet, would be able to raise their vibration. The hope was they would evolve spiritually alongside the Atlanteans. That did not happen. The Laggards poisoned the well.

"It wasn't long before they continued where they left off manipulating the electromagnetics of the morphogenetic field of the Taran Planetary Core. Once they accessed the core, they released an ancient primeval energy that had been used to correct the spin rate of the planet to make it habitable. Once it was released on the surface of the planet, they began experimenting with it, altering and manipulating it with chemical DNA to create new life forms. The energy became self-aware and hungered for its own evolution. It would become a force that would rampage throughout the solar system, the galaxy and then consume the universe itself. This catastrophe was foreseen along the timeline. The various alliances understood that this event could result in the unraveling of the universe itself. It could not be allowed to stand.

"Plans were drawn in light of the potential that the Taran planet would need to be sacrificed to prevent the spread. Preemptive rescue strategies were put in place to preserve the evolving Atlantean culture that had been on an Ascension path to the 7th Dimensional planet, Gaia."

Alison allowed this information to settle in for a moment. Lightworkers were used to calling Earth 'Gaia', the concept of an evolution to a 7th Dimensional planet was a new idea for many... as was Atlantis not being an island somewhere in the Bermuda Triangle.

"The more highly evolved beings could access Star Gates and wormhole technologies through the inner realms of Tara that could enable them to evacuate quickly to ships or even back to other planetary systems. This was part of the Amenti network of Star Gates that exists on many planets. But those between physical incarnations, cycling as consciousness through the Taran crystalline grid, caught between the physical and etheric realms would be dispersed and vented out into space when the grid was blown. Those souls would be lost. The planet would be knocked off its axis and crash through the dimensions into a three-dimensional space. Then cataclysmic events would render the surface of the 5D planet uninhabitable. As Earth was already prepared to accommodate human life, the particles of soul essences drawn in through the newly forming morphogenetic field of the planet would have to manifest again beginning as a monadic soul within the mineral kingdom. Over eons of time, the souls would have to reincarnate in spiral of evolution to the level of individual incarnated humanoid experience."

The room fell silent, save for the hacking coughs of students as they released more Atlantean cell memory.

"This is why so many of you are having respiratory issues."

Alison recounted the evacuation of Tara. "I have a memory of Grace's, of the deployment. It is my translation that they 'parachuted in'. They had been receiving dispatches and it appeared as if everything was set.

"Everyone was jubilant because we 'had this' and we could turn it around. Then from a strategic position at the edge of a vast desert landscape, I saw a detonation. I knew that something must have gone badly wrong. I remember accessing the Halls of Amenti and running through the passages to an awaiting ship. Lisa has a memory of crashing through the dimensions. Other people that we've had in our classes have memories of boarding ships or putting their loved ones on ships and choosing to stay behind."

As though reliving their own memories, several of the students had begun to weep.

"The darkest moment was when the entity, that had been created by the Laggards, saw an opportunity for control and possession. We have seen this as a very black, oily, thick choking smoky substance that killed many in that process. The coughing that you each experience is releasing the cell memory of your death in that lifetime.

"We all carry the cell memory of that. Grace gave the order to detonate and Ariel carried it out. Ariel was branded as 'the Butcher of Atlantis'...

"We have all played our parts in this and we're here to seek redemption. That's what this is! The reclamation and closure of the Atlantean rescue project which began 56 million years ago."

After Alison finished claiming responsibility for ordering the destruction of Tara, and named Lisa as the destroyer, they both stood there with tears streaming down their faces. The emotion of it felt like being hit head on by a runaway truck. Looking from face to face among the students, they noted too, there was not a dry eye left in the house. They all felt it. They all knew the truth of it. As Lightworkers, they volunteered to be here, now... they asked to be a part of the rescue mission, both as 'rescuers' and as 'the redeemed.' This was their mission too, and they were awakening to it. They only needed to align.

After giving the class a lunch break, they spent the rest of the afternoon at the massage tables running energy. Alison invited Robin on to the table. Robin felt pressure on the top of her crown, which she described as feeling like 'something sitting on my head'. Alison took the opportunity to demonstrate The Crowning again to the students. Of all the wild, weird, and wonderful things they had heard and experienced, The Crowning could not be denied – it was witnessed by every pair of eyes in the room. As the energy came in, Lisa heard 'Hathor' and knew that the Egyptian had arrived. She was quiet and waited for Alison. Without speaking the name aloud, they both knew whom Robin had received and acknowledged it by an exchange of look. Robin was going to need some extra time off of work.

"Do you have a sense of who it is?" Alison asked with an eyebrow raised.

Looking from Alison's expectant face to Lisa's, she grinned, "No, but you two obviously do... tell me!"

Both women smirked and shook their heads. They made it a policy to not tell if they had a sense of the individual integration. It was more powerful for the integration experience when the incarnate claimed their own 'I AM'.

Just like in the Level I & II class, the students all began to report a similar signature experienced during The Crowning as the Higher Self energies began integrating. From table to table the energies were icy cold and there was pressure at the back of the practitioners' hearts.

A shy petite woman who had delivered a huge energy to the student on the table whispered to Lisa, "I'm hearing a word, but I don't know what it is... It's hyborean or hypoborean?" Lisa smiled and shuddered with her usual 'confirmation chills'.

"Alison, we have another guardian race!" Lisa called cheerfully across the room, "Hyperboreans!"

During another integration, one of the students sat bolt upright and proceeded to take off his shirt. Lisa went flying over to the table, "Woah, Woah, WOAH" she shouted laughing. "Hey, Wayne, this is not that kind of party!" she chided. Sometimes the Higher Selves did some funny things. This one, identifying himself as an Arcturan Ship Commander, was not impressed with the choice of attire his incarnate had donned. Wayne smiled sheepishly at Lisa and shook his head.

At another table Skye and Ian were working together. She was wearing a head scarf with which she had artfully tied her long hair into an elongated beehive. Alison tapped Lisa's arm; they looked at her dumbstruck. She was a dead ringer for the famous bust of Nefertari. Skye had finally received her integration and was sure that it was Hathor. She signaled for help.

Alison approached the table, aware immediately that something was amiss. "What's going on Skye?" she asked, observing Ian's laboring breath.

"We have those beings from Alcyone ready to come in. But Ian says the frequency isn't high enough here. We need to raise it."

The rest of the team had gathered. "Okay then, alright... let's just support the space by beaming energy," Alison offered.

"Lisa, come over here please," Alison called with urgency in her tone.

Lisa moved swiftly from the other table where she had been supervising. "What's going on?" she whispered.

"He needs the frequency higher..." Alison whispered back. They exchanged another look. Something was definitely amiss.

As they began beaming Ian started chanting, "Alcyone... Alcyone... Alcyone..." Skye joined him. One by one, the other members of the team and several students began chanting as well. Alison and Lisa remained silent both of them seeing this spectacle was getting quickly out of hand.

From the command room Grace marveled. "How is it that they find playing with matches so attractive?"

"Do we need to be concerned about these two," Ariel asked gesturing to Skye and Ian in the hologram.

"Free Will," Grace responded. "They are being 'romanced' by opposition. They cannot discern the frequency."

She and Ariel both pulsed their own incarnates, their Free Will had already been relaxed, as they had already aligned.

Lisa had taken up a position at Ian's feet and grabbed his ankles. Without knowing why, she synced her breath with his and began energetically blocking whatever it was that she could see pushing through the portal that had opened in the vaulted ceiling above them. She repeated in her head, *'NO, NO, NO.'*

Alison began snapping the others out of the strange trance induced by the chanting. She could see the portal too, and the huge strange blackened face that was pushing against the membrane between the dimensions. "Okay, that's ENOUGH!" she commanded. Skye and Ian both stopped the chants. Ian sat up abruptly, pulling in his feet. As he wrenched himself from Lisa's field, she doubled over at the foot of the table and let out a yelp.

"Okay everyone, let's all take a break," Alison called, noting that several onlookers were totally confused by what they had witnessed.

"What the hell was that?" Alison said to Lisa as she helped her to her feet.

"I don't know, but it was off, and I was blocking it. I couldn't chant with the others," Lisa said softly.

"Whatever that was, if it was supposed to be in this realm, it would have come in through The Crowing..."

Lisa jerked, the chills confirming, "Yes." After a moment, "Could you see the portal?"

"Yes – yes, that's why I put a stop to it."

Upon returning from the break, Alison addressed the class and explained the deviation from the protocol, which they were normally so strict in teaching. Taking full responsibility for it to use as a teaching moment, she told them curiosity had led them to experimentation, which was something they should not have done.

Deciding to lighten the mood, Alison asked how Wayne's Commander was getting on. He told the class that on the break he tried to light a cigarette and 'The Commander' demanded, "YOU PUT THAT OUT!!! It hurts me." Wayne imitated how he spat the cigarette out and the class laughed.

It was a perfect end to the night.

*   *   *

"So, Little Lady," Lisa called affectionately to Robin, "Why don't you ride over to the restaurant with Alison and I?"

The team were meeting for dinner. Robin's eyes narrowed. She could see the ulterior motives written all over Alison and Lisa's faces.

"Do you know yet who you integrated?" Alison quizzed.

Robin thought it was Hathor, but she was conflicted because Skye had been so positive that she had integrated Hathor. Robin's confidence had suffered slightly in Skye's presence. "I'm not sure."

"Come on Robin," Lisa urged her, "Who is it?"

"That's right Robin, claim the I AM!" Alison encouraged.

"Well I thought it was Hathor… but…"

"But what?"

Robin hesitated, "Well, Skye was really convinced that she had taken in Hathor."

"Yeah, NO." Lisa blurted. She and Alison both turned in their seats to look at Robin in the back seat.

Robin shook her head, "But – well then… who did she take in?"

"Nefertari… did you see how she was dressed today? The head wrap?" Alison asked.

Though they made it a habit never to tell someone who they'd integrated, Robin was going to need a push. "Robin, I saw Hathor with you back in June, remember?" Lisa asked her, referring to one of their classes the previous summer in New Hampshire.

"Robin, I want you to claim the I AM," Alison instructed.

The three women sat quietly. Robin fidgeted in the backseat. Lisa pressed the door lock button and the ka-chunk sound broke the silence. Lisa smirked, "You can't get out of the car until you do."

They laughed. "Okay," Robin conceded. She took a deep breath. "I am Hathor," she mustered in the weakest, most lackluster way.

"Seriously!?!" Alison and Lisa chimed in unison.

"Robin, love, you are going to have to try a little harder than that." Alison said.

Robin tried again, "I am Hathor."

"Again Robin," Lisa encouraged, "but with feeling!"

"I am Hathor."

"Again!"

"I AM Hathor." Robin called, closing her eyes.

"AGAIN! Robin, say it AGAIN!" they called together.

Robin's voice was deep and booming as "I AM HATHOR!" escaped her lips and rippled like a sonic wave through the car.

"Yeah you are!" Lisa hooted.

"Yes, you are!" Alison said satisfied.

When they sat down at the table in the restaurant Gina asked what had taken so long. "We thought you girls got lost in the parking lot." She joked.

"Alison and Lisa kidnapped me, locked me in the car and made me claim my integration."

"Oh well, when you put it like that - !" Alison quipped.

"Yes, that makes us sound terrible!" Lisa laughed.

The team had piled around the table to celebrate on the eve of the last day of class. They had made it through five intense days, and now they would be preparing for the unknown with Ian's crystals. As the conversation flowed from students to integrations, to the interns, Mary Pat pointed out Vicky's absence.

"She's got that workshop tonight with the students," Lisa commented.

Chapter 20
The Vilkriss

Ariel and Raffé stood flanking Gabriel as he pulled up the image of Vicky in the yoga room. They winced at the dissonant 'harmonics' pouring through as several crystal bowls were struck and rung.

"Look at that one," Raffé said indicating a woman who was holding her head in her hands. Several others were beginning to react in the same way. As the playing went on, the frequency coming through the hologram felt as though it could fracture the humans they were observing. "How are they able to stand it?" he wondered aloud and then one of the women began coughing. It accelerated so violently, within a few moments she was gasping for air. She lifted herself from the yoga mat on the floor, staggered outside the room and vomited.

They watched with concern as several others began to cough as well, a deep raspy choking. A few more excused themselves from the classroom.

"Is *it* actually in the room?" Ariel asked, looking more closely at the hologram. It was nearly impossible to detect it with so many energetic signatures in such close proximity. Unlike when it was loose on Tara, it would not show itself in the same way. Its genetic markers included an ability to shapeshift, and it was aware; a dangerous combination.

As the students filed out, taking their light and the protection of their Guardian integrations with them, the vibration of the room shifted. "Stay on her," Ariel told Gabriel, referencing Vicky.

"There it is," Raffé pointed. In the absence of the higher light frequency, they could see the blackness all around Vicky, though not within her or infecting her. It was moving, morphing from a single mass, into individualized fist-sized spiders. She was the host.

*   *   *

The end of each class is always a bittersweet mix of success and sadness. There are hugs and tears as the students prepare to depart. After having spent days together healing, shedding and being with their tribe, it is hard to leave and return to the density of 3D life.

Alison and Lisa met with Vicky in the first floor lobby of their hotel across the street. Over the course of the training, they realized that Vicky was not going to be a match vibrationally for them or the team. She might be perfect for the occasional guest appearance at some of their larger events to teach nutrition for those developing Lightbody but she was not willing to let go of her shamanic background. They had already experienced the friction between stellar and earth grid energies and knew they were not a mix.

They were seated when Vicky arrived.

"So tell me how you think the volunteering went, Vicky?" Alison ventured, "What was your impression of working with the team?"

As Vicky spoke at length on her opinions and impressions, her tone became melodious and hypnotic, her gestures drawing both women in. Suddenly a red flashing light, like a soundless siren sparked in Lisa's mind.

*   *   *

"We're monitoring it," Ariel said as Grace entered the command room like a clap of thunder. "I just pulsed Lisa."

"Do we have confirmation that it's with her?" Grace demanded, looking down into the hologram.

"Yes, Grace, it is." No words needed to pass between them. After thousands of years the Taran crystals were finally in reach and now everything was at risk. Grace wanted to ask how, but the question was pointless, it was there. They would have to stay on top of it for the next few hours on the linear timeline.

"It was hiding in the light and they couldn't detect it." After a moment she added, "It's evolving." Seeing Grace's jaw tighten, Ariel assured her, "but it hasn't crossed over to any of them… it's still with the host."

Then Ariel boomed to Lisa who was still leaning forward in her chair, "SIT BACK!" Clearly she was slow on the uptake; the red warning light was not enough.

They watched together as Lisa jolted out of Vicky's trance and sat back in her seat. Lisa blinked and looked at Alison who sat back as well. Vicky appeared surprised at the change of their body language. Grace poured down frequency to Alison, who was suddenly not feeling well.

Ariel pulsed Lisa again. They heard her say, "Alison, we really need to wrap this up, we have that *thing* with the team…" Ariel nodded to Grace, they were responding.

"Can I join you? Aren't you going to work with the crystals now?" Vicky asked.

"Oh, Vicky, we're sorry, we were made to understand that only those with the Egyptian integrations can be present," Alison responded gently. They were all three aware that Vicky had not received any integration. She had been on the table and they had both remarked how she had 'glowed' white; it was as though a shadow had been lifted off her, but there was no increase in the energy, none of the usual indications that a Higher Self energy was even waiting to come in.

Grace and Ariel watched as their incarnates said their goodbyes. As they put on their coats, Vicky turned from the doorway and called out, "You know," she said slowly, "I have traveled such a long way to see you ladies, can I get a goodbye hug?"

"NO!!!!" Grace and Ariel shouted in unison.

The two women froze in their tracks.

"Oh, uh…" Lisa managed to stammer.

"Oh, okay…" Alison added, feeling that she couldn't be rude.

Grace and Ariel wore identical expressions of shock and dismay as they watched both women hold their breath and lean in for an awkward group hug.

Once Vicky departed, the women walked across the street to a local restaurant and took seats across from each other at a table by a bank of windows.

"Alison, I don't feel good."

"Me neither. We'll have a cup of tea and something light." Alison looked up and saw Vicky standing at the window staring in at them. They had no idea how long she had been there. Then she smiled, nodded and moved on.

Grace and Ariel watched as a dark shadow moved across Alison's shoulder.

Alison lowered her head and then looked at Lisa. "I think it was in the hug."

"I'm already on it, Grace." Ariel sent an interference wave before Grace could stop her.

Lisa suddenly stood up, crossed over to Alison and embraced her where she sat. Not wanting to embarrass her friend, Alison hugged her back.

* * *

"That was foolish and reckless!" Grace hissed rounding on Ariel.

Ariel turned from the hologram and locked eyes with Grace. "You know I had no choice," she said softly as a flood of emotion passed between them. It was not within Ariel's being to stand by and allow harm to come to Grace on her watch; she would always step in the line of fire. It was not within Grace's being to allow Ariel to sacrifice herself; she would always find a way. Ariel knew Grace was more worried than angry.

"Are you going down?" Grace's concern marked by the deep furrow in her brow.

"Yes, I'll be on the ship." It was closer dimensionally. Grace nodded, her heart heavy.

Ariel began to departiculate into shimmering flecks in a cloud of grey-white smoke. Then there was nothing. As particulates pulled together into form, she materialized on the deck of a small ship flying under the banner of Ashtar Command. A few moments later, Grace could see her on the secondary holographic screen that she would now monitor alongside Raffé and Gabriel.

Ariel watched the hologram as the Vilkriss scuttled across her incarnate's energy field.

"What did you do?" a resonant male voice spoke from the recesses of the room.

"I sent an interference wave," Ariel's eyes were still set to the screen.

An interference wave was a violation of Free Will, but Commander Sheran was not going to point that out. Instead he asked, "What did she hear?"

"She heard Alison say, '*I think we need to hug*.'"

* * *

They were partway through miso soup and tea when the color drained from Lisa's face. She looked at Alison, eyes wide. "What is crawling on my back?" She whispered, a hint of alarm in her voice.

"Turn, let me see."

Lisa shifted in her seat, showing her back. There was nothing visible. Lisa's adrenaline began to spike. She could feel something that she imagined to be tarantula sized, and with a comparable number of legs, crawling up her spine and over the back of her head. "I can feel it," she whispered, unable to conceal the fear. She touched her head, indicating where it was on her skin, in her field, but according to her fingers there was nothing there.

"What the heck?" she whispered. Her voice cracked slightly.

"Don't get upset. We are going to walk back over to the hotel and get a better look at what's going on. Okay?"

The waiter appeared with more tea. "Check please?" Alison asked.

They stood up and began to make their way from the back of the restaurant to the exit. Lisa felt her strength leave her and she grabbed the back of a chair at one of the tables they were passing. "Sit down a minute, I'll be right back," Alison insisted and was gone before Lisa could argue.

Alison rushed across the quiet street and into the hotel. The team would all be assembled in room 151. She knocked on the door urgently. Robin swung the door wide with a big smile that quickly faded as she read Alison's expression. "What's wrong?"

"I need help to get Lisa. She's across at the restaurant and she's sick."

Moments later, Alison flanked by Robin, Ian and Skye exited the hotel and made their way into the restaurant.

Robin and Skye moved in to help Lisa to her feet. "Don't touch me!" she insisted, "I don't want to pass this on to you!" Skye ignored her and helped her to stand up.

They made a diamond formation around her, Ian took point, Alison and Skye flanked her on either side and Robin held up the back. As they entered the hotel, Vicky was standing at the reception desk talking to the clerk.

"Hold on Lisa, we're almost there." By Alison's estimation they had just a few more feet to go.

As they passed Vicky, the *thing* on Lisa's back reached for her, wrenching Lisa's field. Lisa yelped as it tugged her backward, like a huge fisherman's hook between her shoulder blades. Vicky had turned to watch the strange processional head down the corridor.

Gina opened the door as they approached. She, Mary Pat, and Diane had set the massage table up and were awaiting their arrival. Again Lisa growled, "Don't touch me, please, I don't want any of you to get hurt." She was in pain. They managed to get her onto the table.

The team watched as Lisa lifted off the table, her back arched as the thing pushed against her field from underneath and then dropped her onto the table with a thud. She was lying on top of it.

Alison called on the Galactic Federation, beginning the process of invoking protection and enlisting aide. Together the entire team drew in the energy of Marconics and began to expand their fields.

The arachnid moved through Lisa's field, she could feel that it had settled on her hip. The team had her surrounded on the table. They began to beam her, which made her cry out. The 'tarantula' dug into her field as though it had iron claws; the energy was agitating it and it was emboldened. Lisa could feel it moving as if on her skin.

Alison demanded, "Who can see it? Can any of you see it?"

"I can see it, right there," Skye pointed to Lisa's right side.

They directed the energy to the being. In response it sank long, sharp tendrils into Lisa's hip and pulled hard, flipping her 180 degrees in the air and dropping her on her stomach, face down on the table.

Then it scuttled up her spine again and clawed between her shoulder blades. She screeched as it 'bit' her.

"We've got to get her on her back," Alison demanded. "Okay Lisa, we're going to flip you over."

"Please... don't touch me," she whispered. She was more afraid for them than she was for herself. She didn't want anyone else contaminated.

As they turned her over, Alison decided to raid the energetic arsenal. In her early days of practice, Alison had become proficient with entity and low soul removal. She decided to approach it with logic and reason. She spoke to it. "We are aware that you are here, and you must realize that you cannot stay." She tried concern and empathy, "If you stay you will ultimately be destroyed, it would be best for all concerned that you leave and go now."

Lisa let out a whimper as it dug in more deeply, like a tick burrowing into the skin. The energy was antagonizing it and Alison wasn't sure, but it seemed to be getting stronger. It wasn't responsive to direct commands, or requests either. This wasn't a typical low soul or entity attachment. Alison mentally scanned her past client experiences looking for something else to try.

Lisa called softly, "Please help me, Ashtar, Ariel, someone, please help me." Then she was still for a few moments.

A wave of inspiration washed over Alison as she remembered the last time she and Lisa had to deal with a breach of such severe magnitude. Several months earlier, they had assisted a woman who had been compromised by several Zeta energies. They had breached her field by her invitation. The team had thrown everything at it, with limited results. In the end, they telepathically connected and journeyed to the ship where they were able to employ the help of the Galactics. What had taken the humans hours to achieve, the Galactics addressed instantaneously.

Lisa had been on the table now for an hour and she was deteriorating. Alison knew they needed to change their approach. "Lisa, we're going to try hypnosis. Let's deal with this thing telepathically."

"Okay," Lisa agreed, knowing what Alison was hoping to accomplish. Alison directed the team to move Lisa to a chair. The Vilkriss wrapped itself around Lisa's left hand. "Get off of me!" she demanded, as she grappled with it.

Lisa took in each of their faces as she settled into the chair. Robin's face was drawn tight with worry. Though Robin had been with Alison and Lisa at the Zeta exorcism, this was uncharted territory for the others. Gina stood to the side, deep in thought. Diane and Mary Pat stood at either side of her, ensuring she didn't fall. Skye stood with Ian holding hands, faces solemn. Alison wore a look of determination; she was not about to surrender. If they were afraid, none of their faces betrayed them.

In that moment, Alison felt all eyes on her. How could she possibly know what to do next? This was not a three-dimensional entity. *'Grace,'* she thought, *'Where the hell are you?'*

She couldn't even see this invader; just perceive the damage it was wreaking in Lisa's field. She didn't even know if this assault was survivable, or if Lisa's heart would just eventually give out. If there was one etheric spider, were there more? Something shadowy had caught her attention in the bathroom earlier. Could the entire team be compromised?

*   *   *

Grace was magnetized to the holographic screen, watching intently as Alison began to count Lisa down into hypnosis.

"Do you think she'll choose to come up?" Raffé asked, breaking Grace's trance-like stare. The Galactics could not enter the 3D hologram, not without trapping themselves in density.

"It's possible. But she is very like Ariel…" Grace didn't have to finish the thought… Raffé knew Ariel was equal parts loyal and tenacious. As it turned out, the incarnate had a healthy dose of the same, a recipe for unconscionable stubbornness.

The intervention Lisa required meant she would have to board the ship. "What if she doesn't? … Grace?"

"Then, they will have to deal with it themselves. She already has a sense of what it is and what it wants. Neither Ariel nor Lisa will risk letting it loose. If it breaches the incarnate too badly, it will kill her." Then she closed her eyes and searched with her mind until she detected Ariel's frequency.

At the console aboard ship, Ariel's consciousness was flooded with pale violet. *'Grace,'* Ariel acknowledged her. She too was waiting for Alison to guide the clear connection with Lisa.

Ariel awaited Lisa at the bottom of the staircase Alison was leading her down. When Lisa stepped off, Ariel called to her.

They listened as Lisa recounted to Alison, "There's a circular portal that's opened above me." She continued at a whisper, "I can see Ariel and some others... oh, I think they want me to come up."

"Are you able to go up and come back?" Alison's voice vibrated through the hologram.

They could see Lisa's vibration change as she thought about projecting her consciousness to Ariel... to the ship. This was hopeful. She was relaxing into the idea.

"Good," Grace encouraged. "Good, now come on up."

Suddenly, Lisa's frequency plummeted into the fear bandwidths. They could read her racing thoughts like pages in a book.

'I can't risk this. I can't take this thing up there. I know that's what it wants. It's going to consume everything. If I bring it up there how can you contain it? How can I put you all in jeopardy? I will not come up.' And the cycle of thought repeated itself.

Grace lowered her head. It was as she suspected, Lisa would not risk the spread of contamination.

Ariel pulsed Lisa's field of internal vision. *'Come up,'* Ariel pulsed as her form came into focus. Lisa felt a wash of love flow over her and knew this was her last opportunity to go. Ariel urged her again to let go of fear and come up.

'I can't.'

The Seraphiam saluted her incarnate. Lisa understood the finality of that gesture and returned the salute in kind. Ariel hesitated, and then closed the portal.

"Alison," she called softly, finding her awareness back in the chair in room 151. She opened her eyes. "They're gone... Ariel... The connection is gone."

"What? What do you mean *gone*?!" she was incredulous.

"Ariel said goodbye, she said *'If you can't clear it, Kid, you come up'*."

Alison was furious. How dare they just leave them like this! How could The Galactic Federation just abandon them? What was Ashtar Command doing? And where the hell was Ariel?

The Vilkriss had tightened itself around Lisa's chest like a boa constrictor. "It's trying to get into my heart chakra," she placed her hand protectively over her heart center.

"Let's get her onto the bed!" Alison instructed.

There was a knock on the door of 151. "Who the fuck is that?! NO ONE opens that door!" she commanded.

Lisa groaned.

"Alison, it's me, Vicky" came a muffled voice from the other side of the door. "I wonder if I could speak with you and Lisa? I tried calling but she's not answering her phone."

They had forgotten Vicky was staying an extra night in the hotel. Alison just looked at Gina, her face spoke a thousand words.

Gina called through the door, "Vicky, Lisa is really sick right now. I can't open the door, but Alison will find you later."

Lisa began gasping for air, and reflexively brought her hands to her throat.

"What's happening Lisa?" Alison demanded.

"It's choking me," she gasped, sobbing. "It's choking me," the words were strangled as she struggled to breathe. It was trying to breach her either by entering through the heart space, or by coming in through the nose and mouth. If it was successful, she realized that it would kill her. She heard Ariel's words reverberating in her head, *'if you can't clear this, Kid, you come up.'*

She began to telepathically connect to the team one by one. *'Robin, Gina, Mary Pat, I love you all... Thank you.'* She pulsed to the others, *'Thank you all for trying to help me.'* Then she turned her awareness to Alison. *'It's okay,'* she pulsed, *'It's okay. I love you, and it's not your fault. I love you and thank you for everything. If you have to let me go, I'll still be with you.'*

"Oh no you don't!" Alison scrambled up onto the bed beside Lisa. She clutched her hand tightly. This was not happening. She girded herself and prepared to fight fire with fire. "Now you HEAR me," she growled through tears, "You let her go right now, *you let her go*! Or so help me!"

Then Grace boomed through Alison, "...I will scour the universe for you. I will hunt you down and eradicate your SPECIES. I will destroy your lineage! And I will not rest until there is nothing left!" Her voice was pure venom.

After a long pause, Alison directed Lisa to visualize opening a portal in her third eye.

"This is your last chance. Go now, and I will grant you safe passage through this portal. You can return to your own dimension, your own space and time, with my assurance that no harm will come to you."

After a moment Lisa's throat was released and her breathing was less labored.

"Lisa, where is it now?" Alison asked.

"It feels like it's receding."

They were all hoping that Grace's threats had encouraged the 'tarantula' to leave. Then Lisa felt it move again. "It's back on my right hip."

Alison had always admired the huge blue Aqua Aura pendant Lisa was wearing. It was a fist sized clear quartz cluster that had been super-heated and fused with 24 carat gold vapor. Now she noticed how it had settled right over Lisa's heart center. She suddenly realized, the crystal was repelling the entity from access. Alison thought about one of the last hypnotherapy clients she saw in private practice. She had asked the woman's snarky subconscious personality where the negative imprints drawn out from her client's body had been placed. "It's in your rocks," it responded with irritation. Rocks being crystals Alison had used in her healing practice.

"Does anyone have a crystal? A clear quartz?"

Everyone began checking pockets, purses and bags. "We have one," Ian handed a long clear quartz laser to Alison. "It's the one I told you about, it's an Atlantean crystal."

Alison inspected it. There was a smaller protrusion that had grown alongside the laser, which she recognized to be an inter-dimensional bridge.

"Okay Lisa, we are going to cut it out of your field."

Lisa nodded.

"I can't see it," Alison reminded them, "let me know when I'm there." Then to the being she declared, "This is your final chance to go on your own."

"It's still just above my right hip…"

Alison wielded the quartz like a weapon, eviscerating Lisa's field with slashing motions running horizontally, vertically and diagonally. Then she began to circle the point of the laser through the wounds creating a vortex. Lisa gritted her teeth against the pain.

She took the crystal and placed the blunt end to Lisa's body. Skye pointed to where she could see the spidery, dark shape. Alison spoke again, calmly and directly, "This crystal contains a cross-dimensional bridge, which you can use to transport yourself back to your point of origin."

Lisa could feel the 'tarantula' tense, and then release slightly. She held her breath. Alison called on it again to go or be destroyed. Suddenly Lisa felt an extraction, like something was being plunged from her body. Alison felt the crystal jerk in her hand and Skye saw the darkness get sucked into the crystal.

Alison looked up at Skye, "Is it gone?"

"Alison, here," said Robin, holding out a freezer bag of sea salt. She dropped the crystal in the bag and Robin sealed it. Mary Pat opened the sliding glass doors, and Robin placed it on a table on the balcony, in the snow. She closed the door and locked it.

Alison collapsed on the bed next to Lisa. "How do you feel now?"

"I'm in a lot of pain, here." She gestured toward the area where Ariel had been wounded. This was the weak spot in her field that the being had exploited, like poking your finger in an open wound.

Gina leant down and offered, "Alison, I don't know if this would help, but in energy school I learned how to repair and seal auric fields. I could try to stitch Lisa's wound."

"That's brilliant Gina, give it a go."

Gina was precise and methodical, like a surgeon. She energetically cleansed the area and told Lisa that she was packing the wound with a healing gel. She created a shape that she described as an open weaved golden dream catcher. She took a golden thread and began to stitch. Lisa could feel the tugging on the skin and in the field with each suture as Gina's nimble fingers worked deliberately to close the wound. That was the moment Gina earned the nickname, 'The Medic'.

*   *   *

It was late in the day now, and they were all exhausted. "Someone needs to go and see Vicky," Gina reminded them.

"I'll go," Alison said, resigned. She felt compassion for Vicky. The woman clearly had no idea what was happening. She had traveled so far, bombed her internship, and now they wouldn't even open the door for her.

"She can't go alone," Lisa insisted, "I am not in any condition to go." Skye and Gina volunteered immediately.

As they exited the elevator on the 4th floor, they were met by a strange odor. "What is that?" Gina asked. "Do you smell that?"

"It smells rancid, like meat or something has gone off." Alison wrinkled her nose.

"It smells like brimstone," Skye added.

As they got to Vicky's door it was overpowering. They knocked. Skye had positioned herself in front of Alison, Gina beside her.

Vicky greeted them and stood with the door wide as though waiting for them to enter. Skye simply stretched her arm across the door frame creating a barrier between Alison and Vicky. Clearly they were not coming in to sit and chat.

As Alison began to explain to Vicky what had happened, she seemed genuinely unaware. She had observed how sick Lisa looked when they escorted her down the hall, but had not connected that it had anything to do with her. Skye was keeping a sharp look-out, she was watching the being moving in Vicky's room. It was morphing, adapting; one minute a black shadow, the next, scurrying spiders were moving in every direction. Skye kept pushing Alison back, who was now on tip-toes trying to speak to Vicky over her outstretched arm.

Alison's compassion for Victoria overcame her and she pushed passed Skye and into the room. This was not the incarnate's fault and she couldn't let her feel as though she was some kind of outcast. She wanted her to know she needed to take care of herself.

"The biggest issue here is spiritual hygiene Vicky. You are involved in many different things that are conflicting with the stellar energies... Especially the telluric work."

Vicky took it all in stride. "What do you think I should do?"

"I think you should go home. Get with your team and try to get yourself clear." Alison had briefly considered an intervention on Vicky's behalf and realized that it wasn't appropriate. It was one thing with Lisa being under attack, she hadn't invited it. She hadn't broken the cardinal rules. Vicky was involved with calling in ancient earth energies that she did not understand or could hope to control. "You need to stop channeling, and stop running energy. It seems to get stronger in the energy."

"You know Vicky, Ian and I used to be heavily involved earth work. We understand the attraction to it, but you have to be really vigilant in your protection and cleansing," said Skye, as she continued to engage Vicky. Gina took the opportunity to push Alison in the direction of the elevator. Gina doubled back to tell Skye that she was taking Alison back to the room to check on Lisa. "I love you," Vicky affirmed to Gina. Unsettled, Gina didn't know how to respond, so she nodded and said nothing.

* * *

Lisa had no memory of the drive back to the house that night. As they sat side by side on the couch holding hands she admitted to Alison, "I really thought I was going to die today."

"I know. It wasn't looking too good there for a while."

"When we were cut off, that was so scary."

"I still don't understand why Ariel left? How could she leave? If they are integrated, how can she just bugger off?" Alison was still irritated over what she perceived to be abandonment.

Lisa gathered her thoughts, "No, she didn't leave, it was more like she was saying to me that they could see I wasn't going to come up, they couldn't come down… So if we couldn't clear it, she'd be waiting for me."

"Well, I get that. Grace goes on lock down too when there is something that she can't be exposed to. I felt that when we did that work with the Zeta infiltration. It's like she steps into a vault."

Lisa nodded. She had heard Alison describe that before.

Noting that it was almost midnight, Alison suggested they get some rest. "We've got to figure out what we're doing with those pigging crystals tomorrow."

Lisa smiled.

As they walked into the bedroom they noticed a large black spider on the ceiling. Lisa screamed and jumped up and down. "KILL IT! KILL IT! KILL IT!"

Alison started to laugh, "Commander of the Seraphiam afraid of a teensy, weensy spider?"

"No, that is NOT a spider, that is a minion of Hell – KILL IT! KILL IT! KILL IT!" she shrieked, laughing but at the same time totally serious.

"I'm going to catch it, and toss it outside." Alison said in a superior tone. Her eyes twinkled and she was trying to suppress a grin.

"No! No! Don't *catch* it! It's an assassin, kill it!" Lisa howled.

Once the offending arachnid had been tossed out the front door, both women lay in bed. Lisa's eyes were wide in the darkness. *'I'll never be able to sleep now,'* she thought. "Alison?"

"Yes?"

Lisa grabbed for her hand and squeezed it. "I love you... Thank you."

Alison wasn't used to people telling her they loved her. She found it a very American thing to do – just blurt out to people that you love them. The phrase was overused in her opinion. But she could feel the emotion behind Lisa's words were authentic and genuine.

"Well, I suppose I'm stuck with you now," she teased. Then she added, "I love you too, Butcher."

*   *   *

When Ariel arrived in the control room, Grace was waiting for her. Ariel bowed and then they embraced. They were both relieved but not ready to celebrate. It was premature. They had learned the hard way, 'Pride goes before the fall.'

"We had to employ a maneuver that may have some unintended consequences," Grace informed Ariel.

Ariel sighed, looking from Grace to Raffé. "Timeline?" From their expressions Ariel could see it was something a bit more aggressive than a shift to a comparable timeline. She waited for Grace to bring her up to speed.

"In their linear time, it will be a reset of Zero Point." Grace was solemn.

"They are currently on different timelines then?"

"We have them suspended, they are presently in a pocket without time."

"For how long?"

"Until we can get them unified again. Until Alison decides."

Chapter 21

I Will Wait

As they pulled up to the restaurant, it looked deserted; a casualty of the Cape Cod winter. They sat in the parked car for a few minutes. The morning was beautiful, cold and crisp but sunny and clear. The sky was a shade of blue that could deceive you into thinking it was summer, but there were still patches of snow and ice all over the ground. The women had agreed to meet a few of the students from the west coast that were interested in bringing Marconics to their communities.

After the previous day's 'demon spider' fiasco, breakfast with aspiring Lightworkers immediately followed by a meditation with some crystals sounded very appealing. Still though, both women couldn't shake the feeling that something was seriously off. It felt as though at any moment they were going to wake from a dream.

"How much time do we have?" Alison asked, breaking the trance.

Lisa produced her phone from her pocket and pulled a strange face.

"What's wrong?"

"My phone says it's 7:38pm... December 31, 2000."

Alison did a double take, "Really?"

"Yes – look see."

Lisa reset the phone, she took the battery out, she reset it again, each time it returned to 7:00pm and always December 31, 2000. "This is bizarre," she mused aloud. Then she checked her email, texts, and social media accounts. Nothing. How could that be?

The gravel and snow crunched under the weight of their footsteps as they entered the quiet pub. The waitress told them to sit where they like. They chose a secluded table for six over by the windows so they could overlook the harbor. They hummed along to the Mumford and Sons song playing in the background, *"And I will wait, I will wait for you..."*

They had a productive meeting with the students, but couldn't shake the surreal feeling of disconnection that continued all through breakfast. The group from the west wanted to open an off-the-grid spiritual community for Lightworkers. It sounded lovely on paper but it was off mission. Alison felt strongly that the 'light' shouldn't be bottled up in one place. The Lightworkers were needed to go out and spread the light. Besides, a Lightworkers' compound sounded like it would only be one pitcher of spiked fruit punch and a silver tracksuit short of being a cult; and that was a perception they were careful not to be associated with.

Lisa obsessively checked and rechecked her phone. Still December 31... still 2000.

They made their goodbyes and sat at the table for a moment.

Lisa tossed her phone onto the table frustrated. "Alison, I have no email. I mean I literally have no email, no texts, nothing!"

"Nothing new?"

"No, nothing. My accounts are *gone*. I even signed in through the web browser and there is nothing. They don't exist."

A very sad soulful song had been playing in the background.

... *'And I will wait for you...'* the chorus had the same lyrics as the song they'd heard earlier, but it was a different song, hauntingly familiar but neither one of them could place it. They asked the waitress, but she didn't know. She told them it was music piped in through an on-line service and not a CD. Alison felt a thought trickle through her mind like icy water.

"Lisa," she said slowly as she leaned in to whisper, "did you die yesterday?"

Chapter 22

Ramses, The Great

They returned to the hotel and entered room 151, still trying to understand what had just taken place in the cafe at breakfast.

Smiles and hugs greeted them. They were overwhelmed by the intensity of love in the room.

Lisa kept wondering, *'How do you thank people for saving your life?'*

Ian had laid out a blanket on top of a dresser that was pushed to one side of the room. Thirty-three of the pink Taran crystals had volunteered to come on the journey with Ian and Skye and be the surrogates for the 467, which Ian had left safely at home.

"How do you feel about us receiving some energy work before we start?" Alison asked Lisa. They were both drained from the previous day. Frankly the whole team looked like they could use an energetic reboot.

"That sounds really great," Lisa agreed. "You first, Lady." Lisa gestured to the massage table so Alison could lay down.

Alison got comfortable on the table, closed her eyes and tried to relax. She was exhausted. The instant Lisa stepped into her field she traveled, and was immediately transported to somewhere in the Middle East. She could make out ancient monuments half buried under bludgeoning, shifting sands, sweeping across barren desert planes.

"It's all in ruins..." she heard a voice say with deep sadness.

Her vision zoomed in like a camera, on a decaying arch made of mud bricks. The limestone covering, which had once been decorated with painted friezes had long since disappeared. She saw flashes of imagery, street scenes, market places; civil unrest as soldiers dragged people from their homes to be flogged, tossing their belongings into the streets to be trampled by horses. An overwhelming feeling of sadness and regret washed over her in waves.

Pain surged down both her legs and anger bubbled up from her belly as she felt her top lip curl back into a wrinkled snarl of cold contempt she knew was not hers. A sinister growl escaped her lips.

Lisa looked across at Robin, who stood back, wide eyed. She straightened herself into Ariel's stance and demanded to know, "Who is this?"

Alison could feel her hands balling up into claws, her nostrils flared and her face contorted. She felt she was sharing her body. She could still think and reason, but someone else was at the wheel. *'What is this?'* she thought, *'Is this possession?'*

"Who is forward?" Lisa demanded again.

Alison was flashed an image of a humanoid face with vivid, sapphire blue eyes set in a spikey, rubbery-looking, fuchsia-pink face. Somewhere in the room she could hear the hissing of snakes - cobras, slithering from the dark recesses of a tomb as if their sleep had been disturbed.

Lisa watched in dismay as Alison, writhing in pain, cried out.

Ariel commanded, "Answer me! Who is forward?"

The being was unimpressed.

Strangled gurgling sounds rose up from Alison's throat and gave wave to low, slow and almost demonic laughter, "Ha!... heh... heh..."

The being in Alison's body began toning somewhere deep in her lower chakras, like it was hunkering down and settling in.

'Shit!' Lisa thought, *'this is the kind of thing Alison usually takes care of.'* She altered her approach and began to taunt the being. "Don't you at least have enough intelligence to speak to me?"

Filled with contempt, a voice snapped back at her, loud and disdainful. "Yes! I can speak!" it hissed.

"Then answer me! Who is forward?"

A moment passed, then a deep voice said quietly, "I am Ramses."

Alison felt the cobras slither closer in the darkness of the tomb, as memories of a past life in ancient Egypt began to run like a Pathé News reel in her mind.

Memories of being trapped for eons of time underground, surrounded by snakes, and eaten by insects, conscious but unable to move flooded in. Alison knew this was the lifetime she had experienced of being trapped in her body; the one the Pleiadians had told her was the root of her illness. They had said this was the reason why she had been so sick and weak in this lifetime, because she didn't trust her body. She wouldn't ground down into it. They had made her the promise that she could never be trapped like that again.

Lisa could hear Alison connecting with Ramses in a low, pitiful voice, "What did they do to you? What did they do?" She was gagged again, and as if there were hands squeezing her throat, she choked and struggled for breath.

Speaking through her, *his* voice was deep and raspy. He said, "I have come for you, I have come for you... This is not the place for us.... we can be healed, but we must leave. We'll go through the Halls."

She whispered to Lisa. "He's going to take me with him." She could see him depicted as a beautiful, vibrant young Egyptian Prince. Then she saw him murdered, and subsequently tortured! Yes! He was tortured after death. He was deliberately trapped in his body by a botched embalming. He showed her that he could not be extracted and his spirit was imprisoned in decaying remains.

In a hushed voice, Alison whispered to Lisa, "He isn't human! He never was. He came to Earth with a mission. He should have been extracted, and returned to his people, but he was sabotaged by a betrayer and he's been stuck here for all of this time."

Something choked her off and she began to cough and splutter. Putting her hands to her throat again, she uttered, "His throat was cut. He has had no time in the Spirit world so the memory of what happened to him is still fresh! He is so angry he was left behind."

More and more concerned for Alison, Lisa asked her, "Do you want me to bring Grace forward? Alison, Relax, I am not going to let anything happen to you. I love you."

Gently sobbing Alison continued speaking to Ramses, "I am sorry, I am so sorry for what happened to you..." She sounded as though she was grieving for him. "Please go. Release me from your pain." Speaking softly, she added, "You cannot take me with you."

Lisa became Ariel. "Ramses stop! You are hurting her! She is the incarnate of Grace Elohim. You are not a match for her vibration and you are causing her physical pain. I will extract you from her body with my bare hands, if you do not cease and desist!"

"Now you're talking!" He growled.

Lisa continued, "Our mission in this incarnation is not in alliance with-"

"With what"? He snapped.

"Reptilian agenda."

He let out a deep contemptuous laugh.

"And what is so funny?" Lisa asked.

"You are, ha ha ha ha..."

"Please tell me what you find so amusing?"

"Hummm...." He mused, breathing heavily through the nostrils. Then he spoke, "I have been here on this planet since the beginning..."

Ariel cut him off, "And it was your choice to not come through the Gate with me when I came for you. Your Queen, your children, your kingdom do not exist anymore!"

"They do," he insisted.

"Not in this dimension or time. You saw your own kingdom reduced to ruins."

"And what makes you think you won't see the same?"

Lisa answered him gently, "We understand that, we are on a dying world. You have a unique opportunity to move up through the dimensions and leave the density of this planet to return to your own space and time. Why won't you take it?"

"I am not finished here!" Then his voice softened. "She needs me."

"What work do you have left to accomplish here?"

"Same as yours."

"Our work is for the ascension of humanity. The Reptilians do not want to be part of this agenda..."

"There are other ways to skin cats." He snorted.

"If your mission is the same as ours, you would be most invested in Ascension and salvation for the Lightworkers. Is that what your mission is?"

"Yes."

"Are you speaking the truth?"

"Yes."

"Are you lying to me?"

"YES! Ha!" He laughed a real belly laugh, which amused Lisa. To her surprise, in a moment of brevity between them, Lisa realized she was warming to him. And she could sense he liked her.

She flattered him, "Well, I admire your style." She smiled and waited for his response.

"I am having fun..."

"I'm sure you are." It was like playing chess with a sociopath.

"Why would I want to go?"

Lisa was more comfortable now that she had established a rapport with him. She pushed on, "I understand the power and the richness of all that you have seen and experienced in this material realm – the good, the bad and the ugly. But your time here is done. I don't know how you managed to enter into this body, but I promise you, I will bring down upon you the wrath of all that is at my command, of all that is at Alison's command..."

"That would be interesting, wouldn't it, that would be interesting," he mused, "Go out with a bang, or with a whimper...?" It was as if he were considering whether to have the turkey sandwich or the ham.

Alison's hand reached up towards Lisa's face as she stood over her. "I can see Grace, and I can see pink...pink..."

He chuckled, as though he thought it was just getting interesting.

"All vibrations except Grace will recede, I call Grace Elohim, please come forward," called Lisa.

Grace answered, "I can hear you."

"Grace?"

"Yes."

They were both relieved. "It is so good to hear your voice," said Lisa,

"I need to be sure it is you. Tell me something that only I would know about Alison."

"He will know everything."

"What do I need to do to remove him from the body? Can I...? Can you...?"

"No." She answered, calmly. "He is her Higher Self, you can't remove him without damage to her. Ramses is sad and *afraid*. A lot has changed. He doesn't want to leave the material realm, and he doesn't know it's over. He feels truly that he could be of service to Alison. He came to be healed by her. We are talking to him and flooding him with frequencies of love."

Alison could hear Grace and Ramses in her mind.

She said, 'You must trust me now and recede from this dwelling. No-one wishes you harm, you can feel that. But it can't be allowed to continue Ramses. You must release her in all dimensions and free her in all of her bodies.'

He countered, 'There is work still to be done.'

'We can seek to find ways that she can retain the memory she needs of you going forward, but you need to be on the other side and you must go now.'

'I didn't finish my mission.' Alison detected the regret in his tone.

'You can finish it now Ramses. You have been waiting all this time, come up and we will finish it together.

There were deliberations that went on for some minutes that Alison could not hear before Grace said aloud though her, "He has agreed to go to Amenti with you and will assist your mission there."

Alison's body relaxed, her hands unclenched and her face softened. As Ramses' snarl faded, she began to open her eyes.

"So much for you getting a little energy work on the table," Lisa sighed, looking down into Alison's face.

* * *

Ian stretched a piece of canvas on the floor in the center of the room. He and Skye gently placed the crystals down and began arranging them in an intricate geometric pattern.

Alison was sitting in the 'comfy' chair beside the bed. Lisa handed her a cup of tea and sat down beside her. They waited as twenty minutes ticked slowly by.

"What are they doing?" she said quietly so that only Lisa could hear.

"They are making a grid of some sort."

Skye and Ian moved crystals from place to place, checking angles, feeling the crystals with their palm chakras, questioning placements and conferring with each other in a tone that was barely audible to the others. Alice, who had joined them for the day, entered the fray and was making suggestions. The others observed, nodding when they felt something was 'right' and silent when they weren't sure.

Alison's patience was wearing thin. "This is unnecessary," she whispered to Lisa.

"What do you mean?"

"It doesn't matter how the crystals are placed. It's impossible to know how they should be laid out in this density. Truthfully, it doesn't matter because this is symbolic, and regardless, we don't have all the crystals present."

"I know..." Lisa agreed, "but this is their moment. We can let it go on a little longer."

Twenty more excruciating minutes passed and Lisa could see by the expression of Alison's face - she was done waiting.

"Guys," she said quietly, "It doesn't matter... like Alison said, it's symbolic."

Skye, Ian and Alice were still entrenched in the gridding. "We're done!" Skye proclaimed triumphantly, placing one more crystal to the far left.

Lisa threw a sideways glance at Alison, who cranked her eyebrows up a little higher.

They each stretched and were about to take a quick break before preparing to take the journey, when Ian dropped like a stone. Skye steered him as he collapsed back on the bed in a full trance. His body began to tremble like he was experiencing a spiritual rapture. As Skye attended to him, he began whispering to her.

"Skye, is he okay?" Lisa asked.

She looked up, visibly shaken. "It's not Ian... it's his integration, Ra."

Still seated in the chair, Alison had closed her eyes. She had been simultaneously transported and was viewing a scene as it began to unfold before her.

Realizing that Alison and Ian were connecting, Lisa and Skye stood between them and clasped hands. Skye was beaming Ian and Lisa beaming Alison. "We're bridging them," Skye said.

"I know." Lisa confirmed. "And we are anchoring for them."

"My beloved, can you hear me?" Skye spoke gently to Ian.

"I am Ra..." Ian said, his voice no louder than a hum. *"Ah-A-el-RAY-ah."* He said, pronouncing each syllable deliberately. Ian had left the building.

"Is he Elohim, Lisa?" Alison asked. She got an immediate yes and then asked Skye.

"Yes! He says yes!"

"Why is he here? What is his role?" Lisa relayed Alison's question to Skye.

Ra was speaking more forcefully now, stronger as he came more forward. "I am the keeper of the crystals. I have been waiting for this time to be realized. I have been keeping Tara safe for Grace."

Lisa relayed Ra's message to Alison, then asked Skye to find out where he was from.

"I have traveled from outside of this universe. I arrived here at the Fall and I have waited..." he murmured to Skye.

"What were you waiting for my love?" Skye asked.

"The Gates are reopening. We can reclaim them all now. They can go home."

Alison whispered to Lisa. "I'm in a vast open air market." Her eyes surveyed rows of tables heavy with pastry, meats, fish, fruits and vegetables. She began to describe the scene, "Merchants have displayed jewelry, pottery, clothing and tapestries... I can hear music and the blend of many voices speaking at once... The air is fragrant." She took in a slow, deep breath, "It's a perfume of exotic flowers and sea spray... I can see people moving through the market." Alison lingered, taking it all in. It was perfect, the quintessential bazaar.

Alison observed that time had momentarily speeded up, and then slowed again at the next juncture. "Something has shifted."

She kept her voice at a whisper as she explained to Lisa what she could see and feel. The gaiety of marketplace had been replaced by a sense of urgency. Alison could detect the hint of something sour on the wind, like rubber tires burning in the distance. There was a gathering crowd around them on their soapboxes.

"We were evangelizing." Then the realization of what she was seeing dawned on her. "Oh, we were evangelizing to draw them in, to get them into groups." She could see them, men, women and children, dressed in Grecian style clothing and huddled together in a mass. Their frequencies were a blend of fear, hope, anger, relief and confusion.

"I can see a white smoke moving through the crowd... it's traveling from person to person, entering them through the thymus..." As Alison wondered what the smoke was doing, she heard herself say, *They were moving among them as smoke,*

"Who is moving among them?" Lisa whispered.

"You and your Legions were moving as smoke, from one to the other, capturing their soul essences."

Lisa and Skye whispered to each other about what Alison and Ian were seeing, and relaying the information back to their respective partners. It was like a strange interdimensional game of Chinese Whispers.

Alison was walking through the crowd as an unseen observer, eventually she realized, "Oh Lisa, *they're all in the crystals.*" Alison sighed heavily. They both understood in that moment who they were and what they had done.

Ariel had shared with them that the Seraphiam could be the Angels of Death, Angelic Destroyers that moved through density as smoke. They had captured the soul essences and downloaded them into the crystals.

The picture changed. It was now the modern era. There was a sadness in Alison's voice as she recounted what she could see. It felt to her like she was their witness.

"I can see people going about their everyday lives. Sitting with friends around tables, at pavement café's, chatting and laughing on a warm, spring day. It reminds me of Paris, or any of the other cities in Europe. They are enjoying a semblance of a normal life, but it's artificial. It's all contrived for their experience."

As she watched, suddenly every pair of eyes turned and looked directly at her as though they knew she was there. They had been awakened and were aware. It unnerved Alison.

Skye whispered to Lisa, "He said when the grid blew, he captured and preserved as many of the soul essences as he could, before they were totally lost. He said he contained them in the crystals."

The frequency that had felled Ian and enabled Alison such clarity began to subside, enabling them both to return to the present moment.

When Ian finally surfaced, he looked at Skye and touched the pink crystal that hung from her neck. He had wrapped and fashioned it into a pendant for her. "We are to build a ship of light," he said softly, "they are going someplace different."

After months of questioning, they now knew what they had to do.

Chapter 23

Amenti

"Okay," Lisa called to the team, "Everyone get comfortable. I'm going to need you to stay with me as I do this. We have to all go down together; it's going to require all of us so... no drifting off – everyone got it?"

Lisa perched on a massage table with her back against the wall. The others took up stations on the floor and in chairs, encircling the crystal grid.

She began the process of bringing the group and herself into a deeply relaxed and meditative state. As they breathed into their bodies and cleared their minds, she felt the energy shift as something deep inside her took over.

Lisa stood alone in a grassy field and waited as one by one they each appeared beside her, forming a circle under the night sky.

A husky voice issued forth from Lisa, "Each of you will now claim your Higher Self alignment."

Lisa could feel the energy amplifying exponentially as deep resonate voices reverberated from each of the incarnates. One by one, they called forth their Egyptians causing sonic waves to ripple through the room. She shuddered with chills and goosebumps erupted down her arms.

Isis waited as the incarnates were each overlaid with their Egyptian essences. Lisa watched intently as each member of the team was slightly obscured by a column of translucent energy. It was as though they had been enveloped by beings of light that were significantly larger than them as individuals. They were finally joined by the essences of other Egyptian beings that had banded in support of the mission, including Ramses, who Lisa could see shimmering alongside Alison and Horus.

"And I AM Isis. Follow me...

"In the center of our circle are the crystals. Breathe into your hearts and direct your energy into the central stone... See it fill with golden light, and begin to vibrate... See it illuminated from within as it becomes brilliant... Allow the light to enter into each of the surrounding crystals – those that are here in this room, and those that they represent. There is no space and time."

Lisa could hear the breathing change as the Egyptians directed their energy towards the crystal grid. The metallic pyramid shape inside each one glowed and came alive within the matrix of each Taran point. Satisfied that they were all activated, Isis continued. "In the center of our circle there is an octagonal platform. Can you see it?"

Eight voices answered, "Yes."

"Step onto the platform with me."

They were no longer the team Lisa knew; they were Pantheon. She could see them now as they were, in the magnificence of their Egyptian 'I AM'.

The masculine energies of Horus – The God of War, Ramses – The Great, and Osiris - The God of the Dead, were drawn in golden light. Horus wore a Modius; a flat-topped, cylindrical headdress, similar to the famous bust of Nefertari. Osiris donned the crown of upper Egypt, the Hedjet. Lisa recognized its shape. Ramses' head was round, smooth and bald. They all displayed bare chests, with strong muscular physiques, and broad shoulders, with the classic triangular torso; narrow at the waist and hips. Each wore traditional dress, pleated linen loincloths secured by decorative painted leather belts. Thoth presented himself as a wizened old magus, tall and thin, with a long beard that in the light, looked white with age. Ra was different from the rest. He was represented as a vibrating column of gold and green light that intermittently took on humanoid form.

Equally spectacular were the Goddesses, Hathor, Ma'at and Sekhmet. They too were drawn in gold light; Hathor, like Isis, wore the Head Horns Crown, with the sun disc, Ma'at wore a simple Ostrich feather, representing truth, order and justice. Sekhmet was adorned with a gold headband, a Seshed, with a serpent attached. Queen Nefertari, a Hybrid, was drawn in blue light. They were beautiful to behold, regal in stance and almost blinding to look at. No wonder they had been perceived as Gods.

Each of the Pantheon carried in their hands several pink, Taran crystals.

"The platform is descending... down... down... down... see it sinking through the grass, through the soil... going deeper and deeper through the layers of earth containing minerals and gems... we are beginning to take on speed as we lower further and further down... still traveling through underground caves... moving faster, passing underground rivers and lakes, until finally breaking through the layers of earth's crust and mantle strata as we go deeper, and deeper, and deeper...

"Feel the descent now as it is beginning to slow and then finally allow the platform to come to a stop."

A symphony of sighs confirmed they all felt the platform settle deep within the Earth.

Lisa could see that they were in the entrance to Set's underworld. "You will follow me," Isis commanded. And she led them from the platform, to a doorway that had been cleaved from the rock.

They followed Isis down a long limestone corridor. It was narrow but tall, and illuminated by torches chained to the walls along either side The sounds of their footsteps were muffled by a layer of soft sand that covered the flagstone floor. As they emerged from the passageway, they found themselves in a vast atrium overgrown with all manner of tropical plants and palms. Birds of Paradise in every imaginable color and species called to each other from wide leafy Hostas the size of elephant ears. The rushing sound of water indicated there was stream or small river somewhere out of sight.

As they trailed deeper into the atrium, Lisa heard them gasp as they took in the majesty of a huge Golden Sphinx. The corner of her mouth turned up, as Isis allowed a small smile.

Between the front paws of the Sphinx a doorway appeared. "Follow me please," Isis called again. She waited for them on the other side as they filed into the great Hall of Amenti.

The domed rotunda was accentuated by rows of layered archways, reminiscent of the Roman Coliseum. In the center of the hall was a 4-sided, stepped pyramid. It looked like a raised stage with a vast stone archway at the center. Lisa observed the shimmer in the open space of the arch and realized it was a Star Gate.

"Can you all see the pyramid?"

"Yes," they said in unison.

"Please step up. We are going to cross through the archway together... place the palms of your hands against the membrane of the gateway." It felt viscous yet firm. It reminded Lisa of the thick layer of 'skin' that develops on the top of gelatin left in the fridge too long. "Push with your hands until you feel it give... then your arms... continue pushing forward until you feel it against your chest, your face, your thighs... now step through and feel the membrane passing over the top your head and beneath your feet... Feel it close up behind you as you step fully through to the other side..."

Isis waited.

Lisa felt a strange tugging on her field. She had stopped in the middle, straddling both dimensions. She knew immediately that one of them was lost. "Who's missing?"

"Me." Robin's voice called, "I can't find you!"

"I am right here." Isis held out her hand to Hathor, Lisa held her physical hand out to Robin, though she was sitting on the opposite side of the room.

"Got it," Robin called as Lisa felt her come through.

Chapter 24

Liberation

On the other side they could see that there were two doors. The left door was marked by a carved, solar disc with rays ending in ankhs. Lisa recognized the symbol as the 'One' God – Aten. *'Unity consciousness,'* Isis explained to Lisa, *'Through that door is a return to Source.'* The markings on the right door were more intricate; an octahedron in the center surrounded by star tetrahedrons. *'A return to their point of origin; this is how they will regain their Ascension trajectory.'*

Lisa felt a pang of pain on her right side. She knew Ariel was warning her. She took a deep breath and allowed the words to flow, "None may enter through either door without pure intentions to return to Source, or to Tara. Nothing may enter here that may cause harm. Nothing may enter here that is not sanctioned."

"Ra," Isis called aloud. "You are aware of your mission? You and your bride?"

"Yes."

"Enter to the left," Isis instructed. Lisa watched as their light disappeared through the portal marked by the solar disc. The others Isis led through to the right.

They found themselves in a cavernous room, like a huge warehouse lined with arched colonnades stretching around and above them, as high and as far as they could see. A beam of light appeared through the arches spiraling down toward them. As the light approached they could see the varied shapes of different merkabas hanging like suits of clothes on a drycleaner's conveyor belt.

The crystals began to hum and vibrate, the metallic triangular discs within them glowed white hot; they were releasing the trapped Atlantean souls.

White smoke began to billow out of the crystals with orbs of pink, blue, and golden light. Lisa could hear sniffles and the whimpers of soft sobs coming from the team as they were overwhelmed by the flood of emotions emanating from the lost Atlanteans. Had they known the whole time they were trapped? Had they given up hope? They could equally feel the Egyptians' regret and the acceptance of forgiveness; they had waited these long years for the chance at redeeming their failed rescue mission.

"GO!" Isis roared, "Go, go, go!"

The conveyor belt began to move, and the Pantheon began placing the orbs inside the geometric shapes of the merkabas. Like the deployment of paratroopers over their target, the souls merged with the merkabas and took flight one after the other in rapid succession. The conveyor belt speeded up, ushering the populated merkabas toward the apex of the chamber and shooting them through the oculus and out through the dimensional structure. The room was heating up from the friction of the energy required to propel the merkabas through the Amenti Star Gates.

As they watched the last of the merkabas depart through the oculus, Isis called out to Ra. "Ah A el RAY AH," she bellowed, annunciating each syllable as he did.

"We are ready." He responded.

Isis led the processional to support Ra and Nefertari. They connected telepathically and could see the gigantic elongated octahedral merkaba Ra had engineered. The crystals they carried contained the soul fragments too weakened or damaged to return to pre-cataclysmic Tara, or those that had simply requested to return to Unity Consciousness. His ship, a giant shared merkaba, was to take them back to Source so they could be reabsorbed into a pool of bliss.

"Alison," Ramses smiled as he left her side, and whispered the words of a wartime love song, *"I'll be seeing you in all the old familiar places..."* It had been her Father's favorite.

Skye had believed her crystal was the key to the ship. Whether it was or wasn't, their intention made it so. Nefertari held the crystal and together, the full pantheon beamed it into ignition.

They watched as the ship harnessed their gifts of quantum energy like a space shuttle preparing for launch, and then it shot off through the dimensions heading back to Source.

Alison and Lisa both were overcome; the sentiments of gratitude, relief, joy, pain, grief and elation belonged to the women, to Grace and Ariel, and to their Egyptians.

Isis led them back through Amenti to the antechamber for their return. As they rode the platform back up, Isis spoke to them all.

"We thank you. Together we have redeemed five hundred thousand souls... we send you onward now in gratitude." Though Isis left her signature, a gift of essence in Lisa's blend, she never spoke again.

Chapter 25
Stay

One by one the team surfaced, returning their consciousness to their bodies and opened their eyes. Hours had flown by like minutes. They each sat there in stunned silence.

Five hundred thousand souls? And yet, there were so many more... sleep walking through their current lifetime; disconnected and unaware. Would they hear the call?

Lisa looked from face to face; they were tear-stained and weary, but smiling. Alison was very pale; Lisa could tell by the look on her face that she wasn't feeling well. "Alison, are you okay?" Lisa asked, "Is Ramses gone?"

"I can feel him, he is drawing himself up through the body; he's going!"

"Let's get her on a table!" Lisa urged. Lisa grabbed her under one arm and Mary Pat the other and they lifted Alison so she could recline on the massage bed.

Alison saw Horus come for Ramses and greet him as comrade in arms. Time speeded up as she watched him heal and grow young again. The emotion she felt for him flooded her senses, as if she was parting with kin she knew she would never see again, at least not on this plane.

Lisa called on Grace to confirm that he had left Alison's body.

"He's going," she said. "He's going."

Alison felt the sensation of his energy pulling in from every cell and atom of her body, drawing slowly up through her feet, legs and arms and drawing into the hands, like an integration in reverse.

Ariel was monitoring the timeline, and noticed something of an anomaly. She called Grace to the console and pointed at readings of Alison's bio- feedback.

"Her vital signs are all over the map," she said, "there are massive fluctuations in all recordings of essential life support."

Lisa watched Alison go from pale to white as the color drained from her face. *'Oh, no – no, no,' she thought, 'something is very wrong here.'*

"Alison, what's going on?"

"I'm so cold." Alison whispered.

Lisa felt her forehead; she was cool and clammy. Beadlets of sweat had broken out on her face. Her eyelids were at half-mast.

"Yes, I see it," Grace was already monitoring Alison. She had seen the sensors light up one after the other. "Her blood pressure is rising, she's in danger of overheating," she said as she scanned readout after readout, which all pointed to the same outcome.

"This is going to be too much for her...she is melting down and if we don't reduce her temperature now she'll burn out." Grace looked on in dismay as the situation went from bad to worse... She paced and checked and re-checked the data screens. Eventually, she conceded to Ariel with a heavy heart. "I'm losing her."

"Alison," Lisa called.

No response.

"Alison!" she shouted.

No response.

Alison's face had taken on a strange grey pallor and now her skin was ice cold to the touch. "Alison, answer me! Are you okay? What's happening?!"

"Something's wrong," she answered. Her voice was feathery and weak. Alison could feel herself draining out of her own body.

'Help me, help me help her!' Lisa called to Ariel and Grace both. Alison was struggling to breathe.

Grace lent forward resting both hands on the console and spoke in a low voice to Ariel. "We're hollowing her out. Ramses was integral to her life force we can't leave her in a vacuum like this she will simply disintegrate. I have to go in."

Ariel looked up at her incredulously, but before she could speak, Raffé appeared behind them. Grace signaled her to secrecy and she stood down and watched as Grace spun around to encounter Raffé, grabbing him by the forearms, "Help me!" she pleaded.

He looked back at her, her eyes wide and vulnerable. He hadn't seen her like this since they were young, in the early days of the Lyran conflict. Were his fears being realized? Would this be what breaks her? She couldn't take another loss.

Only he and Ariel, her true confidents, really knew Grace. They had witnessed the sacrifices she had made. They knew all that she had risked, all she had promised, and the heavy price she had paid on her quest for redemption.

In that moment he felt something he couldn't begin to describe. He felt helpless. "Grace... what can I do?" She detected the sound of defeat in his voice. He thought there was no more to be done.

"She's stroking out." Ariel broke in, still observing the timelines, as they snaked and coiled towards another nexus point.

Grace kept eye contact with Raffé, tightening her grip on him as though she was afraid if she let go she would fall. There wasn't time to tell him what she must do now. No time to petition the usual channels for sanction. And she knew she would answer for the decision she was about to take. Grace wouldn't sacrifice him too, and she knew that for that he would never forgive her. He saw something in her eyes he'd seen only once before. It looked like 'goodbye'. Still clutching his sleeves so he couldn't reach for her, she began to dematerialize before his eyes.

"Ariel, what is she doing? Where is she going?!"

Ariel knew Grace could be anywhere or nowhere at all, and her loyalty ran deep. Raffé didn't wait for an answer he had already disappeared. This was not like Grace. Ariel tried to focus on Lisa, and what was happening in that hotel room. She knew this was the only way she could help Grace now.

If Grace was still aboard ship there was only one place she would be. Raffé tried to put himself in her position. What would he do in the same circumstances? Something flashed across his mind that he immediately rejected as being too reckless, too dangerous and uncharacteristically irresponsible. He re-materialized on the floor of the matter transfer terminal in Grace's staterooms; Grace was already partially submerged, in the bio-plasma tank.

"No! Oh, no... Grace," He cried out when he saw her. He kneeled beside the tank and took her hand in his. She pulled it away slowly and he watched as it sank beneath the surface of the thick, iridescent green liquid. He stood by as she became fully immersed; her hair, her eyes and finally her mouth dissolved into essence.

Back in the hotel room, Lisa climbed onto the massage table. She positioned herself to sit astride it, cradling Alison's limp body in her lap, holding her close to try to warm her with body heat. Alison was failing.

"Lisa, there's a portal opening up in my third eye..." Alison felt pulled toward it... "They want me to go." Then as though she was pleading with someone unseen and unheard, Alison reasoned, "No, not yet. It's too soon, they're not ready, it's too soon."

Lisa's heart turned over as she realized Alison was bargaining for her life. *'Don't you fucking take her from me!' she screamed at the Galactics in her head.* "Alison, you can't leave me. I love you, do you hear me? Don't go, Alison, Don't go," pleaded Lisa with wet hot tears streaming down her face. "I stayed to do this with you, I need you," she whispered.

Alison could hear her friend's voice but it seemed very, very far away.

Grace's face suddenly appeared more clearly and more beautiful than Alison had ever seen. She drew in so close that her eyes appeared to be no more than a few inches away, and she began to lower herself into Alison's body. Alison could see the pupil of Grace's left eye open like a portal and another face emerge from it. She knew she had never seen this face before but understood immediately that this was Prime Creator. He didn't speak; just knowing he was there made her feel safe.

She heard, *'Alison, your physical vehicle has been greatly weakened by the friction of Ramses departure. Biological systems are breaking down and inner pathways of the vessel are losing integrity.'*

"Am I dying?" Alison asked.

"No Alison!" Lisa called to her, but Alison did not hear.

She felt Grace descend even further into her multidimensional structure. A surge of energy flooded her body, electricity shot through her heart and electrified every cell, every atom and molecule. She twitched and vibrated as though being shocked back to life. The heat intensified and she slipped quickly into semi-consciousness.

The team watched as breaches began to appear in Alison's field, trying frantically to seal them, but as soon as one was closed another opened.

Alison was now aware that her consciousness was hovering inside the physical body around the area of her thymus and not, as she was used to perceiving it, inside her head.

"You've locked me out of my brain?" Alison questioned. "You've locked me out of my brain," there was an undercurrent of anger in her voice. Lisa looked at Robin and Gina, none of them understood what Alison meant.

She watched the geometric structures of the etheric and ketheric templates begin to warp and melt. Holes appeared in the layers of the subtle bodies, like Swiss cheese. She knew she could disappear down one of them at any moment and clung to a column of light that ran parallel to her spine. She couldn't see the portal anymore; she wasn't in her brain. Why would she be locked out of her own brain? Then words came as a warning, *'Don't slip, don't let go.'*

She repeated them out loud to the room, "Don't let me slip," they heard her say, "if you see me start to slip, catch me."

Gina stitched up the holes as quickly as they formed, but they were morphing as others were opening. Alice and Robin knew they couldn't seal them all, not in time

"Don't go, don't go." Lisa whispered.

Her pleas had fallen on deaf ears. Lisa's tears were freely flowing. She felt helpless and angry. Where was everyone? Alison's hair was plastered to her head in wet stringy clumps. She was fading out, about to slip into unconsciousness.

"Alison STAY!" Alice shouted in a drill sergeant voice. Alison's body jerked in response. Realizing that the command 'stay' had a totally different vibration, Alice shouted again, "Alison STAY!"

She jerked again. The team screamed a chorus of 'stay's at her.

Suddenly Alison was sucked up her spinal column through a tube of light and landed back in her head.

To her, it looked as if she was on board a ship, with slick black obsidian floors and a Tesla Mushroom sparking in the distance. It resembled the laboratory of a mad scientist. A chair appeared and as she sat down, a blanket was draped around her. There were several beings working hurriedly on a brain. She could see that there were wires coming out of it, and it was overheating and smoking, like a transformer that was about to blow.

They instructed her telepathically, *'Alison, turn yourself into a coolant and pour yourself over your brain.'*

Alison thought of a cold pitcher of heavy cream. Something that would coat like latex, and bring the temperature down. As she poured herself over her brain, she could see the liquid bubble and sizzle from the heat.

Raffé appeared beside Ariel. He knew why she hadn't betrayed Grace's plan, but that wouldn't keep him from blaming Ariel for not stopping the madness. "What's their status?"

"I'm losing them both!" Ariel raged from the console rounding on him. "I need your help." Hearing the urgency in her voice, he put his grievance aside and leant forward to look at the unfurling timeline with Ariel.

"The higher percentage of Grace's essence should have filled the vacuum Ramses left."

"Alison's vehicle was too damaged," she breathed, "Grace can't stabilize her, it's too much. She needs more time, more linear time. Can I split the frequency between my incarnate and hers?"

Raffé assessed the data, "You're going to put them both at risk. Lisa is physically stronger, but you've only just got her stabilized."

"I have an idea… but I will need your help…"

Chapter 26

The Reset

Lisa leant back against Skye who was holding her up as she continued to hold Alison. Though Alison had calmed a little, Lisa could feel her life force draining away. They were running out of time. Nothing they tried was working, and they couldn't beam more energy at her, she was overheating as it was. *'Ariel, where are you? What do I do – she's dying?'*

Ariel connected. Lisa felt the surge of energy as Ariel came forward in her mind and in her body.

'How do I help her?' *Lisa asked telepathically.*

Ariel knew the fastest way to make Lisa understand was to show her. She rifled through the memory of a movie Lisa had recently enjoyed, it featured beautiful imagery where the lead character is assisted and saved by his friends because they share the burden of an energetic overload. Ariel pulsed the scene to her.

Lisa smiled and nodded.

Ariel turned to Raffé, "She's got it."

She slid backward off the table and gently rested Alison's head on the massage table. "Alison, Ariel just sent an image. I have an idea. Can we split the frequency beam?"

Alison thought of the ray gun with 'resuming frequency modulation' written across it. "Yes, okay," she whispered weakly.

Lisa looked at the team, "Here's what we're going to do. I am going to split the beam with Alison-"

Before she could finish, Robin jumped in, "I'll take some too."

"Me too," chimed in Gina and Mary Pat.

"Yes here too," Diane added, and Alice.

"Alright then. Let's make a circle around her. I'm going to take it first and then I will send it to each of you, okay?"

They all nodded and moved quickly into place.

Lisa stood over Alison at the head of the massage table. "We've got this," she said, "I need you to stay with me and focus. I'm going to put my forehead on yours, and then I want you to siphon off all the excess energy to me. You just keep sending it to me, and I will pass it to the others. Okay?"

Alison nodded.

Lisa leant over and connected third eye to third eye with Alison. She was immediately jolted as lighting flooded her field through her third eye. She drew it in and anchored it into her body.

"Mary Pat!" Lisa yelled.

"GO!" Mary Pat replied and prepared to receive the energy from Lisa. She began to vibrate in her seat as she breathed deeply to anchor.

"Gina!"

"GO!" Gina accepted the flood of energy in her field and anchored it down into her body.

Lisa repeated with the others.

"Don't forget Robin!" Robin yelled.

"Robin!"

"GO!"

They stayed connected, entraining to one another and anchoring the frequency as Alison began to stabilize. The color returned to her face as her shallow, rapid breathing slowed to become deep oxygenating breaths, and her temperature began to normalize.

"Alison, Ariel says that when you feel the energy start to back up and overload, you can send it out to us. We can stabilize you. Then when you are ready and able to assimilate it, we can release it back to you, one by one," Lisa whispered.

Slowly Alison came back to them. Somewhere in the background she heard the kettle boiling; it was like music to her ears. *'Too bad no one drinks,'* she thought, *'a nip of brandy in the tea would slip down a treat just about now.'*

Spirits were lifted with steaming hot mugs of 'builder's tea' and copious amounts of chocolate.

Robin was deep in thought, and after a moment asked earnestly, "So, if you two die on the tables, what are we supposed to do?"

"Wipe everything down so you don't leave prints," Alison answered without missing a beat.

"Yes, and then walk out like you didn't see or hear a thing," Lisa added.

Laughter, as it turned out, was the best medicine. Everyone felt better as their laughter raised the vibration.

"Alison, look at this..." Lisa said curiously, presenting her with the phone. The white plastic cover on the back of the phone was scarred with a spidery black mark. But more importantly, as Lisa pointed out, it was no longer New Year's Eve in the year 2000. The date and time had been reset to the present day. All systems restored.

They looked at each other as the significance of the numerology began to dawn on Lisa. "Alison, I think we reset the triple date Star Gates..."

"What does that mean?"

"The switch from 1999 to 2000 marked the planet's return to Zero Point. That's when we began the countdown to Ascension on December 21, 2012. Every year of the new millennium the planet passed through a Star Gate created by a specific Galactic alignment, each one occurring on a triple date. The 'triple dates' are when the day, month and year are the same number. Each Gate brought us closer to the Galactic Core, and exposed the planet to increasingly higher frequencies in preparation for reentry into the Photon Belt. It began on January 1st, 2001 - 1/1/1. Then in 2002, it was in February, 2/2/2. Then the following year it was, 3/3/3... leading all the way up to December 12, 2012, 12/12/12."

"Right," Alison nodded for Lisa to continue.

"If I died yesterday, then this morning, you and I were on different timelines...they must have returned us to Zero Point. That's why I had no email accounts, texts or anything, why everything disappeared from my phone. None of it existed on that timeline, because I didn't exist." She watched Alison nod.

The thoughts were crystallizing in Lisa's mind. "We were suspended somehow... we were suspended in the Zero Point... that's why it was New Year's Eve in 2000. They positioned us to be able to reset the Star Gates beginning with January 1, 2001 – 1/1/1."

Alison could feel the confirmations in her body. "That's right!" she agreed.

"That's how they enabled us to release the souls through Amenti. They used the alignment for us to be able to access all of the 12 Star Gates simultaneously..."

The lyrics to the songs from breakfast played through both their minds, 'and I will wait for you.'

"So... if the timeline collapsed when I died, they maintained us in limbo at Zero Point to complete the work ... we must have traveled back through the Gates together..."

Alison drew the only reasonable conclusion, "You and I are back on the same timeline again!"

They looked at each other incredulously, struggling to grasp the enormity of the situation.

Chapter 27

Sacrifice

Ariel stood at the console watching the plume of light erupting from Earth's Amenti Gates and piercing the dimensions like a rocket. She felt Raffé materialize behind her. His expression was grave.

Together, they maintained their focus, and monitored the upload of the precious contents of the long lost Taran crystals to the Fifth Dimensional planetary Matrix. Then they synchronized the timelines with Orly, and initiated the final stage of the Galactic Reset.

Volunteer forces from various Galactic Federations, including the Alliance of Free Worlds and the Interstellar Alliance, the Guardian Alliance, the Paladin and Ashtar Command, had all worked together in preparation to receive the retrieved souls for assimilation back into the Taran matrix, at the culmination of eons of linear years of planning.

Tara had been prepared well in advance. The lost Atlanteans had used the Amenti Star Gate, to loop back in time, and were being reinstated at a point in their own history before the Fall of Tara.

Thousands of years of being trapped in a simulation of life, in 500 pink crystals, would appear to the survivors as nothing more than a momentary lapse in concentration... the sort of thing that happens every day.

The effects on their energy fields would be more difficult to disguise. Their emotional bodies would carry a new vibrational signature, evolved through their experiences of the time-loop, as it was programed into the matrix of the crystals.

They would have no conscious memory of that existence; all they would know would feel like the distant memory of a dream. A remnant of an emotional overlay would impact future choices, decisions and actions, ensuring they remain on a timeline that would eventually branch off from the original one of cataclysm, and follow the path of a new future away from the potential for disaster.

Later, following the withdrawal of the Egyptian pantheon, Ariel and Raffé stabilized the biological vehicles and all physiological responses among the team. But they too had been under surveillance.

The Argen Guard opened the door and escorted Ariel and Raffé to the Council's small meeting chamber.

Ariel closed her eyes and felt for Grace. Her energetic signature was faint.

'Were they released?' Grace called softly upon feeling Ariel's vibration. She was drained and fading from the transfer of energy.

'Yes, five hundred thousand were reclaimed… We had no recourse, Grace. It's justifiable.'

Neither of them would have allowed the crystals to fall into opposition hands.

Grace's absence had been noted. Whispered accusations of 'Dereliction of Duty' contributed to the momentum her enemies were gathering against the Elohim. She had broken protocol, openly flaunted Galactic directives and intervened in Human affairs without sanction. All directly contravened the Laws of Free Will as established by the Council of Ur.

For her own protection she was now in solitary confinement at Allied Command, in Central City, outside of Free Will Universe One.

Ariel looked around the table acknowledging the members of the Council. Before taking her usual seat beside Grace's empty one, she could not conceal her surprise at the presence of the Alpha and bowed deeply.

The successful execution of this inter Galactic rescue mission, so long in the making, was indeed the cause of great celebration among all those involved. This was Creation at work in a Free Will Zone. The in-breath and out-breath of God.

The Council's spokesman directed Ariel to recount the events leading up to the release of the Atlanteans and their return to the 5th Dimensional time matrix on Tara.

The Council's spokesman questioned Ariel, "You have been monitoring the Hybrids?"

"Yes."

"What is their status?"

"Hybrid I is still stabilized. Hybrid II and the other incarnates are helping her to hold the frequency. Their vehicles had been prepared to withstand the higher frequency through their integrations with the 'Original Clan'."

Unfolding in the hologram was an intricate golden web, spiraling outward in every direction, collapsing and reforming as it wove around Hybrids I and II and the other incarnates.

They watched silently until the Alpha spoke, "The time lines must be stabilized. Plans for the Ascension are not myopic, Hybrids I and II will need to be prepared for other realities."

Ariel knew this meant one thing. The Alpha was descending, and that meant the Omega would not be far behind.

* * *

Alison and Lisa returned to the house to rest. It was late but before they finally clambered into bed Lisa reached over and grabbed Alison tightly. "I never felt so helpless." She said, with her head on her shoulder. "I was so scared today. I thought I'd lost you," she confessed, suppressing a sob.

Alison put her arms around her and stroked her back, the way she would soothe a child, with what little strength she could still muster.

Grace was desolate. She had sent down a greater portion of her energy to save Alison and was now unable to assume form. She existed only as disembodied consciousness, isolated and contained. It was like being locked in a box, alone, with no light and no sound. She must retrieve the energy that was divided among the team when the beam was split, or before long her condition would filter down to Alison with catastrophic consequences for them both.

Lisa turned out the light, and Alison rolled over and closed her weary eyes to sleep.

Grace's voice reverberated softly but clearly in her head. "We have 4 days..."

Epilogue

Subject: FW: To the Seven Seasoned Warriors, thank you
On Feb 10, 2015, at 11:40 PM, "Lisa Wilson" <marconics444@gmail.com> wrote:

To the Seven Seasoned Warriors,

How do you possibly thank someone for saving your life? For putting themselves in harm's way without thinking, flinching, or fearing the outcome? How can you even say "thank you" when those words don't even come close to expressing the gratitude and awe and humility you feel?

How can we even begin to express our heartfelt appreciation and love to have you all there to surround and support Alison and I both as we each went through those extreme trials with your love, your courage, your strength and your fearlessness? Your love filled us with love – and I silently called out to each one of you to tell you that I loved you. Your love in calling to Alison to STAY ensured that she did. Your courage helped us to stay connected to our own. Your strength reminded us of what we could each endure as surely we were both pushed to the limits. And your fearlessness helped us to step out of fear and into possibility and hope.

Alison and I spoke about how amazing you are.

You are each, in your own right, stunning and powerful beings of light and love. We are honored and humbled by your actions and your demonstration of faith in us, in each other, and in what we have been called together to do.

With much love and thanks,
Alison & Lisa

Book Three

Marconics: Wrath of Angels

An unforeseen and devastating turn of events in the Galactic Arena changes the face of humanity's Ascension. The Archangels are outlawed.

Please enjoy this brief excerpt from our next book, 'Marconics: Wrath of Angels'.

*   *   *

Alison opened her eyes slowly to the bleakness of this new day. News of the devastating attacks had settled overnight to form a blanket of cold resignation wrapped around her. She had accepted the truth. She felt like she did the morning after her father died.

Lisa was still sleeping, so Alison dressed quietly and crept into the main living room of the seaside apartment they had rented for the weekend – the worst bridal shower ever - and pulled back the curtains. The beach was grey and steely, not like the day before at all. It was damp and she hadn't bought clothes for the sudden chill that was in the air.

The wind was picking up as she walked alone over the dunes to the water's edge, and began replaying some of the things that Metatron had revealed to them the night before. His last words played over and over, on a loop in her mind, "The final victory for the dark is if you lose hope in a hopeless situation."

If it was possible to even imagine, the Alpha himself burdened by grief, and such disappointment… they could almost picture him sitting alone in the gloom of an empty bar in the middle of the day, perched on the edge of a stool and hugging a warm beer.

Her chest tightened as she relived the moments of his revelations, and she found it hard to take a breath. She began to sing. It always helped her to relax. "You call me out upon the waters, that great unknown, my feet may fail…" She filled her lungs and sang it as loud as she could for all beings, anyone out there who may still be able to hear her. Especially Raffé and the Seraphiam.

"We are still here" She called out, fighting back the tears. "And we will do whatever is necessary. Just tell us what that is! Please, don't give up!"

At that moment she realized she had never spoken to Grace, not properly. Not like Grace was her family, someone she loved… She knew that she needed to be there for her now.

Bursting with emotion, she found the words, "I am so sorry Grace, so sorry… I can't imagine how desolate you all must feel. But you can't let this pain turn you into something dark."

Tears fell from her eyes into the sand at her feet and were washed away by the lapping waves.

She heard with her soul, *'What Raffé did is Treason.'* It wasn't accusatory; it was filled with love for Raffé. How could he come back from this?

"What Raffé did and why he did it is still to be determined, Metatron said so!" she insisted. "He didn't betray you Grace. Please, don't let this turn you…" She pleaded, "You cannot allow Ariel to become your WRATH."

Printed in the United States
By Bookmasters